or

Brigadoon

Revisits

a reflection by

Andy Drummond

Copyright © 2014 Andy Drummond

All rights reserved.

ISBN-13: 9781500675691

CHAPTERS

		page
	Preface : With Love, Anything Is Possible	i
1	Him and His Fancy Dancing	1
2	Like the Famous Actress, But a Little Larger	7
3	Witches? We Say the Word Kind of Different	16
4	A Murderer and An Adulterer	28
5	Democrats All	36
6	Foreigners - in Edinburgh !	40
7	Etymologies	51
8	Mr. Ebenezer Erskine and the Anti-Burgher Party	57
9	Mr. MacReekie's New-plucked Fowl	64
10	Is His Tadger Being Tugged?	72
11	The Italian Government Never Lasts Long	78
12	New Warning About Climate Change	91
13	Mr. Campbell Puts on His Best Waistcoat	98
14	The Marrow of Modern Divinity	103
15	Catering Packs of Maltesers	112
16	Bunnies and Sabbatarians	119
17	Cheese-Boards or Social Housing	125
18	They're Not in the Union	132

19	The Scarlet Woman, The Scoffer and The Succubus	137
20	He Came From a Long Line of Giants	148
21	The Pumpherston Chipper	156
22	Fleeing the Close Company of Fornicators	161
23	Fleeing the Close Company of Fornicators	173
24	Americans, Nothing But Trouble	182
25	The Oil of Gladness and the Tappan Presbyterian Association	193
26	Four Doctors and an NHS Dentist	201
27	Petrol-Heads with Powdered Wigs	204
28	The Macy Deming Memorial Library	209
29	Lustful Looks, Intoxicating Drink and Immoderate Dancing	216
30	Very Smart, Troll, But No Smarts	224

With Love, Anything is Possible

In the still morning air, a heavenly choir softly sings: 'Brig-a-doon, Brig-a-doo-oon...'

On the other side of the ancient bridge over the brimming River Doon, Mr. Lundie emerges, his shirt unbuttoned. He peers into the clearing mist, where two figures stand uncertainly.

'Tommy, lad - you!' he exclaims with a smile. 'My, my: you must really love her! You woke me up.'

Tommy Albright and Jeff Douglas hesitate on the far side of the bridge. Tommy feels his heart flutter and then a wave of pure devotion overwhelms him. He takes a few steps forward.

'Come, lad,' says Mr. Lundie encouragingly, waving him on.

Tommy runs up to the top of the bridge and pauses beside the old man, gazing eagerly forwards into the still-sleeping village of Brigadoon.

'You shouldn't be too surprised,' explains Mr. Lundie kindly, seeing the young man's joyful confusion. 'I told you - if you love someone deeply enough, anything is possible.'

Tommy nods.

'Even miracles!' adds Mr. Lundie as he points the way into the village. 'Go, lad!'

Oh, how Tommy runs! Somewhere, just through the early morning mist that evaporated before him, is his sweetheart, his one, his own true love!

From Mr. Campbell's cottage streams a light, and then the figure of a young woman appears. She is tall and raven-haired. She wears a simple cream dress and a primrose-coloured shawl that she pulls around her against the cold air. She has heard something, something in her dreams that has woken her up. She dares not imagine - no, it could not be possible. Could it? Fiona Campbell takes half a dozen faltering steps on her bare feet, into the dawn.

Yes! There, there is dear, darling Tommy! She runs across the market-place. He runs in from the road. They stop and gaze at each other, as if unable to believe what is happening. It is, as Mr. Lundie said, a miracle! Their hearts soar, love bursts through their veins like a magic potion. They run again and throw themselves into each other's arms, together at last, forever. True love, reaching effortlessly across space and time, has found its home.

And on the still morning air, the sound of a heavenly choir softly singing 'Brig-a-doon, Brig-a-doo-oon!'

~ 1 ~

Him and His Fancy Dancing

'Brigadoon - I hate the very sound of it!' complained Harry.

'Yeah?' muttered Jeff, no longer interested.

'It is all the fault of Mr. Forsyth,' Harry grumbled.

Jeff groaned and shook his head. 'Hey, buddy,' he said, 'Forsyth's dead and gone. Move on, can't you? What's the point? Don't give me that Forsyth. Here, have another shot.' He passed the bottle to Harry. Harry, his chin resting in his left hand as he stared glumly into the early morning mist, stretched out his right hand, took the bottle, applied it to his lips, and screwed up his face as his throat was assaulted by the roughest whisky that James Maclaren had ever distilled. James Maclaren only ever sold the worst dregs from his still to Jeff Douglas. James Maclaren considered Jeff Douglas to be a godless ne'er-do-well. James Maclaren was correct. Harry passed the bottle back to Jeff, hacked a cough and spat into the bracken.

'Gross,' muttered Jeff, curling his lip in disgust. 'Your problem, buddy,' he returned to the matter, 'is you're living in the past.'

'Aren't we all?'

'Some of us more than most,' said Jeff. 'All I'm saying is, you've got to put some things behind you. Enough with the regrets. Face it, buddy: Jean's not for you any more, she's Charlie's girl now.'

Harry turned his head slowly to the right and glared at his companion. 'Jean?' he demanded, 'Jean? What's she got to do with it? It's not Jean.'

Brigadoon Revisits

'It was Bonnie Jean yesterday, buddy, and the day before that and the day before that,' countered Jeff, measuring how far the dregs in the bottle would go. Until breakfast, maybe, then he'd have to go and unearth a new bottle from his cache on the hill. If his neighbours hadn't got there first. 'And the day before that,' he added.

'Man, I'm over Jean,' replied Harry belligerently. He kicked viciously at a lump of sheep dung, sending it flying into the bracken. 'Jean means nothing to me. The woman didn't want me, she went for Charlie Dalrymple. That's all history now.'

'Fine, fine,' drawled Jeff, his attention wandering. He'd had a pain in his gut for the past few days - years even. He wondered if Meg could fix him something to ease it. Meg was a gypsy-woman's daughter - sure, she could fix his gut. It stabbed him now, a sharp pain in the side. He caught his breath, shut his eyes, and lay back on the damp heather, only half-listening to Harry's drawn-out dawn lament.

'Jean can do what she likes. But the woman is no fool. She'll see through Charlie one of these days. Mr. Charles Chisholm Dalrymple, him and his fancy dancing. If she wants to come back to me then, that'll be fine.' Harry paused. 'But I'm not saying I'll take her.'

'Spoiled goods,' said Jeff agreeably. 'Or is it soiled?'

Harry darted a malevolent glance in Jeff's direction. Jeff, with his eyes closed and pleased with his latest barb, did not notice. Harry took a step and picked up Jeff's bottle, quietly turned away and drained the last few drops. He carefully replaced the bottle by the older man's side and hobbled back into position.

Harry was a handsome man, in his late twenties, black hair, slim fine features. His chest and arms marked him as an athlete, but his legs were wasted and he walked with a pronounced limp, dragging his right foot. His eyes, when you looked close, had no sparkle in them, just a murky blur which shut out all life. His face bore the lines of a smile which had nothing of cheer and laughter in it.

Jeff, by contrast, was heavily-built, with sandy hair, a permanent sneer on his lips, his cheeks and nose ravaged by the ruddy traces of over-indulgence. He lay like a rock on the hillside, his chest rising and falling as he fought with the pain in his side. When his eyes were open, the world-weariness was plain to see, etched upon them as if by a master's hand.

'So, if it's not Bonnie Jean, then' said Jeff after a few minutes, since Harry had fallen silent, 'what did Mr. Forsyth do to you? What was his mistake that you can't forgive him after all this time?'

Harry stared at Jeff for a long, long while. Jeff stared back, quite able to hold those eyes and to turn them away. He felt nothing inside when looking at Harry, not any more. Once, in the early days, he had felt shame; then it had turned to pity - for himself, mind, not for Harry; but now, if he felt anything, it was the enjoyment of the challenge of facing him down. It was like a marriage that had gone sour years before. Jeff and Harry, bound together, for better and for worse, by their own tragedy.

'Mr. Forsyth locked us up here,' said Harry at last, 'and God took away the key.'

'God!' exclaimed Jeff, sitting up suddenly. 'It's God now, is it? It was Mr. Forsyth a minute ago. Make up your mind who to blame, can't you? You double-crossing son of a bitch,' he added, noticing the emptiness of the bottle, 'you finished the bottle!'

Harry nodded. 'What are you going to do about it, Mr. Douglas?'

'I could whip you from here to MacConnachy Square, and then some,' growled Jeff. 'But you're not worth it, buddy, you're not worth the effort. Neither's the booze. So I'll just lie here, thanks, and wait for sun-up.'

'Coward,' said Harry. Jeff ignored him.

'Braggart,' said Harry. Jeff closed his eyes.

'Adulterer,' said Harry. Jeff smiled to himself.

'You were only ever Tommy Albright's best man,' said Harry. At this, Jeff got up slowly, padded purposefully over to Harry, and lashed out hard with his boot. He caught the younger man on his right foot. With a groan, Harry keeled over. Jeff padded back to his bed of heather and sat down.

The mist swirled around them. It was cold and clammy, and it set both of the men coughing, grimacing at their individual pain and at the cold. Jeff sat and clutched his ribs, Harry leaned back against a stunted birch tree, feeling the rough lichen that coated the trunk, and massaged his leg.

'If,' said Harry at last, more to himself than to anyone else listening, 'Mr. Forsyth had not prayed to God, God would not have listened. God would not have locked us away in this prison, and we would not be living now under this curse. I'd have gone to Edinburgh and studied the law and been a great man in Scotland.'

'A great man!' echoed Jeff's mocking voice. 'Oh, a great man indeed, Harry Beaton. All the way to Edinburgh, by jiminy! The ends of the earth! Couldn't make it to America, then? New York not good enough for you, Harry? Afraid of being third-rate? I tell you - you wouldn't last an hour in New York, they'd chew you up, spit you out, and take a slug of rye to wash away the taste.'

'I could have run off to Edinburgh with Jean, maybe,' speculated Harry. 'No,' he re-considered, 'Mr. Campbell would not have liked that for his daughter: I could have gone to Edinburgh, made my fortune and come back to take bonnie Jean away with me. Not a word could Charlie Dalrymple have said to that. The uncultured fop - he's only ever been to Aberdeen. Not one word, I tell you: Mr. Campbell would have seen to that. So would Jean.'

'Well, well,' said Jeff at last, 'Harry goes to seek his fortune. In Edinburgh. Jean marries him. They all live happily ever after.' He laughed bitterly. 'Listen, buddy, you've been feeding me this line forever. Day after day, the same old crap. If only this, if only that! If only I'd run off with Jean, if only Charlie had broken his leg at the dancing, if only Tommy Albright had turned up earlier -'

'If only you'd not fired the gun that almost killed me,' interrupted Harry.

Jeff was not to be silenced. 'If only he'd not fired the gun that almost killed me, if only I'd not climbed that tree and looked like some kind of bird for Jeff to shoot at. If only, if only! You got eyes, Harry? You got eyes in your head? You seen marriages, have you? I tell you, buddy, I've seen marriages by the score and not one of them was worth the price of the licence. Not one. I've seen it in New York, and I've seen it here. Just take a look at Tommy and Jean, won't you?'

Him and His Fancy Dancing

At that moment, there was a shout from somewhere nearby in the mist.

'Harry Beaton!' It was high-pitched and excited. 'Harry Beaton!'

Harry listened keenly, glad of the interruption to their long-running, repetitive, useless debate. 'Is that you, young Hamish?' he called.

'Aye, sir,' came back the shrill voice. 'Where are you, Mr. Beaton?'

'Up here by the Witch's Tree.'

Jeff snorted. 'Witch's Tree, my ass. You're a simpleton, Harry Beaton. Mr. Forsyth believed in witches. Look where it got him. Look where it got you! Believe in witches? I told Mr. Lundie once - Witches? I said to him: sure, we know the word - only in New York, we -'

'- pronounce it kind of different.' Harry completed Jeff's only joke for him. 'Give us a rest, Mr. Douglas, from New York, you and your world-weariness. Hamish!' he called again, 'I'm up here!'

At that moment, a tousle-headed small boy, dressed in a kilt and a linen shirt several sizes too large, burst out of the mist. A very large and hairy sheepdog bounded along at his side. The boy's face was a healthy red and he was out of breath.

'The bridge, Mr. Beaton, sir!' he exclaimed. 'It's broken down. Something terrible has happened!' His eyes were round with excitement. 'Do you think the witches have found us?'

'Jesus!' exclaimed Jeff. He hurled the empty bottle towards the young lad. It missed by about ten feet and slid harmlessly into the undergrowth. The dog drew back its black lips to show its teeth at Jeff. It growled. Jeff ignored it.

'The bridge?' asked Harry, looking anxious. 'What's happened to it, Hamish?'

'It's all broken down,' repeated the boy, running round in circles. He nodded his head forcefully in confirmation. 'Maggie here saw it too,' he added, indicating the dog by his side.

'Great,' muttered Jeff. 'The dog saw it too. What does Lundie teach these kids in that schoolhouse of his?'

Harry took the boy's head in his hands and forced him to a halt. 'Take your time, Hamish, and tell me properly,' he said. 'Tell it to me like I was the dominie.'

The young shepherd took a deep breath, and then another. 'I took Maggie down to the river to look for some sheep and then I saw the bridge and half the stones had gone and they were lying all in the water and the rest of it was all broken and the ground had all turned black on either side, black and steaming like Mr. Lundie says is Hell and Damnation and there was a witch and a wizard standing on the other side of the bridge there and - '

'A witch?' asked Jeff, appalled at this fantasy. 'And a wizard too?'

'A witch,' said the boy, confident in his knowledge of the numberless threats to small boys, sleepy villages and sheep. 'A big one. And a small wizard in a glowing yellow cloak. Or maybe it was a werewolf?' he offered, suddenly recalling another possible threat.

Jeff waved away both the wizard and the werewolf. He rose from his place of rest. 'If it's a dame,' he declared, 'reckon I'll go down and take a look. You coming, buddy?' Without waiting for a reply, Jeff set off down the hill, striding over the heather and through the bracken at an energetic pace. Harry seized a stout walking-stick and hobbled after him. Hamish and his dog ran back and forth between the two men, anxious to be first back at the scene of enlivening devastation, but unwilling to be seen to accompany Mr. Douglas. 'It was a wizard! Or a werewolf, Mr. Douglas!' he yelled after the figure now vanishing into the mist. 'It might be the Devil in disguise, come to fetch us sinners away like Mr. Forsyth said!'

~ 2 ~

Like the Famous Actress, But a Little Larger

It was merely Warren Newcombe and Nana Visitor.

Warren Newcombe was the engineer supervising the construction of the Cleanhill intersection of the new Aberdeen Western Peripheral Route. Warren Newcombe liked to rise early and inspect the land each morning before his ears were assaulted by the noise of machinery and rumble of earth and the complaints of the workforce. He liked to commune with the dawn and in that fresh light to see precisely and clearly what challenges lay ahead of him. In this professional solitude, he found a cocoon which held him safe, secure, untouched by the more troubling things of the world.

Warren Newcombe's life until now had been an endless series of failed relationships. His mother and father had brought him up with the sole aim that he should enter the Diplomatic Service. Young Warren had at the last turned up his nose at the opportunity to serve his country, and as a result had never again been welcome in the ancestral home in Colchester. His wife had left him some considerable time ago and gone to dig herself a foxhole in a protest encampment lying directly in the path of the M40 extension through rural Oxfordshire. His three children, each almost immaculately conceived in the marriage, had all escaped from home at the first

Brigadoon Revisits

opportunity and had concealed themselves in huge cities on the far side of the globe, places that both Mr. and Mrs. Newcombe were unlikely to reach, changing address if it appeared likely that someone would track them down, be it parents or siblings. Mr. Newcombe's recent dalliance with a female engineer from Norway had lasted only as long as the sewage-works contract on which they had collaborated near Hartlepool, after which she took offence at something he had said, or had omitted to say, or had written, or had not written; and was last heard of dating a Lithuanian airborne-weapons specialist. There had been other brief encounters before and after the Norwegian had drifted away like the exhaust of a JCB on an winter's day. And now, as he stood this Friday morning in September at the head of the strips of tarmac which unfolded with startling magnificence across the pristine countryside, he puzzled over the fact that a date the previous evening with a homely lady from Portlethen had ended, at midnight precisely, in yet another rejection. They had found a good many things to talk about during a pleasant evening in Stonehaven's finest restaurant and had parted at eleven, on the best of terms, she to her collection of rag-dolls, he to his gentleman's lodgings. He had nurtured a very small and fragile dream for an hour, until the long-familiar text message had come through from her, declaring that 'it would be best' if they never saw each other again.

Warren Newcombe stood therefore wearily upon the northern bulwark of the Cleanhill Intersection, gazing down upon the silvery waters of the River Dee, those which came down from the mountains away to the west and poured eastwards into the North Sea which sparkled under the rising sun. The day promised to be calm and sunny, as only September can deliver. Here and there, and in the field directly in front, patches of mist lingered, hemmed in by the surrounding woodland. Across the broad Dee valley, the lower hills rose up again; in the distance he could see the odd wind-turbine catching the early light. To his left he could just make out, behind a narrow screen of trees, the cement figures of fairytale coachmen and the Disney characters that populated 'Storybook Glen', that children's theme-park which would soon be by-passed, at a distance of not less than twenty metres, by the new four-lane highway. In a sensitive re-

Like the Famous Actress, But a Little Larger

alignment of the road, the designers had preserved a cultural icon for future generations of children and their grandparents. Mr. Newcombe considered the sensitivities and certainties of road-building and found them more reliable than the ways of other human-beings; he drew a deep breath, and then another and another.

As he did so, the mist in the field before him drew back a little and revealed a bridge. An old, hump-backed bridge, long pre-dating General Wade.

A bridge?

The engineer frowned and peered at the sight which, in just another moment, was concealed again behind the ever-shifting vapours. He waited for a few minutes, still quiet and self-contained, his eyes fixed upon the spot where he had seen something rather unwelcome. His patience was rewarded when, under the pressure of another breath of wind, the mist shifted again to reveal the bridge. Or the ruins of a bridge at least. It seemed to be in a poor state of repair - the parapets broken, large stones dislodged and lying in the middle of it and in the dark brown waters of the small river that ran underneath it.

A bridge over a river?

There was some kind of stream which ran through Storybook Glen, but it had no bridge. None at all. Warren Newcombe suddenly felt a shiver run down his spine. He needed urgently to relieve himself. After looking cautiously around, he unzipped and pointed at the brisk morning air. As he waited patiently for the flow to stop - for he had come to that age - he looked more carefully at the scene opening up before him. A bridge - certainly; ruined and therefore no obstacle to the Peripheral Route. He had seen plenty of ruined bridges on this project and on other ones: it was the price of progress. Bridges were functional things, and like anything else, they outlived their usefulness. But not here. It was not on any maps or plans that he had seen. It had not been here yesterday or the day before, he was certain of that.

True enough, one of the bulldozer drivers had complained about running into something in the mist last night. But that had had to be a tree or bush, not a bridge, where no bridge should be.

This was not good.

Warren Newcombe clambered down from the earthworks and made his way across the field to the bridge and its accompanying river. The posts which marked out the future route of the highway stretched off in a pleasingly straight line, into the mist and thereafter down the hill. They ran parallel to the stream. Already the earth had been exposed by the heavy plant, trees felled, the turf stripped back to reveal the dark earth underneath. And the bridge was now right in the middle of this cleared area.

'*Ha*-llo!' a voice rang out from behind him. The accent was on the first syllable, and Warren's ear immediately detected a European, female. He turned round, unexpectedly finding himself thrown back to heady days in Hartlepool. A figure stood at the edge of the trees which screened Storybook Glen from the march of time.

'*Ha*-llo!' the person shouted once more, waving in a manner more imperious than deferential. She was heading towards him rapidly. Warren returned the greeting, cautiously, then thought he had better prevent this person, who had no hard hat, from trespassing upon the site. He strode purposefully towards her, increasing his stride as he perceived that she would meet him more than half-way. He gesticulated wildly, trying to indicate the danger of her situation. She paused briefly, raised her shoulders and held out her hands in a gesture of surprised inquiry; and continued apace. It was true: there was no live earth-moving machinery, nor any sign of men with the accoutrements of modern road-building. Nevertheless, she must not be permitted on to the site. At last they met.

"Good morning, my friend," she shouted, reaching out towards him with both arms. She was taller than Warren by about a head, and of muscular build. She was dressed in some kind of army fatigues. Or was it civilian - was that a designer label coming away from the sleeve? She was in her late thirties, and bore a look of extreme dishevelment with considerable charm and ease. Without waiting for a formal introduction, she threw her arms around Warren and bore down upon him in heavy embrace. Then she released him. He fell back three steps with the recoil. She grinned hugely. 'Now, my good man - may I ask where I am actually? I have been lost this whole night, dammit again, and wish at once to return to my hotel to bathe. And eat a hearty Full Scottish Breakfast. And file my story. At once, do your hear? Would you like to come with me?'

This direct approach threw Warren completely. He floundered for a moment or two, trying to find some form of words between polite helpfulness and officious repudiation. He failed.

'I was so enchanted by the fairytale figures,' boomed the woman carelessly, gesticulating expansively back towards Storybook Glen. 'Such a completely charming idea! So wonderful for the children, not true? Ah, the children - do you not just wish to have a dozen or more?'

Mr. Newcombe could not find it in himself to agree. 'I regret,' he was finally able to say sternly, 'that you should not be here. This is a construction site. Very dangerous. Very dangerous, indeed, madam.'

'Oh you goodness! Danger!' shouted the woman, pretending - amateurishly - to look wild-eyed. 'You say there is danger! But from what?' She looked around amiably. 'I see nothing very dangerous around here. And I love danger, my friend, I adore it, I lust after it - it is danger and the thought of danger that makes of me a true woman, dammit!' She smote her bosom several times with a fist, to indicate just how a true woman should appear. 'But I guess I must yield to you. You wish that I wear a security hat like yours, yes?' she smirked. 'One on which one might go tap-tap, tap-tap-tappity-tap?' She illustrated the idea by drumming rhythmically on Warren's yellow hat.

'Well, yes,' agreed Warren, flinching under the onslaught. 'But only if I permit you to enter the site. Of course you must wear a hard hat. A *hard* hat,' he repeated.

'A *hard* hat, a *hard* hat,' acknowledged the woman, gracefully accepting the new item of vocabulary. 'But, sir, I have just the very thing!' From her large bag, she pulled out a witch's hat. She displayed it, blushed and giggled. 'I found it back there in the fairytale-park, and thought I might take it as a remembrance. It was attached to a witch, but was very wobbly, you know? It fell off straight away. In Germany, we do not make so jerry-built with our witches.' She placed the hat on her head, where it slipped cheekily to one side. She held on to it with one hand and twirled. 'You like?' she demanded. Suddenly she stopped and peered past Mr. Newcombe. 'Oh, a real old bridge!' she observed enthusiastically. 'And a little river. These belong to this - this fairytale place? You are the manager of this wonderful park, yes?'

Warren shook his head strenuously. 'I am an engineer, madam, and -'

'*Ach so*, an engineer! Excuse!' she exclaimed, shooting her hands to her rosy cheeks in horror. 'I forget myself. Fool that I am! My father always told me that I was as rude as I was tall. He died of shame when I was twenty-one. Shame at his daughter, and at the end of the Democratic Republic. The poor man! But that is of course another story. My name is Visitor.'

'Yes, indeed,' said Warren, understanding her to have a poor command of the English language. 'You are a visitor, and -'

She exploded in laughter, and slapped him hard on the shoulder. 'Oh no, no, not a visitor! Visitor is my name, Mr. Engineer. The name comes from somewhere in the Carpathian Mountains, where my ancestors lived. Visitor, Nana Visitor: like the famous actress in *Deep Space Nine*, you know, but a little taller.' She considered the comparison seriously for a few moments. Then she hauled a photograph from her bosom; it depicted a slim woman with a very bumpy nose. 'This is the other Nana Visitor,' she whispered conspiratorially. 'I know which one you will find the more attractive?' She tucked away the photo and did not wait for his answer. 'And you are called actually?'

Warren automatically introduced himself by name, and then swiftly cast a glance over his shoulder, lest any of the workforce had assembled itself for the purpose of mass observation of his embarrassment.

'Mr. Warren!' exclaimed the visitor, grasping both his hands in hers and shaking them vigorously until his teeth chattered. 'I am honoured! I was of course abandoned here last night by some colleagues. I am really a journalist. From Germany, sir. You know Germany a little? A completely beautiful country, far more beautiful than this one, I think. More trees, better roads. My newspaper sent

Like the Famous Actress, But a Little Larger

me here to cover the Independence Referendum. You have followed of course the Independence Referendum?'

The Scottish Independence Referendum - it was hard to avoid really. The construction-site had been invaded by campaigners for both "Yes" and "No" for the past four weeks, each camp trying either to appropriate the kudos, or distance themselves from the shame, of the Peripheral Route, according to their lights. The Referendum had taken place last week, and he had had some small disagreement with the homely lady from Portlethen, on the matter. He paused - perhaps that was the reason for her surprising dismissal of him: she had been most enthusiastic about one political party or other, he could not determine which; while he had found the whole thing quite tedious and had, perhaps wrongly, said as much.

Warren had little time to reflect on this sudden revelation of his continuing failings. The visitor kept on speaking.

'Get some good story for me, said my editor. Some gossip, some scandal, some low-down maybe. Mr. Warren,' she grumbled, 'my editor has never seen the British political machine in action, or he would never have sent me already. The Referendum is so completely dull! Like the graveyard. No one was ever a Nazi or a *Stasi*, no one insults a defeated opponent, no one smiles with the smile of treachery. The women pretend they have testicles and the men pretend they have hearts. But they are all without hearts and without testicles. *Drecklöcher*! My ancestors come from the Carpathians. Do you know vampires, Mr. Warren, you have them in this country? A vampire has more charm than these ones.' She bent forwards slightly and tapped him firmly on the chest. 'It is my advice, Mr. Engineer - vote only for what the vampires say. They have hearts and they have testicles also. Dammit one more time!' she proclaimed, clapping her hands together, thereby shooing off a large gathering of crows and seagulls from the scarified earth. 'My editor is a complete fool. He sends me here with the strict instructions I should get him a good story - ah yes, and some bottles of your Scotch Whisky that he can impress his friends at the shooting-club. He is a member of a shooting-club in Frankenstein - can you imagine? Frankenstein - it really exists! So, he thinks everything British is such a fine thing. I

Brigadoon Revisits

must absolutely send him stories that will please him. But that is no concern of yours.' Warren shook his head momentarily in agreement. Miss Visitor continued regardless.

'It has been a long week, Newcombe - I may be so intimate as to call you Newcombe? - a long week truly. How many times do they recount the vote? I forget - three, four, maybe. Yes, three certainly. It does not want to end. So last night at midnight we set off from Stonehaven. It was six of us in a small car. Can you believe that, six of us?'

Warren found it difficult to believe it had been a small car, but was circumspect enough not to mention it.

'Six of us - we do that in Germelshausen, in Saxony, where I grow up. Six in a Trabi, eighty kilometres in the hour, then it blows up. Pure crazy! Here, the small car just keeps going.' She shook her head in wonder. 'I do not know who is the driver. I think it was any kind of woman from Ireland. We lost her in town already. She stopped to buy some French fries - chips, she said. Got out and left us. My friend Sydney drove us further. He is not a good driver. You know Sydney?'

Warren shook his head, baffled.

'We drove over the hill - oh, somewhere behind us here, I do not know any more. It was dark. Dark like in our forests. There were some houses, not many. We stopped at one when the two complete idiots from Finland decided they needed to interview some ordinary people. We left them there, I and Sydney and someone else - who was it? Who was it, Newcombe, dammit?' She glared at him as he stood ignorant before her. She slapped him lightly with the witch's hat. 'Never mind, it was actually a man. That was good enough for me - in the dark, in a car with my good friend Sydney and another man. Sydney was not paying attention. He was not holding the wheel. His eyes were closed. He was singing Wagner to me, he is such a good man, dammit. He drove us off the road into a field. The car broke down. The field was full of - *Vogelstrauss* - how do they name themselves the big birds already, Newcombe?'

'Crows?' suggested Warren tentatively.

Like the Famous Actress, But a Little Larger

'I may be an *Ossi*, but I know myself with crows, Newcombe. These were not crows, these were - yes, ostriches! The field was full of ostriches. They ran through the hole in the fence that was made by the car. We chased them but they were too quick. Totally speedy. What a major story that would have been for my stupid editor, yes? A story about the Scottish Referendum - who needs it? Ostriches in the wilds of Scotland, dammit, that's a real story. No matter. We chased them down a small track and came to the fairytale park. No ostrich. So we drank a bottle of whisky that we found in the car. Sydney and I, we went of course in the fairytale coach. The other man, I do not know where he went: I have last seen him dancing with a bear. We do not see him again. And this morning when I wake I see no one at all. Sydney is completely gone! And I am in the centre, as one says, of nowhere! I must go and sit on that beautiful bridge, that is truly mad!'

So saying, she rammed the witch's hat tightly upon her head and pushed straight past the engineer, striding out towards the tumbledown bridge. Warren Newcombe paused a moment in doubt; and then hurried after Nana Visitor.

~ 3 ~

Witches? We Say the Word Kind of Different.

'What happened to the bridge, Jeff?' asked Tommy Albright. 'It's all tumbled down.'

'Hey, buddy!' exclaimed Jeff, 'you're sure wide awake this morning! Didn't notice it myself.'

'Sure you did, Jeff,' said Tommy, 'you're just kidding me! Put a cork in it.'

Jeff did not reply. He was too busy peering across the bridge at the two figures who stood there, still partly concealed by the mist. There was a commotion behind him. Young Hamish had arrived with his dog.

'See, Mr. Albright? I told Mr. Douglas it was a witch and he didn't believe me!'

'Sure looks like a witch,' said Tommy gravely. 'Maybe, just maybe, that Mr. Forsyth got it right after all? What do you think, Jeff?'

Jeff stood with his hands on his hips, staring into the mist. At length, he turned round.

'You lost your mind, Tommy?' he demanded. 'There's no such thing as witches. Sure, witches - we got them in New York, only -'

'- we just say the word kind of different,' said Tommy wearily. 'Yeah, Jeff, I know what you think. But that sure looks like a witch to me. Got a hat and everything. Say,' he said further, looking around

Witches? We Say the Word Kind of Different.

in amazement, 'what in hell happened to the heather and the hillside? It's all churned up and black. Fiona will be heartbroken, all that heather gone. How did that happen? That and the bridge? It's like a bomb hit or something.'

'Beats me,' said Jeff. 'Reckon I'm going across there to ask that dame that very question.'

He reckoned without Harry, who had just hobbled up behind the two men, out of breath and red with rage. Harry grabbed Jeff's sleeve. 'You're not going anywhere, man!' he hissed. 'It wasn't right for me to cross the bridge. Did they not say the entire village would vanish forever if I did? Did you not shoot me out of the tree when I tried? Aye, so I'm not going to let you away. You stay right here!' With those words he whipped a large knife from the folds of the blanket draped over his shoulder, and placed the point carefully in the centre of Jeff's chest.

Jeff did not say a word, did not look at the knife, did not flinch, just looked into Harry's eyes. The two men stared at each other for a long time, neither of them yielding until at last Jeff took a step back.

'What the hell, Harry, whatever you like,' he growled, the voice of a man who had lost the battle too many times. 'You win. You always win. After what I did to you, you can never lose.'

Harry kept his knife in his hand and followed Jeff's every movement with his blazing dark eyes.

'If you cross that bridge,' he began; but got no further.

'Mr. Albright, Mr. Albright!' came Hamish's excited voice, 'the witch and the wizard are coming across the bridge!' Hamish's dog barked in warning, and the young shepherd peered anxiously round Jeff and Harry. For his part, Tommy Albright advanced easily towards the bridge and stopped some five yards short. He watched the two figures emerge from the last trails of mist and ascend the far side of the bridge.

'*Ha*-llo!' shouted the witch, taking her hat off and waving it eagerly. 'What is this place? I think this is part of the fairytale park, yes? The Storybook Glen?'

'This is no fairy-story book, lady,' muttered Jeff. 'Might have been one once, but it's more like H.P.Lovecraft now.'

Luckily, Nana Visitor could not hear him.

'This is Brigadoon, ma'am,' said Tommy cheerfully. 'Come across and be welcome. And bring your little friend,' he added as an afterthought.

Hamish wailed. 'The witch is coming, the witch is coming!' He prepared to run off into the mist that still ghosted the ground behind them.

'Oh!' cried Nana. 'The young boy thinks I am a witch ! Listen, my young friend, I am no witch. Vampire might I be perhaps, from my ancestors down, but no witch.'

Since Hamish had no idea what a vampire was, he changed his mind about running away. But he sensibly remained behind the protective wall of the three men. He watched the visitor come down the gradient of the bridge, and kept his eyes on the smaller figure who followed, a person wearing a bright lime-green jacket and some kind of yellow hat. It was clearly a familiar spirit - that was the term he had often heard Mr. Lundie and Mr. Forsyth use: a Familiar. They appear in many guises - cats, dogs, small people. The cloak and the hat gave it all away.

'Brigadoon?' asked Nana. 'Like the Gene Kelly movie? *Scheisse !* what a completely great movie! Actually that one I have at home. In Russian, of course.' She hummed a bar or two of the melody.

'They made a movie?' asked Tommy Albright, startled. 'They made a movie of this place? Well, what do you know? Jeff - you hear that?'

'A movie?' said Jeff. 'Sure as hell would like to see one of those again. Saw *On The Waterfront* just before we came back again - wasn't that one helluva?'

'What's a movie?' demanded Hamish.

But no one paid him any attention. Tommy was shaking Nana's hand and then Warren's, and Nana was eyeing up both Jeff and Harry.

And at that moment the village came to life. Oh, it was a grand sight! In every thatched cottage in the place, the doors and windows were flung wide open, blankets were shaken out, dogs and children gambolled, young ladies danced prettily into the open air, old men

Witches? We Say the Word Kind of Different.

strode out with never a care in the world, their jolly wives shooing them into the fresh air before they got down to the real business of housewifery. And every one of them was dressed from head to toe in tartan - red tartan, yellow tartan, green and blue, a riot of clans, an advertisement for an indigenous and obviously healthy cloth industry. Here a young fellow in tight green trousers and a tartan shirt that would not have looked out of place on a lumberjack. There a girl with a dress that billowed around her like a parachute, her black hair bobbing in the summer sunlight - for the mist had finally cleared. And as they met and greeted each other with such delight, as if they had not seen each other for a hundred years or so, they formed up into small groups of dancers and waltzed and jigged their way down the main street of the village and came at last to the bridge over the river Doon.

Where they stopped dead, the songs dying from their lips, the dance ebbing from their legs, a frown creeping down upon their brows.

One of their number stepped forward, an elderly gentleman. He pointed at the two visitors with a trembling hand.

'Are you witches, or what are you?' he demanded.

'I am just a girl from Germelshausen,' boomed Nana cheerfully. 'I have a witch's hat, as you see, but witching is not my profession.' She took the hat off and tossed it to Warren Newcombe, who dropped it on the muddy ground.

'If you be witches, then begone from here - we want none of your kind!' repeated the elderly gentleman.

'Oh, Mr. Mackintosh,' said Tommy in a placatory tone. 'These are no witches, these are visitors from the outside world. They should be made welcome.'

'We'll no welcome their kind. They'll be witches, you'll see, Tommy Albright. A witch and her familiar, aye!'

'That's right, Mr. Mackintosh,' piped up young Hamish eagerly. 'Just like Mr. Forsyth warned us - a witch and her familiar!' Hamish's dog growled at this and began to bark. 'See, Maggie can tell! Here, Maggie, quiet - the witch will turn you into something nasty if you don't!' He pulled the dog back to his side and crouched down beside her.

'Are you all nuts?' demanded Jeff, rounding on the frightened villagers. 'This is no witch, like Tommy says. You see any broomsticks? This is a dame from the outside world. What's your name again?'

'Visitor,' she replied smiling bountifully at the panorama of fashion disasters. 'Nana Visitor. I come from Germany!' She waved cheerily at everyone.

'If you are not a witch,' said Andrew Mackintosh, unappeased, 'then how can you explain this familiar of yours?' He stared accusingly at Warren, who stood, utterly confused, at the end of the bridge, his eyes blinking. Never, in his lengthy career as road-builder and civil engineer, had he come across a protest encampment such as this. Dimly aware that he was all of a sudden the object of unwelcome attention, he straightened his hard hat and tried to give the appearance of being in control of the situation.

'Who is in charge here?' he demanded.

There was a silence at this. Mr. Mackintosh looked at him doubtfully. Tommy Albright turned easily and scanned the assembly. At last there was movement at the back.

'There he is!' cried Tommy. 'Mr. Lundie, we have some new visitors! They want to speak to you.'

An old man was pushing his way through the crowd. He was dressed more soberly than the rest of the villagers, in tight black breeches, and with a large white shirt open half way down his barrel-chest. His white hair stuck out at all angles.

'Oh,' said Mr. Lundie once he stood before Nana and Warren. 'I was told you were witches. But clearly you are not of that kind?'

'I am naturally a visitor to your theme-park - that is the word, is it not?'

Mr. Lundie looked at Nana blankly. 'Theme-park? I do not understand one word.'

'Dammit again, Newcombe,' replied Nana, turning to the engineer for assistance. 'What does it call itself? This place where I spend the night with Sydney?'

Witches? We Say the Word Kind of Different.

'That would be Storybook Glen,' replied Warren, resigned to losing control of the situation again.

'Yes, yes, exactly so! You are the manager of Storybook Glen, sir?' she asked the old gentleman. 'It is a totally wonderful place and -' she peered over this shoulder and beyond the crowd of villagers, '- and I can see that there is much more for the visitor. Will you give me a guided tour, perhaps? And maybe you will do me the honour with an interview and a few pictures for my useless editor back in downtown Chemnitz? I think he finds it much more interesting than the results of the Referendum.'

'Before I let you into our village of Brigadoon, madam,' said Mr. Lundie, steadfastly ignoring all other matters, 'I must know what your companion is? Is he, as some have said, your familiar?'

For answer, Nana burst out into a fit of uproarious laughter; and ended it by enfolding Mr. Lundie in a warm embrace, from which he struggled, in vain, to be free.

'My familiar?' she said at last, wiping tears from here eyes. 'Not at all, sir: I would not let him be familiar with me. He is but an engineer on the highway.'

'A highwayman? O, will the Good Lord preserve us!' exclaimed Mr. Mackintosh fearfully, clutching at the purse he kept concealed in his shirt.

'Not a highwayman, Mr. Mackintosh,' said Tommy reassuringly. 'In the modern world we have proper roads and respectable men who build them. This fellow is no doubt one of those?'

Warren Newcombe nodded his head. He thought it best to remove his hard hat. There was a mutter of suspicion among the villagers at this action, but it was quickly replaced by sounds of admiration when Mr. Lundie conceded that he had heard tell of such a profession among the southerners. But Andrew Mackintosh persevered.

'This terrible destruction you have wrought upon our heather and our hillside, then - that would be the work of this highwayman, would it, Mr. Lundie?'

'I fear it may be so, Andrew,' said Mr. Lundie sadly. 'It seems that men of the modern world like to raise their monuments to challenge the works of God. But perhaps we can offer our visitors some hospitality and maybe see if they can do something to repair the damage.'

With these kind words, Mr. Lundie invited the two visitors to his side, and together they walked through the villagers, whose ranks parted before them. And then one by one, two by two, but no longer dancing, the crowd fell in behind, murmuring to each other and speculating pessimistically on the ways of the modern world.

'Can I ask you, lad,' said Mr. Lundie by way of conversation as they walked up the path to the village, 'what day of the week it is?'

'It is Friday,' answered Warren, glad to be able to make a statement that was neither contentious nor doubtful.

'Friday? My, my,' said the old gentleman to himself. 'I thought it might be.' He paused for a moment. 'And, if you would permit me to ask, sir, would you mind telling me what year it is now?'

'The year?' repeated Warren, raising his eyebrows. 'The year is 2014.' He gave out this information rather tentatively, half-fearing it might not be quite so certain as the day of the week.

Mr. Lundie stopped in his tracks, causing the whole procession behind him to shuffle and stumble to a halt also. All conversation died for a few moments, while the old man considered the year.

'Gratifying,' he commented at last, 'most gratifying.' He resumed his stately progress up to the village. As did the crowd behind him.

'Why would this year be gratifying, my friend?' asked Nana Visitor. 'The year has been 2014 for some time now, has it not? Yes, also in Chemnitz!' She paused. 'Well, perhaps not.'

'But not, God be praised, in Brigadoon,' said Mr. Lundie pleasantly. 'I was just expecting, you see, that it would be a Friday and that it would be the year 2013 or 2014. And I was quite right in my prediction. That was all. It was Thursday yesterday, you see. I expect tomorrow will be a Saturday.' He fell silent. Warren and Nana looked at each other, slightly wrong-footed by the old gentleman's meandering thoughts.

The silence was broken by the arrival at their side of Jeff Douglas.

Witches? We Say the Word Kind of Different.

'Don't worry about the old-timer,' said Jeff in a tone which, if it had been considerably quieter, would have been conspiratorial. 'He's living in the past.'

'My grandfather is like that,' said Nana agreeably. 'Wishes for the good old days of Erich Honecker and Karl-Marx-Stadt. We tell him every Sunday when we go to eat with him, grandfather, we say, the old days are actually gone and the better days are here. But he does not want to know this. In the old days, he says, we had an honest man in a position of power and we did not have Pepsi Cola. Now we are *kaputt*!' She laughed. 'You do not have any Pepsi Cola here, sir?'

'No way, not a drop,' said Jeff morosely. 'They don't have much here. It's the boondocks, lady, only much worse. They only have rye and it's as rough as hell.'

'Come on, Jeff,' argued Tommy, who had come alongside as well, 'it's not that bad at all. You said it yourself - New York has gone downhill. Mrs. Visitor,' he addressed himself to her, 'what we have here is peace and quiet, happiness and simple living, dancing and singing all day long. This is an idyll, a place of refuge.'

'Yeah,' said Jeff, 'singing and dancing all the day long. Jeez, Tommy, can you not give it a rest? You know all that dancing and singing and all those bright clothes give me a real headache. Peace and quiet? A crock of - '

'Jeff!' interrupted Tommy, laying a hand on the other man's sleeve. 'Shove it, or I'll sock you one.'

Jeff mouthed something and turned his attention to Warren Newcombe.

'Do you have any whisky on you?' he asked. Warren felt a little threatened. Jeff was a good bit larger than him, and seemed to fill the frame. He shook his head and avoided his eye. Best not to offend these protestors, whoever they might be, but also best not to be seen to be helping them in any way. And he needed, at the first opportunity, to get back and on the phone to security. He had already tried his mobile-phone, but the signal was non-existent on this part of the hill.

At Warren's discouraging response, Jeff grunted and turned away. His place was taken by a young woman. She was bare-foot and dressed in rags, but had well-brushed hair, a pink glow to her cheeks and a twinkle in her eye that, under normal circumstances, would perhaps have attracted Warren; but just now, he felt very cautious indeed.

'I'm Meg,' she introduced herself, and linked her arm with Warren's. 'Oh, you're a winning lad, though, aren't you!' She tossed her head. 'What a glorious day it is!'

Warren nodded dumbly.

'A good day for a walk on the hill and a bed in the heather under the sunshine, perhaps?' She winked lasciviously at Warren and then launched herself into a skip and a jig, forcing Warren to dance alongside her, or look a fool. From behind them came mutterings of disapproval; and then the angry voice of Jeff. 'Leave that man alone, Meg, or I'll give you a good hiding.'

Meg sighed, stopped her skipping and relinquished the engineer's arm. She stood to one side, pouting and kicking the mud with the toe of her dancing shoe.

'And you,' added Jeff for good measure, placing his right hand very firmly on Warren's neck and squeezing hard and harder still, 'you leave that dame alone. She's mine.'

Warren blinked in acquiescence, and Jeff released his grip with a vicious forwards shove. Warren was left wondering how on earth he was going to get away from here. It was his duty as an employee of the company, no doubt, to discover the extent of the camp and try to spot the strengths and weakness of the opposition; but he would rather be doing that from a distance, or in the company of three security guards. As it was, he had one eccentric foreigner, whose main interest, at the moment, was journalism. Journalism, once an honoured profession, had stooped very low in recent years, and Warren had no great feeling that matters were any different in Germany than they were in Britain. This Visitor woman would doubtless find herself obliged to tell the story of the protestors, who were engaged in criminal activity, rather than the story of the perfectly legitimised progress of the Peripheral Route.

As the whole procession reached the outskirts of the village, the villagers struck up again with bagpipes and drums and were soon

Witches? We Say the Word Kind of Different.

twirling and reeling in pairs and foursomes and eightsomes, kilts swinging and Tam O' Shanters jigging. From the first two houses they passed, where smoke was billowing merrily from the chimneys, small children and toothless crones emerged, gazing in wonder at the two new arrivals being paraded past their doors. A good woman peered out, porridge spurtle in hand, as she was momentarily distracted from preparing the breakfast. Nana Visitor waved to them all and beamed upon the small children.

'This,' she advised Mr. Lundie, 'is the totally best theme-park I ever have visited! Completely mad! I spend a day in Disneyland in France - that was my editor again, the man is an idiot, he wants trinkets for his little girl-friend - and it was not so - how shall I say? - not so ethnic as this!'

'France?' murmured Mr. Lundie knowledgeably. 'But that is a fair distance away. You'll have met with the young King over the water, my dear?' he enquired in a low voice, looking around cautiously.

'Kings, Presidents, and money-launderers, sir,' she answered cheerfully, 'I have met them all. What would be the name of your one?'

'No matter,' muttered Mr. Lundie quickly. 'No matter at all. I made a mistake. Now see, here are Fiona and Jean come to greet us!'

Two young women emerged arm in arm from a house a little set back. They whispered to each other, scanning the crowd. There was a shout from a young gentleman with the brightest tightest tartanest costume of all bright tight tartan costumes. 'Jean!' he cried, his face bright with anticipation. There was a moment's hesitation and then she walked towards him. There was an audible groan from Harry Beaton, and those around him fell away at the haunted look of despair upon his face. He turned away from the road and went to sit under a birch tree.

'There, is young love not a Godly thing?' said Mr. Lundie, gazing fondly upon the happy scene. 'That's young Charlie Chisholm Dalrymple and his fair wife Jean. I married them only the other day.'

Meanwhile, the other young woman still scanned the crowd. It was noticeable to all that Tommy Albright was lingering at the back of the crowd, on the opposite side to the woman. 'Tommy!' she cried

Brigadoon Revisits

at last, 'are you there? Tommy?' There was a note of fear and despair in her voice, so clear that Mr. Lundie stopped in his tracks and turned to seek out Tommy Albright.

'Mr. Albright, sir!' he commanded, 'Fiona is calling for you. Go to her, man, or feel the wrath of the Righteous God!'

Showing surprise that was clearly feigned, Tommy emerged from the crowd and strolled over to the woman named Fiona. She stood with eyes lowered. He took her hand and said something quietly to her. She did not look up. Slowly, silently, they moved along with the crowd. Jeff Douglas stood and watched the pair for several moments, an expression on his face that was three parts anger and one of pity.

'And are these two also married?' asked Nana, always with a nose for trouble.

'Alas, yes,' was all that Mr. Lundie would say, in a quiet and terrible voice. He remained silent for a lengthy period. 'Now,' he said at length, 'here we are in MacConnachy Square.'

Mr. Newcombe and Miss Visitor looked. It was not obviously a square; Miss Visitor opined that Chemnitz had far grander squares, better-paved than this. My Dear God, even Zwickau is completely grander! Here was merely a wide path, some uneven ground sloping up to the hill, cleared of undergrowth, and it looked to be well-trodden by the feet of women and men and the hooves of cattle. A number of market-stalls, as yet bare, stood around rather forlornly. However, in one corner, one stall was occupied and, as soon as the procession arrived, began doing business. The boards of the stall were weighed down with three large barrels, each furnished with a tap that dripped. Charlie Dalrymple was first to serve himself from a barrel, and was soon brandishing a brimming mug to the accompaniment of a rousing drinking song. Jeff Douglas pushed in and joined him, and then a ruck of men of all ages was clustered around the stall, shouting and joking, and bawling out the chorus of the song. Charlie's wife Jean stood to one side with the other womenfolk, loyally attending the merriment. But her eyes were downcast.

Witches? We Say the Word Kind of Different.

Warren Newcombe looked on appalled at this bacchanalia. By his watch, it was barely a quarter to eight in the morning.

~ 4 ~

A Murderer and An Adulterer

'You see, Mr. Newcombe, it is all the fault of Mr. Forsyth,' said Harry Beaton, one hand clutching a half-empty whisky bottle and the other wrapped around the collar of Warren's safety-jacket. Harry's eyes did not leave the jacket - the sheer brilliance of its lime-green luminescence fascinated him.

Jeff sighed and shook his head. 'Hey, buddy,' he grumbled, 'this man doesn't want to know about Forsyth. He doesn't care. Why should he care? Do you, buddy? The world has no interest in Mr. Forsyth.'

Warren looked from one man to the other, not knowing what to answer. Harry looked the stronger of the two men, but Jeff the angrier. It was a hard choice. He shook his head doubtfully in the hope that the action would be interpreted charitably. His forlorn hope was not favoured. Jeff snorted and took another drink from his own bottle. Harry glowered.

'If you know nothing about Mr. Forsyth, man,' said the invalid, 'then you know nothing about Brigadoon.' He jerked his head towards Jeff. 'Don't you listen to that man. He's a murderer and an adulterer, and what he thinks of Mr. Forsyth, God rest his soul wherever it might be, is of no value.'

'Sure, sure,' said Jeff wearily, rolling his eyes. 'And don't you listen to this wash-out, buddy - he's just sore that he didn't get his girl. Give it a rest, Harry.'

A Murderer and An Adulterer

'I'll give it a rest when I die,' said Harry. His voice was cracked and bitter. 'It won't be soon enough.' He eased his throat with some more whisky. His attention wandered as he looked over at the crowd of drinkers, amongst whom Nana Visitor was a figure of much attention, not least because she seemed able to put down one tankard of beer after another, without the slightest impairment. Warren attempted to use this moment of Harry's distraction to ease himself out of the vice-like grip. Harry immediately turned, grabbed the arm again and looked Warren in the eye.

'Let me tell you about Mr. Forsyth, sir,' he said in a low voice. 'And after you have heard about Mr. Forsyth and have considered his unforgivable actions, you may debate with Mr. Douglas here on what it is right and proper that the world should know.'

The three men sat on a rustic wooden bench in front of one of the cottages. Warren was positioned in the middle, with Harry to his right and Jeff to his left. Hamish's dog lay some three feet in front of them, its eyes fixed upon Warren, almost certainly with the intention of lunging with bared teeth at the first sign of independent thought: it was an excellent sheepdog. The boy Hamish, Warren noted uneasily, was nowhere to be seen.

'It was in the year 1754,' began Harry, 'that Mr. Forsyth determined that the wide world was too dangerous for the likes of us defenceless and naïve villagers. Mr. Forsyth was our minister, you see,' he explained to Warren, 'you will understand that, of course?'

Warren nodded hastily, keeping his eyes on the dog. The beast growled in a predatory manner.

'Mr. Forsyth had his correspondents in the wider world of Scotland, and kept his ear close to the ground. He was known to receive certain journals from high-minded men in Edinburgh, you see.'

Jeff muttered a blasphemy and shook his head sadly. Harry ignored him.

'Witches, Mr. Newcombe, sir,' whispered Harry. 'That's what Mr. Forsyth had heard about. Witches were rampaging through the land and imperilling the very souls of all whom they came across. The cities of Edinburgh and Stirling had already fallen under their evil sway. St Andrews and Aberdeen would surely follow suit. Every Godly man throughout the land was urged to protect his flock from those terrible hordes of women. Mr. Forsyth was hard put to it to conceal his trepidation from us. He confided only in Mr. Lundie there.' Harry waved a hand in the direction of the elderly gentleman who was smiling upon the morning celebrations which continued not a dozen yards from where Harry and Warren sat.

'And Mr. Lundie is - ?' asked Warren, anxious to understand some of the social mechanics here.

'- an old fool.' Jeff whipped in this judgement before Harry could enlighten the visitor.

'Mr. Lundie,' said Harry Beaton, as if his companion had not spoken, 'is our dominie.'

'Dominie?' queried Warren, no more enlightened.

'The schoolmaster,' explained Harry. 'A man of considerable learning. It is said that he studied in St Andrews.'

'Mr. Lundie says that,' commented Jeff. 'Mr. Lundie can say what he wants, of course, because there's not one fellow in this whole village who can contradict him. Mr. Lundie could state that he studied at Harvard, and no one would be able to argue. Mr. Lundie could tell us all that he wrote the Encyclopaedia Britannica and this lot would nod like the wise men. It's like that round here, buddy,' he advised Warren. Jeff took another drink from the bottle, his second of the day: the bottle was practically empty. He eyed the level critically and looked up at the sun, which was coming over the hill. He muttered something to himself, got up and left.

'At last,' said Harry with some satisfaction, 'the man leaves us alone.' He gazed after Jeff's shambling figure as it headed towards the general melee around the beer barrels. 'That man shot me from a tree. With a musket. He made me the cripple I am now. That is the kind of man you see there, sir!' He gripped Warren's arm more tightly for a few moments until Jeff disappeared into the crowd, where his arrival seemed to generate another burst of merriment and laughter. 'What would you do if you had to live in close company with the man who almost killed you, mistaking you for a grouse? What would you do, man?'

A Murderer and An Adulterer

Warren paused long enough for Harry to forget the question.

'Mr. Forsyth determined that he would save Brigadoon and all who lived within it from the witches. It was, he advised Mr. Lundie, his duty as our pastor. His holy task. Accordingly, so Mr. Lundie tells us, Mr. Forsyth went out upon the ben yonder.' Harry paused to point out to the north; there was no mountain in sight. He stopped in confusion. He looked around. 'The ben there,' he repeated. Warren looked around as well. There was a line of low hills some distance to the north. Harry's shoulders sagged. 'Every time,' he said obscurely, 'every time we wake up, the mountains and the lochs have moved around. It's enough to drive a man to drink.' He drank accordingly, then thrust the bottle upon Warren.

'Thank you, no,' said the engineer nervously, 'I'd rather not - this time of the morning - very kind - but thank you.'

'Drink,' commanded Harry, with a look in his eyes that was filled with darkness.

Warren drank, coughed and choked; his eyes filled with tears. Harry smiled upon his discomfort.

'Mr. Forsyth,' he resumed, 'went up the hill on Tuesday, and prayed loudly and passionately to God, asking the Good Lord that the village of Brigadoon and all of Mr. Forsyth's flock who lived here be hidden from the view of all men, women and witches, so that they would remain safe until the danger of the witches should pass. And God granted this one virtuous request, allowing only that the village should re-appear every hundred years for one day only. And as Mr. Forsyth finished his prayer, so the village vanished, the village to him, and he to us.'

There was a long pause, as Harry considered the wondrous ways of the Lord God Almighty, and drank a little to ease the burden of knowledge.

'Mr. Beaton,' ventured Warren at length, 'if Mr. Forsyth was cut off so suddenly from the village, then how - ?'

'- then how do we know what he prayed for and how do we know what the Good Lord commanded?' Another voice completed Warren's question.

Warren Newcombe turned and saw Mr. Lundie standing close by.

Mr. Lundie settled himself down on Warren's left side, and made himself comfortable. He breathed in deeply , closed his eyes and smiled to himself.

'Oh, what a beautiful morning, is it not, lads?' he enquired of his companions on the bench.

Warren nodded as enthusiastically as he was able; Harry Beaton brooded.

'Well now, Mr. - Newcombe, is it? - well now, Mr. Newcombe, many have asked that question and there is only one possible answer. Only one.' He paused, possibly for effect. The sounds of the villagers breaking their fast filled the air. 'The reason we know that Mr. Forsyth sacrificed himself for us, and that the Good Lord answered his prayer and preserved us, is quite simply that Mr. Forsyth confided his intentions to me, his friend and fellow-spirit, just before he went up yonder hill. He discussed with me what he would pray for, and we argued - oh yes, I tell you, I am not ashamed to say that we argued. At first I opposed his plan, stating my opinion that God would preserve Brigadoon from the marauding witches by His own means, and we had no need to hide away; but Mr. Forsyth countered this with many and valid quotations from the Bible and from the opinions of the much enlightened and respected Ebenezer Erskine, of whose sermons Mr. Forsyth possessed more than one handy volume. At last I was obliged to yield to my brother's greater knowledge and wisdom. And when he did not return and when we awoke on the following day, one hundred years further on, I knew that Mr. Forsyth's voice had reached God's ears.' Mr. Lundie paused again, to lift his eyes to the blue sky.

'It is not my belief,' put in Harry, 'that God has ears for the likes of us in Brigadoon.'

'Now, why do you say that, Harry lad?' asked Mr. Lundie reproachfully.

'Why? Why, since I have been begging, these past few days, for God to release us from this prison and to let us live our own lives again, free to move, free to stay in the world for more than a day at a time!' Harry Beaton struck one fist into his other hand. 'Is that too much for a Christian to ask, Mr. Lundie?'

A Murderer and An Adulterer

The dominie shook his head sadly. 'You always were an intractable lad, Harry. But you must not let your present affliction govern your head. God, you know, will always look out for us, providing we are not sinners. You are not a sinner, are you, Harry?'

Harry made no reply. Warren began to fidget, wishing he could go back over the small hump-back bridge and call in for advice. He glanced furtively at his watch. It was just coming up to eight. Too early still for Head Office.

'And we know, do we not,' continued Mr. Lundie, now launched into his favourite topic of conversation, 'the disciplines that God has set upon Brigadoon, and the commandments which we must not break? There is no question, Harry, that we do know them.' The old gentleman was quite certain of this. 'Firstly, that our village will remain concealed from the view of the world for a hundred years at a time, appearing only for one day once a hundred years has elapsed. Secondly -'

'God appears to have broken that commandment all by himself,' observed Harry, pointing his now-empty whisky bottle at the schoolmaster. 'Where does that leave us?'

'Secondly,' continued Mr. Lundie as if Harry had not spoken, 'that no person who lives in the village will be permitted to leave. Not one. Not ever. For if one person leaves, the village will be hidden away for eternity. And that would be - for what reason, Harry?' The dominie looked meaningfully at young Harry, forgetting perhaps that he was no longer in the schoolroom, and that Harry was not longer a boy in short trousers.

Harry sighed. 'Of course, Mr. Lundie: no one may be permitted to leave in case that person reveals the secret of Brigadoon. To the witches.'

'Quite right, Harry,' confirmed Mr. Lundie placidly. 'You have learned your lesson well. Thirdly,' he continued, 'that no person in the village is permitted to regret or speak out against the great sacrifice which Mr. Forsyth made for us all.'

Harry looked up sharply. 'That is never a commandment that I have heard before, Mr. Lundie.'

'Is it not, Harry?' asked the dominie quietly. 'Well, perhaps you were not listening so well. Perhaps you were more interested in your whisky bottle?'

Harry stood up, and tucked the empty whisky bottle in the belt of his tight-fitting black trousers. He expressed the opinion that the works of Mr. Forsyth had been short-sighted, that his actions had been unforgivable, and that God had no business making prisoners of innocent people for all eternity. And then he limped off in the direction of the drinkers.

Mr. Lundie laid his hand upon Warren's sleeve and shook his head. 'The poor lad has never recovered from being shot that night by Mr. Douglas. A sad case, indeed. Mr. Douglas had come to hunt the grouse, you see. At the time we thought that he had slain young Harry, but that was fortunately not the case. Harry, however, has been a man broken in thought and dreams and morals ever since. It is hard for the rest of us to bear.'

Newcombe looked after the shambling figure of Harry and wondered how best to make his excuses to the old gentleman. 'Well,' he began, 'it's time I was getting off.' He made a move to stand up, but found himself held down by a surprisingly strong pressure from Mr. Lundie's arm.

'Well, of course you must go, sir,' said the old man, 'but first I must explain to you just what Harry meant by suggesting that God had broken His own rule. It was decreed, as you will remember, that Brigadoon should vanish for one hundred years at a time, reappearing only for one day at the end of each period. Thus, the village came out of the mists in 1854 and again in 1954 - that would be Thursday and Friday to us, Mr. Newcombe, since we sleep the sleep of the just in between times. We go to bed in one century, and wake up, quite refreshed in the next.' He turned to Warren suddenly. 'Do you sleep well, sir?'

Warren could not well answer this question, and hesitated. His silence appeared not to matter.

'Because, you see, God made allowance for Love. With love, anything is possible. When Mr. Albright there - you see him, don't you?' Mr. Lundie indicated Tommy Albright who was in the thick of the merrymakers, singing his heart out and tap-dancing energetically. 'Mr. Albright fell in love with young Fiona Campbell -' again he paused and pointed her out, a young woman standing on her own in the shade of a tree, giving every appearance of being the unhappiest young woman in the world, '- and came back from over the sea - from America, New York, he said it was - to marry her. And for that reason, God allowed the village to reappear and take in Mr. Albright. That was twice then, in 1954, and very happy days they were.'

'Well, that's all very nice, Mr. Lundie,' said Warren, making to stand up once more, 'but I really do have to go.'

Mr. Lundie's arm pinned Warren down. There was no fighting the power in the schoolmaster's arm.

'However,' continued the old man, 'even I cannot explain why God permitted the mists to roll back and the sun to shine on us on so many occasions since then. Mr. Newcombe,' he murmured quietly, looking around suspiciously, 'would you believe me if I told you that Brigadoon has appeared no fewer than six times since 1954?' He paused for effect. 'Six! That's almost one week, when we should have been asleep. Oh, let me tell you, it gets so tiring! So tiring. When you get to my age, Mr. Newcombe, you need a rest, you do not need to be continually waking up and finding yourself on the threshold of some godless modern country!'

Mr. Lundie paused. 'Godless - like your country, sir. Like your country!'

~ 5 ~

Democrats All

'*Prosit !*, and to your health!' laughed Nana Visitor, as she returned the wishes of good health and long life offered to her by the early morning drinkers. She downed a tankard of heather ale with no apparent signs of discomfort or distaste, although it was quite certain that this was one of the worst alcoholic drinks she had been offered since arriving on the British shore; and she had, as her daily reports to her stupid editor witnessed, been offered some completely insulting beers and spirits already. She intended writing up a report for the travel supplement of the *Chemnitzer Nachrichtenspiegel* on her return. A short series, perhaps, on the worst of English and Scottish hospitality. No, make that a long series already. She had notes enough. It mattered not that her experience of native German hospitality was no better; she had once developed a thesis that the legends of werewolves and vampires were no more than a city journalist's appreciation of the horrors of rural hospitality beyond the city walls. Her editor had spiked that particular story, citing likely problems with the notoriously thin-skinned Saxon Tourist Board.

What she was now obliged to drink, in the cause of investigative journalism, would be the highpoint of the series. It was like herbal medicine, unadulterated; but she doubted it would have any beneficial effect. And yet, none of the people around her seemed to mind the taste. The men, in particular, seemed fascinated by the appearance of so strong a woman in their midst, and stared at her with naked longing. One or two of the more eager ones nudged up alongside her, smiling like idiots.

'And for which side,' she asked, during a lengthy pause in the conversation, 'did the village make its vote yesterday?'

There was a blank silence at this. The men looked at each other, puzzled beyond measure.

'In the Referendum,' said Nana encouragingly. This explanation fared no better.

'The Referendum for an Independent Scotland. *Ja*, you must know already, voting for "Yes" or for "No".'

There was a general look of confusion. The men muttered to each other; the women were scandalised. Some backs were turned.

At last Jeff Douglas came over to the visitor. 'These jerks,' he advised in a low voice, 'don't know anything about referendums or elections. Voting? No way, José.'

Nana was appalled. 'Not to vote?' she exclaimed. 'But they must do it. Did they spoil their ballot-papers, or have they simply not turned out to vote? Tell me, Mr. Douglas, what does it mean?'

'Hell, ma'am, who cares anyway?' replied Jeff. 'Look at them - what do they know? Would you want them voting alongside you? Like hell you would, if I may say so.'

'There have been far worse than that voting alongside me,' replied Nana confidently. 'You, my friend, have never voted in rural Germany!'

'And you, lady, have never voted in the Bronx,' countered Jeff. 'Listen, lady, I'm a Democrat, through and through. Tommy there, he leans the other way. But the two of us, we're like regular Commies, compared with these guys. I tell you, when Tommy announced he was a Republican, they practically strung him up. Would have lynched him if I hadn't have stepped in. Not that a Democrat sounded any better to them - so I told them I was a Royalist. What's the difference, anyway?' Jeff paused for a short slug from his third bottle of the day. 'No, lady, there's no way you want any of these queuing up to vote. Anyways.' he added, 'they didn't get any voting papers.'

Nana was silent for several moments. She looked narrowly at Jeff. Her heart had missed a beat. The journalist buried deep within her awoke. She put down her drink and took Jeff by the collar.

'You say therefore,' she said very quietly, 'that they have never received any voting papers.'

'That's right, lady,' said Jeff cheerfully. 'Someone got that right, didn't they?'

'And these are citizens of Scotland?'

'Right.'

'And in age over 16 years?'

'Right.'

'And not in prison?'

'Right again. Some of them should be in prison, is my view, but no - not one of them just now.'

'Not lunatics?'

Jeff paused for thought. This one required more consideration, he felt. 'No,' he said at last, 'not strictly speaking lunatics. Close to it.'

'In Scotland,' asked Nana, 'is it possible for lunatics to vote?'

Jeff did not know. 'But in the States, sure. Every lunatic gets a vote. Casts it for the Republicans, most times.'

Nana looked around slowly. '*Na ja*,' she agreed, 'they cannot all be lunatics. But possibly that one over there?' She pointed out a man with the wildest look in his eyes, who was engaged in violent argument with a hen.

Jeff looked and shook his head. 'Right as rain, that one,' he stated. 'Would vote Democrat and Republican both, twice over, given half a chance.'

'But no one gave them even one whole chance?' repeated Nana.

'Like I told you, lady,' confirmed Jeff. 'And the world's all the better for it.'

'But you have never received voting papers either?' asked Nana Visitor in a dark tone. 'Neither you nor Mr. Albright?'

'Hell, no, ma'am,' sighed Jeff, who was growing tired of all this political talk. 'We're not citizens of this great and plucky little country. We don't get no vote, no sir. Not even Tommy, who is married to a native. God help him. No taxation and no representation,' he joked. 'Not since 1776.'

Nana Visitor smiled. But it was not at the feeble American witticism, the pricked conscience of an Imperialist. She did not even hear it. She was thinking of other things now.

Much to her disgust, the great Scottish Independence Referendum had ended in stalemate: over the entire country, a margin of merely 33 votes divided the "Yes" from the "No". And that's discounting the people who didn't turn out to vote, and those who did but spoiled their ballot-paper – same number again, give or take a thousand. So the Corridors of Power had been alive with scuttling headless chickens this past week. Neither side accepted defeat. Votes already counted and locked away were turfed out on the tables and counted again, and again, to try to swing a result. Any result. Nana just wanted to get home, but her editor refused point-blank. A stickler for procedure himself, he greatly admired the processes of government.

But now... here was a place where not one of a hundred or so villagers, maybe more, had been permitted to vote. And Nana Visitor had unearthed this. She saw now before her a glittering winter's evening in Dresden, even - yes, why not? - Berlin. The fanciest hotel, a swarm of Germany's finest, cameras and microphones. The prizes for Journalist of the Year were being handed out. And she, Nana Visitor, was first in line. Best Investigative Journalist. Most Influential Story of the Year. Best-Dressed Colleague, if she could fit in some shopping down in London. Her editor would have to give her decent salary now. And maybe even a desk of her own. Not bad for a girl from Germelshausen.

~ 6 ~

Foreigners - in Edinburgh !

'Yes, Bob, that's right. A village. No. Yes. Yes, houses, not tents. No. Well, you can come and see to for yourself if - . No, I'm not. Yes. No. About a hundred people. Yes. No. No. That's not the sound of a pub, Bob, that's -. No. No. No. Yes, I know it's eight o'clock - I've been here since -. Listen, I tell you, I'm looking at them now, Bob. Look, I'll send you a picture. No. Yes. OK.'

Warren Newcombe felt his blood pressure rising as he folded up his mobile-phone. All right, so the story he had to tell was not likely to sound very credible. But to suggest he was playing some kind of practical joke, or was drunk at this time in the morning, was an insult to his professional integrity.

It was unfortunate that the only place he could get a proper signal for the phone was right in the midst of the early-morning revellers, on the market-cross beside the two fast-emptying beer-barrels, where, of course, the noise was loudest. And his attempts to phone proved fascinating for everyone around.

'Yon man's talking to the fairies!' was the general consensus. All of them peered closely at Warren, speaking to him, asking him questions, however much he signed to them to give him a moment's peace.

'It'll not be the fairies,' said Hamish in a panic, 'it'll be the witches! The man's speaking to the witches!' he cried, sending various other children, and not a few adults, scattering in dismay, shawls and caps being pulled tightly over their heads.

Once Warren had finished his brief report to Head Office, he surreptitiously took a couple of photographs of the village, making sure that he had at least one shot featuring, in the distant background, the first major intersection of the Peripheral Route at Cleanhill, the place where the Fastlink from the south would join the road from Charleston. Then he sent them on to Bob Tucker, who would doubtless scoff and send some kind of scathing text-message back. Well, let him try. There would no doubt be some other phone-calls to Head Office now - he could see a crowd of workmen up on the ridge, peering down upon the scene with some signs of interest and unaccustomed liveliness.

'And what would that thing be?' demanded Charlie Chisholm Dalrymple, accosting Warren and poking at the phone.

'It's a phone,' said Warren, recoiling from the stench of beer on Charlie's breath.

'A fawn?' repeated Charlie, much astonished.

'A faun?' demanded Mr. Lundie, drawing back. 'Are you in correspondence, then, with the Reverend Robert Kirk, he who consorted regularly with the fairies?'

Warren shook his head as many times as he felt was necessary.

Tommy Albright came to his rescue. 'A phone, Mr. Newcombe? Some kind of radio-phone, like we used in the war? That'll be,' he explained to the thronging crowds, 'a fine little instrument for talking to someone at a great distance.' The villagers looked blank. 'We had them in New York,' he explained further. Faces, previously clouded, now cleared. A general sigh of understanding went up, and more beer was drunk.

'But it's a very small instrument, Mr. Newcombe,' Tommy continued politely. 'What year did you say we were now in?'

'2014.'

'Well, that would explain it, I guess,' said Tommy. 'Say,' he said conversationally, 'how about a beer?'

Warren shook his head. It had only just gone half-past eight in the morning.

Brigadoon Revisits

'Aw,' said Tommy, disappointed, 'don't be like that. One small beer - can't do you any harm. Listen, friend, I thought the same when I first came here but not any more. You get used to it.'

'And when did you first come here?' asked Warren, anxious to divert the conversation away from alcohol.

'That'd be 1954 - May 28, 1954. Came here with Jeff to do some hunting. Grouse, you know. Didn't find the grouse. Found the village. Thought I'd fallen in love with a girl. Came back in September. Found the village again. Married the girl.' Here Tommy stopped short, and peered into his tankard. 'I'll get you that drink. Don't go away.'

Warren had learned politeness from his parents, good training for the Diplomatic Service, they said. He had never been able to un-learn it. He stayed until Tommy returned. Warren was pleased to note that Tommy had fetched only the one beer, and it was for the American himself.

'1954 - that was,' Tommy thought for a moment and counted rapidly across his fingers, 'that was seven days ago. Strange how time drags here in Brigadoon, Mr. Newcombe, very strange indeed. Mr. Lundie thinks differently. But he's an old man now. You want to know what we've seen and where we've been in the past fortnight?'

Warren did not, but was too polite to say so.

Tommy Albright put his drink to one side, fetched out the fingers of his left hand, and began to count them off.

'Friday - that was when I first came here. Saturday - that was when I came back. Sunday - now where was that?' Tommy paused for thought. 'Oh yes, that was in 1984, March sometime. We ended up in some backwoods mining-town. Bang on top of a coal-mine. No one working though. Mr. Lundie was real put out by that. Quietest place in the world, I reckon. Didn't see a soul at that pit. What kind of mining town was that, I ask you?' Tommy shook his head at the lack of get up and go in Scotland. Then he turned to Warren and grabbed his sleeve urgently.

'You ever have a disturbed night, buddy? You know, when you wake up and can't get back to sleep, and then before you know it you find you've woken up again and it's still pitch black?'

Warren concede he'd had a few of those, particularly in recent weeks.

'Me too,' said Tommy. 'But mine went on for months and years at a time. It sure wears you down.' He shrugged. 'Where was I? Monday?' He frowned 'Oh, Monday, that was a good one.' Tommy laughed. He called out to two passers-by. 'Johnny, Donald, you remember last Monday?'

The pair fairly cackled and whooped, and gleefully saluted with their morning drinks.

'Turned out it was New Year's Eve in 1999,' explained Tommy enthusiastically. 'Millennium. Never thought I'd live to see the day. Never saw so many happy people in all my life. I've never seen such a good time, I tell you! We had a real party in the village that night. And slap bang in the middle of Glasgow we were. Ever been to Glasgow, Warren? Fine, fine place. Fine people, too. They didn't bat an eyelid at finding us.' Tommy shook his head in admiration. Then his face clouded. He looked around.

'You ever been married, Mr. Newcombe?' he asked.

Warren admitted that he had, once.

'Divorced, then? asked Tommy in a low voice.

Warren admitted this also.

'She get to spying on you, did she?' Tommy did not wait for the answer. 'That night in Glasgow, that's when I began to regret what I'd done. The little woman - that's her over there,' he slid his eyes furtively to the right, where Fiona was standing, sadly surveying the scene - 'she wanted me to come home to bed when the party was just getting started. Told her I'd come to bed when the sun came up. She burst into tears. Never saw her again for eight years.'

'Eight years?' asked Warren, much astonished.

'Wish it had been,' said Tommy. 'But eight years - that was just the next morning, wasn't it? Hell of a place, this Brigadoon.

'Tuesday,' continued Tommy, still counting the days and years out on his fingers. He paused, looking confused. 'Tuesday?' He looked enquiringly at Charlie.

'If it's Tuesday,' said Charlie, 'it must have been Dundee.'

'Oh, excellent!' exclaimed Warren with some enthusiasm. He had a soft spot for Dundee. No one ever could understand that, even the labourers and technicians who came from there. They did not know, of course, of a weekend that Warren had once spent there, while still married, in the company of - .

His guilty reminiscences were interrupted.

'Sure, sure,' said Tommy doubtfully. 'Got there in the middle of some kind of national festival of thanksgiving. I tell you, buddy - parties and machinery, that's what seems to wake us up. But mostly parties. This one had fairgrounds, dancing in the streets, fireworks.'

'Aye, it was a wild do,' confirmed Charlie, some of his usual high spirits returning. He put away the knife again.

'National celebration of three hundred years of - what was it again, Charlie?'

'The famous Act of Union, Tommy!' replied Charlie instantly. 'The Act of Union – grand day for the country,!' He toasted his unconscious "Yes" vote with a swig from his tankard.

Tommy shrugged. 'Like the Boston Tea-Party in reverse,' he explained. 'Party night all over again. The folks were overjoyed. Pleased to see us, sure. And that's about it, I guess. Have I got it about right, Charlie?' Tommy looked to Charlie for confirmation.

Charlie looked oddly at Tommy. 'You're forgetting yesterday and the day before that,' he advised.

Tommy brushed away the suggestion airily. 'No matter,' he said. 'Anyway, got to get on - things to do. Can't be idle. Nice meeting you, Mr. Newcombe.'

Tommy turned away quickly and strode off; it was noticeable that his wife did not follow him, just stood still and watched him go. Warren was left in the company of Charlie Chisholm Dalrymple and his rather conspicuous tight trousers.

'Got problems with his wife,' said Charlie in a low voice. 'Fiona's a fine lass, so she is, but she and Tommy aren't getting on at all. Yesterday - .' He paused. 'Are you a married man, sir?' he asked confidentially.

Warren gave the same reply as before, wishing now he'd simply run for it. There were things he really did not want to know. Half the villagers seemed to have marital problems. He did not want the burden of knowing about it. It made him depressed. People should move on.

'Day before yesterday, Mr. Newcombe,' continued Charlie, 'we found ourselves in yet another God-forsaken year in another God-forsaken place. Mr. Forsyth, for all that he was a decent man - .' He stopped abruptly and looked at the ground. 'There now, I should not say these things. What's done is done. Wednesday we awoke to find ourselves in Edinburgh. Have you been to Edinburgh, Mr. Newcombe, at all?'

Warren confirmed that he had.

'Well, nothing much has changed there in two hundred years and more, that's what Mr. Lundie told us.'

Warren raised his eyebrows in perplexity. Clearly, the villagers had not come across that timeless monument to civil engineering, the excellent tram-works of Edinburgh.

'We woke up to find ourselves in the middle of a grand crowd. A huge crowd, man! Hundreds and thousands. Everyone in Scotland, I would say. Very big crowd indeed. All dressed up in finery - all the tartans, all the clans. The pipes, the drums. A big banner that told us they were getting ready for a "Homecoming Festival". Well, we had a good look round, but could never find out who was coming home. But we fitted in just nicely, which is always a grand thing, don't you find?'

Warren agreed with that.

'Some of the more genteel people of Edinburgh talked to Mr. Lundie and made an offer of some sort. What was it now?' Charlie furrowed his brow. 'Now I remember - it was a "Residency" that they offered him, that was it. What is a Residency, sir?'

Warren thought twice before replying. The implications of such an offer might be too much for young Mr. Dalrymple to bear: to see his village treated as an entertainment? No, that would not help at all. He therefore shook his head and said he could not imagine what it was.

Not discouraged, Charlie bent his head close to the engineer's ear. 'There were many foreigners there, Mr. Newcombe.' He pulled his head back abruptly, the better to study Warren's expression of dismay. He was disappointed.

'Really?' asked Warren. 'Foreigners? In Edinburgh?' He tried to look astonished.

Charlie nodded his head vigorously. 'Many of them,' he confirmed, almost salaciously. 'But here's the thing, Mr. Newcombe. I will ask you not to talk about this to anyone. Here's the thing - Tommy Albright spent two whole days in the company of some Americans. To be precise, some American women! From New York. Very beautiful women they were too.'

Warren could now see the problem. He frowned. 'So Tommy's wife - ' He hesitated.

'Fiona,' prompted Charlie.

'- Fiona was not very pleased, I would guess?'

'Heartbroken, Mr. Newcombe. Quite heartbroken. She stayed indoors all the time, and my own dear wife Bonnie Jean tells me that Fiona did not stop her sobbing for a moment. Of course, it's not been right between them for many years now.'

'Would that be years, or days?' asked Warren, trying to clarify the matter.

'Well, both, I suppose.' Charlie frowned. 'No matter - there was no doubt that the pair of them were madly in love last Friday. Saturday even. But Tommy's been cooling off, and Fiona - poor girl - she doesn't know what to do for the best. Tommy doesn't go out gathering heather with her, he doesn't even dance with her any more! Can you believe that?'

Charlie pondered the horrible state of Tommy and Fiona's marriage. And then he pondered something closer to home.

'You know, Mr. Newcombe,' he said, 'marriage is a peculiar thing. Bonnie Jean - that's Fiona's younger sister - she and I got married a week ago now. The twenty-fourth day of May. It was Mr. Lundie who married us, because poor Mr. Forsyth, he was dead and gone by then.'

'So I heard.' Warren remembered the sacrifice of Mr. Forsyth.

'We got married, and then, of course, Harry Beaton, the fool, tried to run away from the village, which would have locked us all away in darkness for the rest of eternity, and then poor Harry was shot by Mr. Douglas, a tragic mistake, and we all thought he was dead. But he wasn't dead at all, only badly wounded, and never able to walk properly again. Bonnie Jean, she takes it very hard. Blames herself, Mr. Newcombe. Tells me that if she had not spurned Harry and married me instead, then Harry would be the same bright, strong young fellow as he always was. And all the days of our life together have been lived in the shadow of that dreadful accident. Then there was Edinburgh!' Charlie's face expressed a deep hurt and sadness. 'Look at her, Mr. Newcombe!' He pointed to the far side of MacConnachy Square where young Jean, his wife, was watching the rest of the village. At her side stood another young woman, her face half-hidden in a shawl. At Charlie's gesture, Jean acknowledged him, a brief single wave. Energetically, Charlie waved back, but already Jean had turned away from him, looking for someone else. 'The pair of them,' muttered Charlie Dalrymple. 'Two sad sisters. Oh, there's a curse indeed upon Brigadoon!' said Charlie boldly. 'I don't know that I can forgive Mr. Forsyth his prayers, I don't think I can.'

At last, Charlie subsided into silence. He drank the dregs of his beer, adjusted his skin-tight tartan trousers which were clearly pinching his buttocks, and headed without another word back to the beer-barrel.

Warren Newcombe saw his chance, and he took it swiftly. He headed for the hump-backed bridge. He glanced at his watch: it was close on nine o'clock. Nothing yet on his mobile-phone - Tucker was obviously busy on some vastly more important matter. A village blocking the path of the Peripheral Route? - that could wait until after the daily management meeting.

No one appeared to notice his departure. At long last, the drinking-party had begun to break up as, in groups of three or four, the men and women of the village danced off - Warren had to look twice: yes, they were dancing, and singing as they went, here and there someone playing a fiddle or the pipes - danced off on their business. From all parts of the village, carts and trestle-tables and baskets of bread, vegetables and other foodstuffs were now arriving. It looked as if some kind of market was being set up. Cattle and sheep mingled with the crowd, while dogs and hens and children agitated..

But as he placed one foot on the leading ramp of the bridge, Warren felt a hand come down hard on his shoulder. The breath went out of him. Lundie had doubtless caught him again. He turned around slowly.

It was Nana Visitor, beaming upon him.

'Well, Newcombe,' she said happily, 'here is a completely strange situation, is this not true?'

Warren agreed. 'I'm just going back to see what Head Office thinks we should do,' he said.

'Head Office?' echoed Nana, looking puzzled. 'They can do nothing. It is clear that your road cannot go straight through the village.' She paused and looked doubtfully at him. 'Or can it?' For a brief moment, she saw a new opportunity arising, which would further her nascent career as campaigning journalist: small but delightful village bulldozed in the path of black tarmacadam Capitalism and the interests of road-hauliers; hundreds evicted from their homes and forced into urban squalor; destruction of a beauty-spot; desecration of Scottish historical monuments – it was Storybook Glen she had in mind. And then she could take it one step further - the fate of eastern Germany as reflected in the mirror of Scotland.

'No, no,' agreed Warren. 'There's no way that can happen.' He, too, paused for thought. Or can it? Much as he found the village untidy, even he could not envisage taking the road through it. They would have to build some kind of bridge or fly-over. Maybe something truly graceful for once, like they sometimes did on the continent - in France or Switzerland. Yes, he could suggest that.

'I must absolutely find a phone, Newcombe,' said Nana in a determined voice. 'I have to speak to that *Arschloch*, my editor; but first must I speak to the authorities here already. Show me a phone, immediately.' She pushed Warren forward and together they crossed the bridge at a fast pace. As they reached the other side, Warren looked back, almost fearfully, remembering what Mr. Lundie had said. He was at first greatly relieved, and then slightly annoyed, that the village did not suddenly vanish. It persisted, busy in its own affairs; the sounds of singing and the clattering of mugs came over the small river to his ears.

'Authorities?' he asked Nana. 'I think it's best that I deal with them,' he advised, rather undiplomatically.

She snorted, and slapped him on the back. 'No, that you will not do, dammit. You deal with your fat-cat boss because of the road. I have totally more important things to discuss. Believe me, my affair has nothing to do with your little road. Not yet, not yet.' She strode forwards, up the hill towards a cluster of Portakabins which formed the command-centre of the Cleanhill construction site. Warren picked up his pace and hurried after her. He could see an ever-growing crowd of workers and supervisors staring down the hill towards them - and no doubt past them.

Nana, in the meantime, had advanced upon a group of navvies and threatened them with unaccustomed intimacy if they did not, immediately, find her a telephone. Immediately cowed by her manner and size, three or four of them offered up their mobiles; she selected the smallest and shiniest of them, embraced the young owner energetically, and took herself off to one side to make some calls.

'What's going on, Warren?' asked one of his colleagues as, breathing heavily, he crested the top of the hill.

Warren tried to keep his explanation simple. But he fought a losing battle against the general scepticism. One or two bolder souls suggested he had been smoking weed with the hippies down there. And then, in the middle of all this, against all expectation, Bob Tucker turned up, his huge and shiny four-door 'Warrior' pickup screeching to a halt right beside Nana. Nana reacted swiftly and gave the monster a mighty kick, demanding some silence. Tucker the Tearless – as his colleagues lovingly named him, playing a curious game with the fricative and the alveolar - Tucker recoiled slightly and took a detour around the angry journalist who peppered him with quaint rural German threats against his manhood.

'What the fuck is going on, Newcombe?' he demanded, from twenty paces. 'What's all this shit you're feeding me? I had to leave the management meeting early because of you. Who's that bloody

Brigadoon Revisits

woman back there, and what's she doing on the site? What kind of shithouse are you running here, Newcombe? This had better be good! You've got ten seconds to convince me!'

In desperation, knowing that words and thoughts cut no ice with Bob Tucker, Warren simply pointed down the hill to where the village of Brigadoon lay peacefully under the thin columns of smoke from thirty or forty chimneys.

~ 7 ~

Etymologies

'Yes, Mrs. Commissioner, that is correct. A whole village. Naturally, houses, not tents. No. Listen to me, if you cannot be bothered - . No, I certainly do not. Yes, of course. No. About one hundred adults, possibly more. No. Not one single one. No. No. No. Naturally I know it's only nine o'clock - I am here already since -. Listen, my dear woman, I will file this story with my newspaper directly after this call, so perhaps it is best that you -.   OK. And goodbye to you already.'

Nana Visitor broke the connection and glared at the borrowed phone. The young men who had offered their services stood around, at a respectful distance, looking worried. Nana consulted with them.

'What is it you say,' she enquired, 'when someone in authority tries to give you total shit? You say he is a wanker, yes? This woman is a wanker.'

The young men nodded, but doubtfully. That, in their shared experience, was certainly the word for a man - but a woman? They fell into a huddle, urgently debating the correct use of the English language.

Nana let them get on with it and fell into deep thought. After some difficulty, she had tracked down the number for the Electoral Commission, and got its local representative out of her bed - some capitalistic hotel in Aberdeen no doubt. The fool had at first refused to accept the call, and only when the magic words 'failure to register electors' were uttered did she deign to listen to Nana. Even then she had found it highly unlikely, highly unlikely, Miss Visitor, that an entire village, which I've never even heard of, should have been forgotten about. It was Nana's mention of her newspaper, *Der Spiegel*, that finally spurred the woman into action. OK, *ja*, so she had omitted to mention that this was the *Chemnitzer Nachrichtenspiegel*, produced thrice-weekly in a town the Electoral Commissioner would not have believed in - but perhaps she should have said it was Karl-Marx-Stadt: that would have stirred her up, *jawohl!!* Wanker, thought Nana with some satisfaction at her grasp of English. Perhaps she could, after her elevation to Journalist of the Year, seek a long-term posting to London? Her English would improve in bounds and jumps. And London was full of shops, clubs, more shops, and cosmopolitan men.

Close by, the peripheral men had not yet found a satisfactory solution to the problem of female definitions. Nana handed back the phone to its owner, who barely glanced at her, so fierce was the semantic argument. She had her own phone, which her cheapskate editor had had configured so that she could receive incoming calls, but make outgoing calls only to him. Her friend Sydney Guilaroff had offered to fix it, but when he found that it was of an obscure Bulgarian make, which admitted no standard SIM cards, he had sulked instead. She took the beige-coloured brute of a phone from her bag and prepared to give the Fool of Chemnitz the shock of his life. She smiled as she pressed the requisite Cyrillic buttons.

Meanwhile, at a very comfortable hotel in Aberdeen, Jane Ashton, international expert on matters relating to electoral cock-ups, sighed and shook her head. That woman on the phone had disturbed her from a very pleasant breakfast in bed. The limey Electoral Commission had called her in from a well-deserved weekend in Madrid at short notice, to help sort out their screw-up. So she had set to and sorted it for them. Were they grateful? Not that she'd seen so far. But her work, she had supposed, was all done here, once these guys got their fingers out of their asses and did the final recount. How difficult could it be? It was rumoured that some jerk had brought in Criminal Psychologists to second-guess which way the ballot-spoilers would have voted. That back-fired, big time: there were 34 more "No"-spoilers than "Yes"-spoilers. Jane Ashton had spent four days knocking heads together, up and down the country, teaching them some basic math and common-sense. Now it was time to relax, maybe some photo-opportunities with the great and the good, and also with the Lord Provost of Aberdeen, or, worse case, Donald Trump, and then she could file her report and head back for a peaceful few days walking her dog beside the river in upstate New York. She'd done some castles and done some shopping, and that about covered Scotland. Next month, she was due in Damascus, which was much the same again, if a bit warmer. But a girl had to take the rough with the smooth, and Peripatetic Fixer with the International Independent Electoral Commission was not such a bad life.

And now this. What was that woman babbling about? A village with a hundred people in it who neither had the vote nor had heard about the Scottish Independence Referendum? Not possible. What was the name she'd mentioned? Brigadoon? Sounded unlikely, very unlikely. She took out her mobile and summoned her aide.

'Tuttle,' she asked innocently, 'would you step in here?'

Will Tuttle took all of twenty seconds to knock on the door and enter. He looked, damn him, neat and tidy and well-rested. Will was thirty but looked about ten years younger. Jane was fifty and, without her makeup, seemed about ten years older.

'Good morning, Jane,' he said pleasantly. 'Sleep well?'

She stiffened. "Ms. Ashton to you.' The boy was getting too sassy for his own good. 'Tuttle,' she shot out, 'what do you know about a place named Brigadoon?'

Will frowned. Then he thumbed through something on his Blackberry. 'Ah,' he said at last, 'that would be Brig o' Don, I expect. Small community on the outskirts of Aberdeen. No irregularities reported there at all, I'm pleased to say. Very well-organised. Sixty-seven percent turnout yesterday. Perfectly average for Scotland in general, according to the latest figures.'

'Bridge of Don?' asked Jane Ashton frowning. 'Not Brigadoon?'

Brigadoon Revisits

'Probably the same place, I'd say,' confirmed Will, who had made a small study of Scottish place-names and their provenance before coming up to Aberdeen. A man who wanted to shoot to the top had to have all the facts at his disposal. 'Corruption and assimilation over the years.'

'Corruption? Show me,' ordered Jane. She went over to a large table in the sitting-room of her suite and stood over a map of the North-East of Scotland. Will sauntered across and immediately placed a finger upon Bridge of Don just at the top of Aberdeen City. 'That's the place.'

Ms. Ashton shook her head. 'I took a phone-call just now. Alleging a major procedural flaw. Some woman who claimed this village was out west somewhere. Near - where was it - Maryculter?'

Will pointed to a completely different place on the map. 'Maryculter - that's there. Not far from Peterculter, I think you'll find. And Culter House and the village of Cults. All good stuff, huh?'

'You can tell me later about Satanic cults, Tuttle. Just now, I'm not real interested. Where's Brigadoon?'

Will bent over languidly and studied the map with some care. Finally he straightened up. 'No such place,' he advised. 'Must be some kind of hoax.'

Jane Ashton shook her head thoughtfully. 'Can't afford to treat it as some kind of hoax,' she said. 'Our job is to investigate everything thoroughly, if only to eliminate all possible doubt. I'm not having anyone take pot-shots at our integrity. Not on my watch!'

Will failed to suppress a groan. He saw a long day ahead of him now. Why did these nutters have to come up with the really out-of-the-way places for investigation? This place looked to be miles out in the countryside. Miles from a decent hotel.

Jane Ashton shot him a sharp look. 'Mr. Tuttle,' she said severely, 'let me remind you about this Referendum. It's your country, not mine. I should not have to tell you anything at all. Or do you need a refresher on your duties?'

Will groaned, but inwardly this time. He paid attention. Ms. Ashton was not one to cross. He knew that. She knew that. You did not get to chair an International Electoral Commission in the home of democracy without having some balls. Or the female equivalent. Will's spirit temporarily joined the huddle of navvies up at Storybook Glen, speculating on etymological matters.

'Are you paying attention, Mr. Tuttle?' demanded Jane, watching him. Will jerked himself back to the present. 'Right now I'm going to ask you six questions, Tuttle. See if you can come up with six straight answers.'

Will nodded forcefully. He had no fear of questions - he always had the answers.

'One: what kind of Referendum was that last week?'

'The Referendum on Scottish Independence, as per the Act of Scottish Parliament, March 2013, to decide whether Scotland should be an independent country.'

'Correct. Two: who the hell gives a shit?'

'Every citizen of Scotland, every citizen of the United Kingdom, and most of the governments of Europe as well.'

'Not bad, Tuttle. You forgot the US President. Three: what was the outcome?'

'As of last Saturday, the vote was split evenly between the "Yes" and the "No". Thirty-three more "Yes" than "No".'

'Good going. Four: who's complaining?'

'The UK Government claims a statistical dead-heat, the Scottish Government claims a statutory victory, the US President calls for an investigation, half of Europe is getting twitchy.'

'Nearly there, Tuttle. Five: how does this get resolved?'

'Recounts and more recounts, Ms. Ashton. Third one on-going as we speak.'

'Six, then: how would an extra hundred uncounted votes swing this? Taking cognisance of that phone-call that got me out of bed?'

Tuttle didn't even bother answering. He just pouted.

'So, Tuttle: what we gotta do?' asked Ms. Ashton in her best low-life New Yorker twang.

'We must investigate,' said Will Tuttle, trying his best to look professional. He failed miserably.

Brigadoon Revisits

'OK – in one sentence. Just so as an airhead like me can understand, you appreciate?'

'Certainly, Ms. Ashton.' Will took a moment to compose himself. 'We have been apprised of a possible voting irregularity that affects the overall outcome of one of the most significant votes in the UK in the past three hundred years. An official and independent investigation must take place immediately.'

Jane Ashton applauded laboriously. 'Well done, William Tuttle. I think we're on the same page now. So, what do we do?'

'We get ourselves the hell out there,' said Will, trying his utmost to sound business-like.

His superior shook her head. 'You forgot something,' she prompted.

Will mentally scoured the procedures. And then: 'We advise the top levels of government, call Stateside, and then we get ourselves the hell out there.'

Jane Ashton now dismissed him with a wave of her hand. 'Get the car organised, Tuttle. I'm going to finish my breakfast and I desperately need a shower. Then I'll make three phone-calls. Twenty minutes, downstairs !'

~ 8 ~

Mr. Ebenezer Erskine and the Anti-Burgher Party

Mr. Lundie sat apart on his bench in his little garden above the cottage, looking at the fading daffodils of which he was so proud, a veritable golden cloud of them across what had once been a heather-filled hillside. He was pleased with his garden. It gave him comfort. Perhaps not surprisingly, God had remembered the flowers when he sent Brigadoon to sleep, and not a single bulb had been lost over - what was it now - two hundred and five and fifty years? Not one bulb, but -

'Mice.'

The Good Lord God, reflected Mr. Lundie privately, had unquestionably forgotten one detail. When He had sent the village to sleep for one hundred years at a time, He kindly thought to send all cats and dogs and sheep and cattle and hens and geese and flowers to sleep at the same time, knowing how attached men and women are to their pets and their animals. It was well done. But He forgot the mice, with the result that, having no cats awake to keep them down, the mice had grown fruitful and had multiplied beyond reasonable measure. And in the long nights had caused havoc to papers and sacks of grain and, indeed, almost anything that could be chewed or nibbled. All the schoolbooks that Mr. Lundie possessed had long since vanished. Even Ebenezer Erskine's Sermons had been consumed. It was, he supposed stoically as befitted a Christian schoolmaster, a small price to pay for eternal protection from the outside world.

Mr. Lundie now prayed loudly three times a day, hoping that God would hear his small, and not ungrateful, prayer that the mice should also sleep.

Mr. Lundie was very tired. He was in his seventies now, a time when a man began to think more urgently of his own mortality, and when, in times otherwise ordered, he should be looking forward to his daffodils and a rocking-chair. In these past nights, all eight of them since Mr. Forsyth slipped out beyond Brigadoon, Mr. Lundie had slept badly. Not that he not slept the full eight hours, or one century, which God had provided for sleep; it was just that he dreamed dreams and heard voices in his sleep. Strange voices, disturbing voices. He could hear the words, but they had no meaning for him, as if he was in a foreign Godless land. What he could hear, echoing through the black nights, were without question the voices of the worlds passing by, rolling by on the wheels of the years. He had spoken about the voices to Sandy Macmillan, who, in his youth, had travelled over the sea, but Sandy could shed no light on the matter. He had spoken to Tommy Albright, as a man who understood the modern world outside, but Tommy had shaken his head and was not at all helpful. That young man had fooled Mr. Lundie, had fooled poor Fiona too, by the looks of things. What sort of love could burgeon in an afternoon? Fiona had been carried away on the emotions of Bonnie Jean's Wedding Day, no doubt, and Tommy - a nice enough young man, in comparison with that hardened sinner, Jeff Douglas - he had thought he was in love. But it was not to be. Mr. Lundie saw that now.

'Witches.'

Mr. Lundie thought back a week or so, to the far-gone days of 1754, when old Mr. Forsyth had first heard of the bands of witches that were marauding across the land. Mr. Forsyth had received a letter from the close followers of Mr. Ebenezer Erskine, the most reverend and evangelical man of his time, as was proclaimed without contradiction across the land, the founder of the Associate Presbytery

Mr. Ebenezer Erskine and the Anti-Burgher Party

and the father of the Secession Church. Not to mention, laughed Mr. Forsyth, in a light-hearted moment, father of fifteen children. It seemed, sadly, that Mr. Ebenezer Erskine was close to death. Mr. Forsyth was a little in the dark about the recent schism between the Burgher and Anti-Burgher parties in the Secession Church, but felt that, as Mr. Erskine was the Professor of Theology of the Burghers, that was where his own heart lay. What was more important in these dangerous times, said he, was to avoid the witches who, stealing down upon a small, defenceless village such as Brigadoon, would tempt the unwary into perdition and cast the innocent into the fiery pit of eternal damnation. Mr. Forsyth was very strong on witches. Very strong indeed. So, Mr. Lundie supposed, was God. But not so strong on mice.

On each awakening since that fateful May day in 1754, Mr. Lundie had endeavoured to find out more about the Secession Church and whether perhaps there might have been a place among the saints of that Church for Mr. Forsyth. He knew that the old minister would have disdained - perhaps even condemned - the elevation of one man over another in the matter of saintliness - but Mr. Lundie did not see it that way. However, when the village had emerged out of night again in the year 1854, they had fallen in with a crowd of labourers constructing a "railway" between Selkirk and Galashiels. Mr. Lundie could not begin to imagine what a "railway" might be, but he was not keen to have it laid down across his village. Among these uncouth men full of alcohol was one who had spun a malicious and unlikely tale of further schisms and contradictory re-unions between Churches with as many different names that Mr. Lundie fair took a headache: Auld Lichts, New Lichts, the Relief Church, the United Original Secession Church, the United Secession Church, the Great Disruption (this was not a Church, but some fanciful cataclysm spawned by the old tramp's corrupted and oozing mind), the Free Church - the list went on and on. At last Mr. Lundie ran out of patience with this man, gave him a lecture on sobriety and chased him on his way. The vagabond had left, but not without raining down curses upon the skinflint village and all its people. Curses, Mr. Lundie knew, that could have no effect upon a village such as Brigadoon.

Brigadoon Revisits

In all of that, not a word of Mr. Forsyth. In the several awakenings that had come and gone since then, there had been no one suitable to ask. Certainly, the two Americans had not heard of anyone of that name. Mr. Lundie feared greatly that, like the schoolbooks, the name of their great saviour was lost in dust and the bellies of mice.

'Mice.'

That American, Jeff Douglas, had had some good ideas about how to rid the village of the mice. Said he had worked for a man in New York whose sole business was the destruction of pests. 'Roaches, rats and women,' stated Mr. Douglas, 'the three greatest pests in a modern city. I've got rid of all three in my time. No trouble at all, Mr. Lundie.' The dominie could not tell how much of this to believe, how much to put down as malevolent fantasy born of the man's ill-humour and fondness for drink. But he urged Mr. Douglas to apply his skills to the plague in hand, and the man had, to his credit, lazily obliged. Gone about it quietly, and without fuss. Recruited Harry Beaton, and James Macdonald, the dairyman's son, to assist. The three were to be seen about their business on several occasions and, sure enough, the depredations of the mice had been greatly reduced.

'Could do the same for the witches, if you'd like, Mr. Lundie,' offered Jeff. But it was already two hundred years too late.

'Witches.'

How was it, thought Mr. Lundie for the hundredth time since 1754, that the village was tossed the length and breadth of Scotland, like some shipwreck in the cruel hands of the seas? Hurled now this way, now that, fetching up against some hidden rock and breaking open in some new age, where all was different, even the very hills and paths and burns. It made no sense. He had not seen his beloved Loch Arrol in many a tumultuous day. Nor the Old Kirk Road. Would he ever see them again? This, surely, was not what Mr. Forsyth had intended. Was it, in fact, witches who played this trick in Brigadoon?

'Witches.'

And why, thought Mr. Lundie for the hundredth time since 1754, why did the village awaken so often? First it was every hundred years;

Mr. Ebenezer Erskine and the Anti-Burgher Party

then, at first glance, it was for Love - oh, but how false was that love of Tommy Albright! And the next few times it awoke to terrible scenes of dancing, intoxication and fornication. Ah, these were sad, wicked shores upon which they had been thrown!

As he sat and brooded this morning upon mice, witches and the Hedonistic ways of the Modern World, the old schoolmaster saw the sad sisters, Jean and Fiona Campbell - now Fiona Albright and Jean Dalrymple, of course - walking arm in arm up the path towards his cottage. He brightened up. It was one of his only pleasures to sit in the company of the Campbell sisters, of whom there were at least eight, all as pretty as their dear departed mother, and to converse with them on matters of so little consequence that they delighted the hearts of young women and lightened the heart of an old man.

'Come along in!' shouted Mr. Lundie, welcoming the two girls into his little garden. 'Come in and spend a few minutes with a lonely old man.'

Fiona and Jean came in and sat upon the rustic bench.

'Ah!' said the old gentleman in a mock tone of chastisement that had so often before caused fits of merry laughter, 'are the two of you playing truant? Should you not be at home, making the breakfast for your men, and the bread and the soup for their dinners, and cleaning the house and washing the clothes? Are you perchance undutiful wives?' He beamed at them.

Fiona looked up. 'I could not care any more, Mr. Lundie. There is little purpose in making a home. It is over for me,' she added bitterly.

Jean looked a her sister and patted her hand. 'I do not care any more either, Mr. Lundie. The world might as well end today.' She fell silent, the two young wives studying their hands, as they lay in their laps.

Mr. Lundie was quite astonished. He sat down suddenly on an upturned bucket and loosened his collar.

'My, my! Are you teasing me?' he asked, without much hope. 'You two girls - I know you from times past. You are making fun of an old man.'

The two women raised their eyes slowly and said in one voice. 'We are beyond teasing.'

There was a heavy silence for several minutes. Once or twice, Jean dabbed her eyes with a very small handkerchief. Once or twice she dabbed the eyes of her older sister. A mouse scuttled in the undergrowth. Mr. Lundie ignored it.

'You poor, poor girls,' he said at last. 'What has caused you to come to this? Tell me about it - perhaps I can help?'

'There is nothing you can do to help, Mr. Lundie,' said Fiona in a low, broken voice. 'It is Tommy.'

'And for me it is poor Harry,' confessed Bonnie Jean.

There was no point in asking. The dominie knew precisely what the trouble was - Tommy and the sudden death of his eternal love; and poor Harry with his wasted legs, an injury that had been caused - yes - by Jeff Douglas, but had its roots in his thwarted love for Jean.

'Poor Charlie,' said Jean. 'He loves me so much and yet I cannot be his.'

'Poor Tommy,' said Fiona. 'He gave up his life for me and now he cannot abide me.'

'Men,' said both the women sadly.

The depth of their charity caused Mr. Lundie's heart to flutter. It was not a good feeling. He took several deep breaths. The girls had cast down their eyes again and did not notice his discomfort.

'But you are married to them,' he managed to say at last. 'I joined your hands myself, and while I am not the minister, we all know that the ceremony of joining hands and declaring your love has made you, in the eyes of the world, wives of good, decent men.' He paused, realising suddenly that his words sounded hollow.

'Yes, we are married to our husbands, for better or for worse,' conceded Jean. 'But we cannot love them as they deserve, and for that reason we can find no reason to look after our houses.'

'But it is your duty!' exclaimed Mr. Lundie. 'It is your duty as wives, whether you will have it or not!'

Jean shook her head. 'Not this week,' she replied firmly. 'It seems that the world has moved on in two hundred years, and women are no longer required to be slaves in the home. We have our own lives to lead, and if we cannot love our men, or if they cannot love us, then

Mr. Ebenezer Erskine and the Anti-Burgher Party

we need not be their servants. We have learned that from some of the outsiders.'

'Especially on Thursday,' confirmed Fiona. 'Yesterday.'

Mr. Lundie thought desperately. Thursday - that must have been Glasgow. No, where was it? Edinburgh. Aye, Edinburgh: dear God, such a wicked place ! And they had seemed such fine people too, all dressed up in their finery.

'And men?' he asked. 'What of men in this brave new world?'

'Men may do as they wish,' said Fiona, 'that is of no concern to women.'

The old gentleman groaned. All at once, the walls of stone which Mr. Forsyth had built up around his flock had come tumbling down.

'It is the witches,' he said firmly. The two sisters looked up and round about, startled.

'The witches have already entered the village of Brigadoon. They have stolen away the souls, and thrown over the shining light of love. And now they are sucking dry the very blood of the village.' Mr. Lundie stood up suddenly, staring down upon the roofs of the cottages below him. 'Oh, when did this start, I wonder, when did this start?' He smote his breast in despair.

But he already knew the answer. He had been keeping it low in his mind for several days: the trouble had started in 1754.

Mr. Forsyth had been too late. The witches were already coiled up like adders in the workings of the universe, like the Serpent in the Garden of Eden, and they could not be removed, however much a man - or God Himself - tried.

~ 9 ~

Mr. MacReekie's New-plucked Fowl

'Have you seen,' whispered Mrs. Maclaren to Mrs. Macdonald as the pair strolled, around the market in MacConnachy Square, weighed down by baskets of shopping, 'have you seen the size of Malcolm MacReekie's what-have-you?'

Jessie Macdonald sighed. 'Not since August 1740,' she admitted. 'It will be much smaller now, I expect?'

'No, Jessie, not that,' replied her companion primly, 'I was referring to Mr. MacReekie's new-plucked fowl.'

'But so was I !' protested Jessie blushing furiously. 'Whatever did you think?'

'Ah well,' said Mrs. Maclaren conceding nothing, just delighted that she had reminded Jessie of a youthful misdemeanour. 'You come along with me and we'll examine it closely. It's a monster!' She steered Jessie in the direction of Mr. MacReekie's stall, where, every Friday from nine o'clock, he was pleased to offer for sale plucked chickens and the occasional duck, grouse or pheasant, according to season. The two ladies had to fight their way through the usual troupe of whirling costermongers, drysalters, haberdashers, confectioners and layabouts, who, by tradition, danced their way around the market before the serious business of selling their goods got under way. Business had been slow of late, ever since Brigadoon

Mr. MacReekie's New-plucked Fowl

had been concealed from the eyes of the world. There was little passing trade and no trade at all with neighbouring settlements. The tinkers and travelling salesmen and neighbours were no more. All that remained for the merchants of Brigadoon was to trade goods with each other.

There was a fair press of on-lookers in front of Mr. MacReekie's stall, and, even from a distance, a sense of awe and wonderment. Whereas, around other stalls, there were either raised voices or no one at all, here a large and generally silent crowd had gathered. And no wonder: the stall comprised a small board normally lightly loaded with the corpses of a thin hen or two, and a perfunctory strip of cloth to shade the dead from the effects of sun and rain. Today however, there was nothing on the board except the enormous corpse of a plucked monster. The thing was the size of a boulder. Malcolm MacReekie in his younger days had been a man of considerable strength and, on certain days of the year, had demonstrated this by lifting from their beds hefty rocks around which most men could barely reach their arms. This bird was of that girth. And the flimsy board which MacReekie used to display his wares was visibly bending under its weight.

It was noticeable, too, that MacReekie's wife, the once-flighty and now-high-and-mighty Catriona, sported a new hat. To the unaccustomed eye, the feathers were astonishing in size, magnificent in sheen, incredible in colour. The gathered women, all covered in shawls of varying size, colour and quality, were of the opinion that it was much like the crown of some fabulous queen. Catriona MacReekie shared that opinion and revelled in it. She paraded up and down behind the stall, while her husband Malcolm gazed in considerable satisfaction upon the sensation of the hour.

'What kind of a bird is that?' asked one brave soul at last.

'That'll be the biggest and strangest bird you ever saw, most like?' asked MacReekie in his turn, well satisfied with the way the day was proceeding.

There was a general murmuring of confirmation, and then the question was repeated. 'Did it come with the witches?' demanded a younger voice. It was Hamish, who had thrust himself to the front of

Brigadoon Revisits

the assembly and was now gazing at the mound of flesh, nose to parson's nose. At this suggestion, there were some dark looks cast upon Malcolm and his bird. Mrs. MacReekie was affronted.

'No such thing!' she said loudly. 'That bird is one of God's own creations. I have it on the authority of Mr. Douglas himself! The bird is an Ox-finch. Is that not correct, Mr. Douglas?'

Jeff, who was lounging at the back of the throng, topping up a hip-flask for a near-empty bottle of spirits, looked up. 'That's quite right,,' he said, 'an ostrich.' He looked around knowledgeably. 'Comes all the way from Africa.'

At this revelation, the crowd immediately split into two camps - the larger party were of the opinion that anything that came from Africa was likely to be the Devil's Own Work, for, even in 1754, the Enlightenment and all of its doings had not yet reached Brigadoon. The smaller party, keen advocates of Novelty, were simply much astonished at the bird's dimensions.

'And how,' demanded a leading member of the Godly Party, 'how the devil did that bird come to be in Brigadoon? Mr. Forsyth would never have permitted it!'

'Aye, how?' went up the supporting cry.

From the Gimmicky Party came a counter-argument. 'If God had meant that the ostrich should not reach Brigadoon, He would have struck it down. Unless you wish to deny the wisdom of the Good Lord?'

This theological argument quickly dampened down the wrath of the Godly Party and the crowd fell once more to admiring the size of the bird.

'And how much does it weigh, Malcolm?' asked one.

'I cannot tell,' replied Malcolm proudly. 'It near broke my scales this morning. However, I imagine it would feed your family for a day or two, Mr. Macafferty, should you wish to buy it.' He smiled comfortably upon his questioner, who had a wife, sixteen children, an aged father and a mother-in-law whose appetite was legendary. For all that, Mr. Macafferty was impoverished. So it was not he who wished to know the price.

Mr. MacReekie's New-plucked Fowl

'I will not take less than ten shillings,' announced MacReekie firmly. This proclamation met with a stunned silence for several seconds. And then disbelief.

'Ten shillings? For that thing, that spawn of Satan himself? Would that be the modern shillings, man?' The crowd had once more sharply divided into the Godly and the Dissidents. But this time, the Godly Party was in the great majority.

'I'll give you a shilling for it,' announced Mrs. Macdonald firmly. 'And not a penny more.'

Catriona MacReekie hooted with laughter, and tossed her head so that the vast superstructure of ostrich feathers danced dangerously. 'Oh, Jessie Macdonald,' she mocked, 'you always were a cheap lassie! Get away with you!'

Jessie Macdonald flushed with anger and would have launched a violent assault upon the proud headgear of MacReekie's dearer half, had it not been for the sudden arrival upon the scene of Nana Visitor.

'*Ha*-llo!' said she. 'Dammit again - that is one of those ostriches, is it not?' She marched through the crowd and poked a finger at the firm pink flesh.

'Please do not touch the goods on display,' ordered MacReekie, waving her hands away with his apron.

'*Ach ja*, quite right, quite right,' said Nana apologetically. 'But how did you catch this bird?' she wanted to know.

'I found, madam, five of these birds standing in my yard at the back of the cottage this morning. Bold as brass. Terrifying my hens and my dog. I managed to capture this one. The rest of them ran off.'

'Ran off?' asked a number of the crowd, now suddenly more interested in the bird than they had previously admitted. At ten shillings a bird, a hunt might be worth the effort. 'Where did they go?'

But Mr. MacReekie was not to be drawn on that matter. He studiously ignored the question. Instead, he now repeated: 'Ten shillings. I will not take a penny less. Just consider the size of it.'

One by one, most of the crowd began to drift off, grumbling, some to take to the hills with the accoutrements of fowling, others to

Brigadoon Revisits

visit the less exciting market-stalls. A small handful remained, two with the intention of driving a hard bargain with MacReekie, the rest to watch the transaction unfold: entertainment was sometimes hard to come by in Brigadoon.

Nana Visitor had come back down the hill feeling satisfied, having made her report to the Authorities and set her editor upon his head, long-distance. Although there was some time to kill before the Authorities arrived, she intended to be the one to greet them and then give them a full picture of the anomalous electoral situation. Her editor, an unrepentant graduate of the Stalinist School, had instructed her to get an interview with one of the Scottish peasantry, 'an old one, one greatly downtrodden by neo-feudalism.' She decided to humour him. Now she looked around for a likely candidate. Her eyes lighted upon an elderly man sitting on a bench next to the stall owned by Archie Beaton, tailor and purveyor of bright tartan cloths. He wore a waistcoat of startling fluorescence and looked, in his stillness, much like an advertisement-hoarding for Mr. Beaton's handiwork.

Nana the journalist approached him busily. 'Good morning, my old gentleman,' she bawled at him breezily. 'How goes it today with you?'

Mr. Campbell, the widowed father of Fiona and Jean and of several other young girls besides, almost fell off the bench in shock. 'You have no need to shout at me, you hussy,' he complained, recovering his balance. 'I am not deaf.'

'I am so sorry,' said Nana in a voice scarcely quieter. 'Is it permitted to sit with you?'

Mr. Campbell said neither yes nor no, but shuffled slightly to one side. Mr. Beaton, however, finishing with a client, turned to Nana and advised her in a loud voice that 'old Mr. Campbell was feeling a little down today, on account of his daughters.'

'Ah, the children,' said Nana sympathetically. 'Always they are a worry!'

'That is the case,' said Mr. Campbell. 'I have heard it said, but never thought to experience it with my own family. Not since my poor wife died have I had any trouble with them.'

'You have many children?' asked Nana, furtively switching on her recorder. 'Boys and girls?'

'All girls, alas,' said the old gentleman. 'Seven in all. Fiona and Jean and Mary and Margaret and Catherine and Jenny and Aphrodite.'

'Aphrodite?' exclaimed Nana.

'I named her after the Greek goddess of Love and Beauty, since reading a review in the *Caledonian Mercury* which Mr. Forsyth brought back with him from Stirling in the year of her birth.'

'And all married, sir?' asked Nana further.

'Only two,' answered Mr. Campbell unhappily.

'Perhaps it would please you to have them all married,' said the journalist soothingly.

Mr. Campbell looked at her crossly. 'Not at all, woman,' he replied. 'I would be pleased to have none of them married. Poor Jean - she is pining away in her marriage to Charlie Dalrymple, because of -' He stopped short.

Mr. Beaton finished his sentence for him. 'Aye, say it, Andrew Campbell, say it: she is pining for my own son, young Harry, on whom your daughter brought so much misery. She should not be called Jean, but Helen, I think, after yon witch of loose morality that started the War against Troy!'

'If you had any learning at all, Archie Beaton,' replied Andrew vehemently, 'you would remember that all the ancient writers tell us Helen was an innocent victim of the untameable male lust of Paris, and that she was a woman of great virtue to whom no blame may be attached!'

'A witch,' hissed Mr. Beaton once more. And when he had had his say; he turned away, wiping a tear from his eyes, to scrutinise his bolts of tartan for blemishes.

'As for Fiona,' continued Campbell after a pause, 'she is married to that no-good American fellow, Tommy Albright. Since those Americans came to Brigadoon, my life has been made miserable. Here,' he said, 'cast your eye upon this.' Pulling from his coat a crumpled piece of paper, he unfolded it and smoothed it upon his lap.

'Mice,' he said, by way of explanation.

'Mice?' echoed Nana.

'This is all that is left of my family Bible, the Good Book which my father had before me, and his father before him. Mice have eaten the rest - yea, even the Book of Job and the Book of Lamentations. A father can have no comfort in the words of those great prophets, since mice have eaten them all up.' Andrew Campbell scowled at the scrap of paper which lay before him.

At length, since the conversation appeared to have ceased, Nana thought to prompt him. She peered at the paper. 'These are therefore the names of the family-members?' she asked politely.

'Aye,' said Andrew. 'Here is the name of my father and mother. My grandmother and grandmother were just above, but are eaten away by the mice. See - here we are - myself and my dear wife Elizabeth, married on the second day of July 1719. She passed away just after the birth of Aphrodite. And these are the names of all my daughters - you will see, my dear, that the name Helen, Helen,' he repeated the name loudly, 'does not appear there. Not at all. Here, however, is Jean born on the 8th day of April 1736, who, on the 24th day of May in the year 1754, married one Charles Chisholm Dalrymple. And here is my eldest, Fiona, born on the tenth day of October in 1732, who was married to Tommy Albright on the 25th day of September 1954. Ah!' he exclaimed, crumpling the paper in a fist, 'what sadness has smitten me about my head!'

Mr. Beaton snorted loudly. 'Mr. Campbell,' said he, 'I would be grateful if you could take your body somewhere else, for you are driving away all my customers with your lamentations. Look, there is not a soul who will come near to my stall this morning!'

Mr. Campbell stood up shakily. Briskly, Nana Visitor took his arm and led him off. She had managed to take a few photographs of the sad old man. With the addition of a caption that stated: 'Elderly Scottish Peasant Laments the Lack of Democracy in the United Kingdom', one of these should greatly enhance her forthcoming series on modern life in England, Ireland, Scotland and Wales.

At that moment, her mobile-phone blasted out a few notes of the Bulgarian national anthem. The International Electoral Commission had arrived in Storybook Glen. Nana Visitor hastily abandoned her

Mr. MacReekie's New-plucked Fowl

charge and hastened to meet The Authorities. No one stood in her way - but many fell.

~ 10 ~

Is His Tadger Being Tugged?

'What the fuck's that, then?' demanded Bob Tucker, peering down the hill to the village of Brigadoon.

'That's the village I was trying to tell you about,' said Warren, getting exasperated. Tucker was no doubt a great boardroom boy, but he was both stupid and unlikeable.

'What kind of shithouse is this you're running here, Newcombe?' demanded Bob, for the second time. 'Is this site being managed or is it an effing shambles? Are you tugging my tadger? Was that village on the map?'

'No, but -'

'Was that village here yesterday?'

'No, but -'

'So it's a protest camp then,' said Bob Tucker triumphantly. 'Hippy bastards,' he elaborated for the hard-of-understanding. 'Tree-huggers. Middle-class tunnel-artists. Weekend swampies. You understand me, Newcombe?'

'Yes, but -'

'So get them cleared out of there, Newcombe, right now, and then we can get on with building the road.' Tucker glared at him, before calling a number on his mobile. 'You don't have a problem with that, do you, Newcombe? Because if you do, I can easily find myself someone who doesn't have a problem with that. Gerry - is that you?' he bawled into the mobile. 'Listen. I'm out at Cleanhill, mate. Got a

Is His Tadger Being Tugged?

bit of a problem with a protest-camp. Yes, you know - the usual? Can you, mate? Phone me back, then. Cheers!'

'Bob,' said Warren desperately, 'that's not a protest-camp. It's Brigadoon. You've got to go down and see it.'

'Don't effing Brigadoon me.' Tucker stared hard at Newcombe. 'I don't have to do nothing,' he said coldly. 'I've got eyes in my head and I see what I see from up here. And if it wasn't there yesterday, it's not going to be some kind of housing estate or nothing, is it?'

'They're from the past,' explained Newcombe. As soon as he said it, he regretted his words.

Bob weighed his words carefully. For about two seconds. 'Come with me, Newcombe,' he said icily. He led the way to the nearest Portakabin, evicted a card-party and slammed the door shut behind Newcombe.

'I'll ask you quietly one more time,' he said in a low voice. 'Are you,' his voice suddenly grew very loud indeed 'Tugging! My! Effing! Tadger!?' He slammed his fist, for added effect, down on a table, which buckled under the force. 'What's that all about - they're from the past, Bob, they're not hippies, Bob, they're just good people, Bob! No,' he said, as an afterthought, 'no, don't tell me any more. Because this is the way it is, Newcombe: if they're from the past, then we clear them out the way, because that's what road-builders did in the past, before nimby-pimby do-gooders stepped in and put as many obstacles as they could in the way of progress. And if they're not from the past, then that means they're protestors, and we just clear them out of the way, because even this nanny-state government doesn't allow tree-huggers to get in the way of progress. Sorted.' With which piece of clean and clear-cut logic, he smiled cheerily and answered his mobile.

'Gerry, that you, me old mate? What have you got for me?' Tucker listened for a moment. The smile whipped off his face like a feather in a gale. 'Christ Almighty!' he exclaimed. 'Am I surrounded by effing idiots or what, Gerry? Yes, pal, I mean you. Who else am I effing talking to? What do we keep you for? I tell you to get the effing police and the local council organised so I can shift these protestors out the way and you come back with excuses? Excuses,

Gerry? You giving me effing excuses? You on a job-share or what? Yes, I have heard of the Referendum. What's that to do with it?' Tucker listened some more, and began to kick violently at the side of the Portakabin. He listened some more again.

'OK, let's see if I understand you, Gerry,' he said at last. 'Just interrupt if I get it wrong, won't you? The Referendum went to a tie. There's a place turned up which claims it didn't vote. The eyes of the world are on this very spot, right in the middle of my road. And none of the political parties wants to authorise any action to remove these squatters because it might get picked up wrongly by the media. So they've slapped an order on us? Right so far, Gerry? What happened to the rule of law, Gerry? We just go in there and move them out, that's the rule of law - we go in and - shit! don't you effing interrupt me, pal ! - and we clear them out. They're only hippies, not OAPs, not the effing SAS or a bunch of terrorists! We don't need help and we don't need authorisation. If the police are too busy with Referendum duties, Gerry, then they're too busy to come out and intervene, isn't that right?' Bob Tucker had a smile on his face again. 'Talk to me, Gerry,' he encouraged. He listened some more to Gerry. Finally, losing patience, he shouted into the phone: 'Cut the crap, Gerry, you just effing sort out your end! Now! We're going in.' He closed the phone with a snap and strode towards the door. He flung it open and turned back to Warren. 'You going to play with yourself in here, Newcombe, or are you going to do your job out there?' He smiled significantly. 'You always have a choice.'

Warren made a move to follow Bob out into the open air. Bob always made him feel very tired. He was now striding about amongst the assembled and thus far idle workforce, unerringly pin-pointing the men who, for an extra fifty quid in their pay-packet, would readily drive bulldozers and dumper-trucks and earth-movers down the hill, into the protestors' encampment, and out the other side. Bob ignored any protests that came from certain mischief-makers amongst the labourers. He stepped inside an equipment-store and came out with an armful of pick-axe handles which he distributed amongst the non-drivers who had gathered round. Then he summoned Warren

Is His Tadger Being Tugged?

with a quick flick of his hand. Warren approached. Bob gave him a pick-axe handle, with a grin.

'You'll be in the front line, then, Newcombe?' he asked, not inviting an answer.

To his shame, Warren took the length of heavy wood without protest and went off to stand, on his own, at the crest of the hill. He looked down upon Brigadoon, contradictory thoughts chasing through his brain, one after another after another.

Meanwhile, Tucker the Tearless had set out the game-plan to his lieutenants.

'Right, lads,' he began, 'the bulldozers go in first, three of them side by side. All you men with the pickaxe handles - you ride on the dozers until they reach the bridge down there. Then you jump off and form into groups of three. Not four, not two, not even six: three. Got that?' The men nodded in a confused manner. 'In groups of three, you encourage these bastards to get off the construction site. Be polite, mind!'

Great gales of laughter. 'That's no fucking sweary-words, you cunts!' shouted one wit.

Bob smiled indulgently. 'And while you're doing that, the dozers are not to stop - not for anything, get that? Not any houses, huts, tents, trees, bushes, walls, men, women or children. And least of all for any dogs. I hate their effing dogs, I do! You get one of their mangy dogs, you get an extra five quid!' Unbridled enthusiasm from the men. 'The dozers don't stop until they reach the banks of the Dee, right? The Dee - that's the big river at the bottom of the hill, not this one half-way down. Got that?' The drivers nodded sagely. 'At the river, you turn straight round and head right back up the hill. And when you get to the top of the hill, everything should be ready for you lazy bastards to start in on the day's work. Something you've never experienced before in your lives!' A good-natured groan of protest greeted these last few words. 'Right, listen up!' continued Bob, now in his element. 'In behind the bulldozers I want those dumper-trucks causing havoc. They're fast and effing terrifying at close quarters -'

'Just like the women in Aberdeen!' shouted someone, to universal amusement.

'The ones I've met weren't even fast!' called someone else, to even greater applause.

Bob acknowledged the outburst of native wit with an indulgent smile, then continued:

' - so they're to head off any attacks from the rear and push any surviving protestors out of harm's way into the trees. The dumpers and the men on foot are to remain on the site for an hour, to make sure none of the bastards tries creeping back.' He paused and then lied: 'The police are on their way as backup.'

'All understood?' he demanded, looking around keenly. There was a general shout of comprehension and Tucker raised his arm as for a cavalry charge. He had seen it done in all those amazing films. The motors of the dozers and the dumpers blasted into life, sending clouds of smoke into the sky and bringing down a flock of passing crows. The noise was deafening. General Tucker leaped aboard one of the huge bulldozers and pointed the way forward. The machinery and men began to move down the slope.

At which point, a large body of people emerged from the trees which screened off Storybook Glen, and began marching across the field towards the hump-backed bridge. At the head of the procession, a woman struggling in heels and a man in a suit, closely followed by people with cameras, microphones, a straggle of skinny girls, and, bringing up the rear, a phalanx of police officers in Hi-vis jackets.

'Shit!' exclaimed Bob Tucker, his voice audible even above the noise of the heavy plant. 'Shit shit shit shit shit!' He waved his arms angrily to signal a halt. Dozers and dumper-trucks lurched and stopped dead. Men who had been clinging on to the larger machines were tossed to the ground, from which they arose to swear profusely and lay into each other with their pickaxe handles. Warren Newcombe breathed a sigh of relief and climbed down from his perch behind the driver of one of the dozers. He made his way to Bob Tucker's side.

Is His Tadger Being Tugged?

'What the fuck's that, Newcombe?' demanded Bob, one more time, his face bright red with rage.

'I think it's the police -' began Warren hesitantly.

'I don't want to know what you to think - I can see what it effing is!' screamed Bob Tucker. 'Get that moron Gerry on the phone. Now!'

~ 11 ~

The Italian Government Never Lasts Long

'Will,' said Jane Ashton in a puzzled manner, as he swerved his vehicle into the Storybook Glen car-park.
 'Ms. Ashton?' he replied distractedly. Much to his surprise, his Satnav had brought him thus far, but now he was disappointed to see no sign of life. Was this whole thing a hoax after all? He had tweeted to his followers just as soon as Jane had dismissed him from her presence, and had advised the world that there was likely some major scandal brewing. 'Watch this space!' he warned them all, 'this could be The Big One for me!' He had tweeted again just as they set off, while his boss was loading all her briefcases into the back of the hire-car. And he would tweet again, just as soon as he knew anything more. Will was a man who liked to keep his profile high, and he commanded a respectable following on Twitter. "Referendum Nation" they called themselves, in honour of Will's current project. Saddos, thought Tuttle, disloyally. More importantly, he was also gathering a sizeable following amongst the media people. This was good.
 'Now, how do we think the press and the TV get hold of this so fast?' Ms. Ashton murmured. She peered out the back window. Will looked in his mirror: sure enough, they were now being trailed into the empty car-park by a host of cars and vans; three of the vans had

enormous satellite dishes on the roof. Bringing up the rear were a half-dozen police-cars. Will shrugged.

'No idea, Jane,' he said honestly. 'Maybe your informant went public?'

'Maybe so, maybe so. But she promised me she wouldn't,' said Ms. Ashton. 'Well, that's disappointing. Still, the police are here as well - I think we'll need them one way or another. It's not looking promising - but we'd better check, for the sake of democracy.' She looked again at Will, suspicion in her clear blue eyes. 'Are you sure you know nothing about this media circus?'

'No idea how they got on to this one, Jane,' he replied, coasting to a halt in front of the entrance-booth. As Jane unbuckled herself and climbed out of the car, ready to face down the media - all part of the job - he sent one last tweet: 'Not looking promising. There's nutters as well as whistle-blowers in this job. But got to check them all for the sake of democracy.'

'Not looking too promising, then, Ms. Ashton?' called out a man in a suit, striding towards her, hotly pursued by a man with a camera. 'Well, you've got to check them all, I suppose, for the sake of democracy. We'll do an interview with you, whatever the outcome!'

Jane Ashton stopped dead and looked at the man, hard. 'Alan Jay,' she said. 'I might have guessed. You're all over this shambles, aren't you, like a rat at a dumpster?'

'Like a maggot,' agreed the man, smiling suavely. 'Got to feed the news to the people, 24/7. So, Jane, what's this then? Possible glitch in the whole proceedings, I hear?'

'And how exactly did you hear, Mr. Jay?' the Electoral Commissioner wanted to know. All the other cars and vans had disgorged reporters and camera-men, and these hastened towards the centre of the car-park where Jay and Ashton stood staring at each other, she with undisguised hostility, he with charm and patience. The police sauntered up at length, watching warily for trouble.

'Got to keep my sources secret, Ms. Ashton. You know that.' He winked at her, and then turned to the camera-man. 'You getting this, Eddie? - we'll maybe do a short intro now and then see what develops.'

Jane Ashton turned on her heel and collected Will Tuttle from the car. 'Let's go and find my informant, Tuttle,' she said, sounding tired. 'If she's wasting our time, I'll have her arrested. And if not, we got work to do before this bunch stick their mikes up our asses.' She marched past the ticket-office into the arena of Storybook Glen. As she proceeded, she used her mobile. 'Miss Visitor?' she demanded in her most officious of tones. 'The International Electoral Commission has arrived. We have no time to waste.' She listened for a moment, then hung up, saying nothing more.

Will Tuttle caught up with her, doing his best to appear to be keeping the media at arm's length. 'Contact made?' he enquired. Ms. Ashton nodded distractedly. Will looked over his shoulder and winked elaborately to Alan Jay and his colleagues of the press and TV.

'We're to meet her at Cinderella's Coach,' added his boss in a low voice. 'If this is a wind-up, I'll have that woman lynched in the centre of Orlando, Florida, so help me. You see Cinderella's Coach, Tuttle?'

Will looked about him - at the Fairytale Castle, the Giant Pumpkin, the Seven Dwarves and their Miners' Cottage. 'Is that the one?' he said at last, indicating a pink conveyance half-way up the hill. His knowledge of Disney films was shaky at best, but he knew a magic coach when he saw it.

'Doubtless,' said Ms. Ashton, directing her steps towards it. Her high heels clicked in a business-like manner on the path. Will used the moment to send a further tweet: 'Heading into fairyland. Is this what democracy's all about?'

Will, Ms. Ashton and Nana Visitor all reached the Coach at the same moment. Will stared at Nana, aghast at her bulk. Close behind him the assembled Fourth Estate clicked and hummed. Alan Jay muttered into a microphone; his camera-man kept on filming. Whatever happened today, there was prize-winning footage to be shot, to sweep the Annual Awards: it did not matter which category.

'Ms. Ashton?' said Nana Visitor, holding out a firm hand for shaking.

The Italian Government Never Lasts Long

The representative of International Independent Electoral Commission shook the hand. 'Now, show me what you've got, and then we'll talk.'

Nana glanced over Ms. Ashton's head. '*Scheisse* ! You have brought the press with!' she said accusingly. 'They should not be here.'

'Indeed,' agreed Ms. Ashton. 'I wonder who called them up?' she said, looking hard at Miss Visitor. 'They're here now,' she continued, 'so we'll just have to live with it. All of us. Now, let's move, shall we?'

Nana Visitor moved, leading the whole group through the trees and on to the muddy field that had, only the day before, been the first few tentative metres of the Aberdeen Western Peripheral Route. She led them steadily towards the hump-backed bridge, where a crowd of people were already standing on the far side, staring in eager and colourful anticipation.

'Oh hell,' grumbled Ms. Ashton, losing one of her heels in the mud. 'I got these in Rome.'

'Never mind,' consoled Will, 'the Italian Government never lasts long.'

At last they arrived at the bridge. The police had made a rapid flanking movement, overtaken the Electoral Commissioner, and now formed a guard of honour for her crossing. On the far side, several officers were pushing back the crowd. Falling back before this assault, the villagers listened intently to a small boy dressed in a kilt, and began muttering, lowering their eyes and surreptitiously making the sign of the cross.

At the top of the bridge, Ms. Ashton stopped. She gazed around, taking in the people, the houses and the smell of peat-smoke. She could see straight away that this was no temporary encampment. If there was indeed mischief afoot, this looked like The Big One. She said so to Will Tuttle. Will Tuttle turned to one side to tweet. Moments later all the journalists brightened up considerably.

'Who's in charge here?' she asked Nana. 'I want to get a clear picture of what's going on. Can you find me someone?'

Brigadoon Revisits

With remarkable restraint, Nana led the way to Mr. Lundie's cottage, saying not a word to anyone. Behind them, the villagers, the police officers and the press and TV crews intermingled, with much astonishment on all sides.

Mr. Lundie was settled on his bench, deep in introspection. He shook his head and muttered to himself. His two young companions had long since gone away, and were seated indoors in Jean's cottage, eating chocolate, a delicacy whose magical powers of healing they had discovered on Thursday.

'Ah, Mr. Forsyth, Mr. Forsyth,' muttered Thessalonius Lundie, 'your Christian sacrifice came too late, for we are over-run by mice and witches, and none can save us now.' As he expressed this great truth, he looked up, and saw, coming towards him, the visitor and a woman dressed all in black. Startled, he stood up suddenly, missed his footing and fell to the ground. Nana rushed to pick him up. As he was being raised from the dust, he peered up at the new arrival. 'And who is this?' he asked Nana.

'Mr. Lundie,' said Nana kindly, 'do not frighten yourself. This is a lady from America who means you no harm. She wishes only to help you.'

'How am I to know that?' asked Mr. Lundie, now that all the old certainties had been swept away by a torrent of unknowing. 'Perhaps she is a witch?'

'Now then: Mr. Lundie, is it?' said Ms. Ashton. She knew how to turn on the charm. 'I am so pleased to meet you, sir. Won't you sit down - we'll be far more comfortable, I think. Tuttle,' she hissed to her aide, 'start recording this - no mistakes. Now, Mr. Lundie, what a lovely garden you have here. Do you look after it yourself?'

The old dominie looked at her blankly.

'The garden,' said Ms. Ashton more loudly, 'a very fine one! All your own work?'

'Aye, thank you,' said Mr. Lundie at last. 'It is and it is. And your name would be what, I am wondering?'

'Jane Ashton,' she replied. 'My friends call me Jane.' She smiled brightly.

The Italian Government Never Lasts Long

'And you would be an American?' he asked, taking note of her accent.

'I am indeed, Mr. Lundie, all the way from the Big Apple.'

He looked astounded. 'The Big Apple? Am I to believe, woman, that there is a place named after the fruit that tempted Adam and Eve? What manner of place is that?'

Ms. Ashton was beginning to lose what patience she had mustered after a long week and a longer night. 'I am from New York, Mr. Lundie, New York.'

'Ah,' said the schoolmaster, his brow clearing. 'The place my father liked to call New Amsterdam. But I have moved with the times, Miss Ashton, and I know all about New York - Queen's and Brooklyn and the New York Yankees. Now,' he said, more at ease, 'how can I help you?'

The Electoral Commissioner sighed with relief, and took out a notebook and pen. Mr. Lundie studied the instruments of writing with great interest.

'Mr. Lundie, sir,' she began.

'My, that is a very fine quill pen you have there, Miss Ashton,' interrupted Mr. Lundie. 'May I see it?' He held out his hand.

Miss Ashton's patience now snapped. 'No, Mr. Lundie, not at the moment, please. I need to use this pen to write down your answers to some very important questions. Very important questions indeed, sir.' She looked at the old man under a heavy brow. Mr. Lundie took the hint.

'It is a pity,' he said, sighing, 'that you have come a few days too late to put these questions to Mr. Forsyth. A pity, indeed.'

'Mr. Forsyth?' asked Ms. Ashton, puzzled. 'Who is Mr. Forsyth?'

'He has left us now, my good lady - but he was a man of deep learning. Anything that you wish to know about God, or Christianity or the Bible - he would answer. And his answer would be a great comfort.'

'My questions are not about God or the Bible, Mr. Lundie,' she said firmly. Will Tuttle tweeted furiously.

'But I understood you that you wished to ask me some very important questions, my dear,' argued Mr. Lundie. 'What can be more important than questions of Faith?'

Ms. Ashton took a deep breath. 'Of course, Mr. Lundie, you are quite right. I did not express myself clearly. The questions I have to ask are not of a divine nature, but more of a secular nature.'

'Oh,' said Mr. Lundie doubtfully.

'Of a legal and political nature,' she elaborated.

'Perhaps, then, I should ask Mr. Dalrymple to attend us, then?' asked Mr. Lundie. 'He has been to Aberdeen, you see.'

Nana Visitor interrupted swiftly. She had already met Charlie Dalrymple. 'Not at all, Mr. Lundie, I think that Mr. Dalrymple cannot help this lady. It is yourself she wishes to talk to. Quite without a doubt.'

Ms. Ashton nodded to Nana gratefully. 'Mr. Lundie,' she proceeded, 'are you aware that a Referendum has just taken place in this country?'

'A Referendum?' The old gentleman rolled the word slowly round his mouth. 'A Referendum? An Accounting or a Conversion, as Mr. Ebenezer Erskine tells us. It is true that he did promise many great and spiritual things for the faithful after his passing. Has it now happened?'

'No, sir, I am talking about a different kind of Referendum.' The Electoral Commissioner had attended many training-courses and seminars which dealt specifically with communications strategies for Third World countries. She felt quite comfortable coping with diversionary religious tactics. 'What we call a Referendum is when all men and women are allowed to cast a vote to choose a new way of living – in this case, whether Scotland should be an independent country.'

'Goodness me!' exclaimed Mr. Lundie. 'The times have indeed moved on, I see! All men, you say? Women too? Goodness me! And there has been one of those Referendums, you say? For the independence of this dear land?'

The Italian Government Never Lasts Long

Ms. Ashton raised her eyebrows significantly in the direction of Will Tuttle, who nodded back gravely. No sooner had she turned away than he applied himself to his Blackberry again.

'Just so that I am quite clear, Mr. Lundie,' she asked, 'you were not aware that there had been a Referendum in the country last week?'

Mr. Lundie pondered this for a moment. 'I must ask what exactly you mean by "last week"? Would that be your last week or our last week?'

This was one question too far for Ms. Ashton. She turned to Nana Visitor. 'Is there no one else?' she wanted to know.

Nana turned to young Hamish, who had followed them here with his faithful dog Maggie, and was currently hiding behind the dominie's wheelbarrow.

'Hamish,' she said, 'run now and fetch Mr. Douglas.'

The boy ran off.

'Another gentleman comes shortly,' advised Nana.

'Have I offended the lady?' asked Mr. Lundie, his face troubled. 'She seems a very circumspect young woman, and I would not wish to have upset her.'

Nana patted his arm. Ms. Ashton scribbled notes in her book and said nothing. Will tweeted. A small collection of TV people were clustering around the wicket-gate to the garden.

As everyone waited patiently, an ostrich streaked past, coming down off the hill and heading for the river. In hot pursuit, a collection of wild-clad Highlanders, howling, and brandishing an assortment of knives that would have put to shame any knife amnesty in Glasgow. The ostrich reached the river, hurdled it in a single step and vanished into the trees. The hunters halted at the river-bank, groaning in dismay and shaking their knives at the vanishing prey. The TV people filmed excitedly.

At length, Jeff Douglas strolled up, examined the journalists with a cocked eyebrow and entered the garden. He tucked a bottle into his jacket pocket, out of sight.

'Hey, Nana,' he said amicably, 'some lulu of party we've got today, huh?'

Ms. Ashton blinked.

'You're from New York?' she asked.

'Sure thing, lady?' said Jeff, surprised. "You too? Hell of a coincidence! Would you believe it? Wait till Tommy hears this!'

'And you live in this village?' she wanted to know.

'In Brigadoon? More's the pity, but yes, ma'am, yes I do. Donkey's years. Ever since 1954.'

'Can you tell me what's going on here?' asked Ms. Ashton, ignoring the figurative turns of speech. 'But first, what's your name?'

'I'll tell you my name if you tell me yours, angel-eyes,' replied Jeff easily, settling himself down beside old Mr. Lundie and putting an arm round him in friendly manner.

'My name is no concern of yours, sir,' replied Ms. Ashton, taking a sudden dislike to her presumptuous countryman 'But your name is important to me. I represent the International Electoral Commission and am here on official business. You are legally bound to answer my questions.'

Jeff looked astonished. Then he stared around. 'Can't see any cops,' he announced.

'They're here, sir, trust me on that. Tuttle, call in the cops.' Will raised his phone to his ear and made an urgent call. 'On their way,' he advised.

'OK, OK, lady.' Jeff made placatory gestures with both hands. 'My name's Jeff, Jeff Douglas. What do you want to know?'

'First, Mr. Douglas, can you confirm the name of this village?'

'Brigadoon.'

'Brigadoon - like the movie?'

'There we go - that movie again. Never saw that movie. But say, did you catch *On The Waterfront*? What a class movie that is, lady - movie of the year, I reckon.'

'OK, Brigadoon. And you're a resident here?'

'An inmate more like,' answered Jeff, grinning. 'Sure, I'm a resident, long-term.'

'And you know all these people - Mr. Lundie here, all those people down by the bridge.'

'Every man jack of them. Better than I know myself by now. You want names? I can give you names.'

The Italian Government Never Lasts Long

'Maybe later, Mr. Douglas. I want you to focus now. Did you hear about the Independence Referendum here last week?'

Jeff pondered his reply briefly. Did he answer what he now knew, or what he didn't know until an hour ago? This dame was a piece of work, though. He decided to look blankly at Ms. Ashton. 'No, ma'am,' he said at last, 'I did not.' He paused. 'Last week, you say? Can we just be clear on what you mean by that?'

Ms. Ashton's notebook slammed shut again, startling Mr. Lundie, who clutched his chest dramatically. 'Last week, mister, I just mean last week. Not too hard for a New York boy, is it?'

Jeff considered the matter for a moment. Then he shook his head. 'No Referendum, lady. Not here. Never heard a word.'

'No one came to record names of people authorised to vote?'

'No, ma'am.'

'No one received any voting cards?'

'There's no mailman here, I can tell you that. Ain't seen a letter in years. Not even a utility bill. That's how far back in the woods we are. Ma'am.'

'And no one instructed anyone here on how to cast their votes?'

'You got it.'

'One final question, Mr. Douglas,' said Ms. Ashton, finding herself comfortably on the home-straight. 'How many people would you guess live in this village, of voting age?'

Jeff paused. He pulled out the bottle from his jacket, took a swig, then replaced it carefully. 'Now what, lady, would you call a voting age?' he asked, looking at her narrowly.

'In this country and for this Referendum, Mr. Douglas, sixteen years of age.'

Jeff whistled, then laughed. 'When I was sixteen, lady, I had better things to do than go out and vote. Poor kids!' He took another swig. 'OK, people in Brigadoon over the age of sixteen? That would be -' He close his eyes and thought. 'That would be about eighty, ninety maybe?'

'That's men and women together?'

Jeff blinked. 'Women too, huh? Ain't that a malarkey? Make that another ninety, hundred maybe on top.'

Brigadoon Revisits

'So, Mr. Douglas, you think about one hundred and eighty voters or more in total.'

'Sure thing,' said Jeff easily, 'that'd be about right, I guess.'

Ms. Ashton made one last note in her book and closed it decisively - but not sharply. 'Thank you, Mr. Douglas, you have been most helpful. Tuttle,' she smiled at her assistant, 'I think we're done here. This is the Big One!'

Surreptitiously yet furiously, Will tweeted one last time - 'It's the Big One!' - and followed his boss back down the hill. They were heading for MacConnachy Square. Nana Visitor strode energetically in their wake, leaving Mr. Lundie to the attentions of the Political Correspondent of *The People's Friend*.

Down on MacConnachy Square, the Friday market had petered out, due to lack of enthusiasm. This was regrettable: when every day was another year, or another century, somehow daily life seemed pointless, daily purchases seemed pointless, buying and selling seemed more like a chore than anything else, and not all the singing and dancing in all the world could stir the enthusiasm any more. The market suffered. However, the arrival of the Electoral Commissioners and all the TV and newspaper crews sparked a whole new life into the place, and within minutes, every able-bodied person in the village - and those not at all able-bodied as well - had crowded into the open space to watch what would happen next.

'So, Jane: this is the Big One, is it?' demanded Alan Jay, before Ms. Ashton had had time to say a word. She ignored him as best she could, stood on a convenient rise in the ground, just in front of a primitive notice-board that held a tattered map, and proceeded.

'I have a statement. I will make this statement first, and then you may ask a number of questions. However, I will point out that the work that has to be done here is of a very serious nature, and I will not - repeat not - tolerate any time-wasting, any repeat questions or any harassment. You may take notes.

'Early on this twenty-sixth day of September, the International Independent Electoral Commission was advised of a procedural problem in the allocation of votes to a community in the local government area of Aberdeenshire. On initial verification of this claim, it has indeed been established that upwards of one hundred and eighty citizens, who were entitled to vote, were omitted from the electoral roll, never received any voting papers and so were unable to participate in the democratic process.'

The assembled hacks muttered excitedly, then fell silent under the glance of Jane Ashton.

'It is the intention, therefore, of the International Independent Electoral Commission to ensure that the affected citizens are able to register as voters, are permitted to receive and digest all pertinent information issued in a fair process of campaigning, and then be allowed to cast their votes without further interference. The Commissioner will discuss a timetable for this with the registered participants, and then determine how these arrangements should be monitored.

'That is all I have to say at this time. My colleague, Mr. Tuttle here, will take any relevant questions. I have phone-calls to make.'

With that, Jane Ashton stepped down from her makeshift podium and hobbled off in search of an office. As she did so, a rather fat old lady dressed from head to toe in lurid purple tartan approached her. Her large bonnet, tied up with a huge green ribbon, would easily have covered the head of a troll.

'Good day, miss,' she said quietly enough, but standing stoutly in the way.

Ms. Ashton gave the old woman a smile and tried in vain to side-step and go past.

The woman introduced herself. 'I am but a simple shoe-maker. At your service.' She stared meaningfully at Ms. Ashton's broken Italian footwear.

'You think you can fix these?' she asked, astonished. 'But have you any idea how much these cost?'

'Oh, a pretty penny, I'm sure, miss,' replied the old lady with the air of a connoisseur. 'A fine, fine pair of shoes. I made a pair like those just the other week, fit for a princess, they were. So,' she urged, 'if you'll leave them with me, I'll have them repaired in no time at all. And I will only charge sixpence.'

'I'm real sorry, ma'am,' replied Ms. Ashton, trying not to offend the old lady. 'I'll take a rain-check on that. I got a pile of stuff to do right now. Perhaps some other time?'

In reply, the old woman simply whisked a pair of remarkable shoes from behind her back. They were made of crystal, and had the most elegantly slim high heels. They glinted in the early summer sunlight and were quite alluring. 'You can wear these, miss,' said she, 'while I repair yours.' Without a further moment's delay, she bent down, slipped Jane's Italian shoes off her feet and fitted the new ones. Jane had no idea how this was achieved. But she did know, immediately, that the new shoes were a perfect fit, and were very comfortable indeed.

'Just give me one hour,' said the old woman, 'and your shoes will be as good as new.'

Jane Ashton walked on, as if in a dream, her glass heels clicking against the stones. She walked on over the bridge and back to Storybook Glen. Two police officers followed her at a respectful distance, deep in admiration of the sparkling footwear.

~ 12 ~

New Warning About Climate Change

'Nice shoes,' said Will Tuttle, when he arrived back at the place which Jane Ashton had requisitioned as the on-site operational headquarters for the IIEC.

Ms. Ashton sneaked another look at them. They were indeed nice. 'Aren't they just?' she said. Then she recollected her deep-lying mistrust of Will Tuttle. She was not about to make small-talk with a bum who, she had every suspicion, was violating all known procedures.

'Did the press have anything to say?'

'Oh, just the usual,' replied Tuttle in off-hand manner. 'How had it happened, whose head was going to roll, are there any more places like this. They felt they should be told. The usual crap.'

'What did you say?'

'Say?' For a moment, Tuttle was genuinely astonished at the question. 'Nothing of any substance. We are investigating, the Press will be kept fully informed, this is a matter of the gravest national interest, yadda-yadda.'

'You made them no promises?' demanded his boss, eyeing him without the least sign of trust.

'None, of course not,' protested Tuttle. He lied, but only to a small degree. And a small degree of untruth was quite permissible. All he'd told them was that they should keep an eye open for any tweets, which might, or might not, provide an insight into the development of the crisis.

'OK,' said Ms. Ashton, knowing that Tuttle lied. 'I've contacted London - they're sending a team up on the next flight. And Edinburgh - they're already on their way. All the political parties have been advised by Edinburgh. Expect them to turn up wailing and gnashing their teeth very shortly.' Ms. Ashton smiled grimly. She looked out of the window of the Cinderella Coach, in which the two of them now sat in splendour. 'I think it'd be neat to watch them fight over the wonders of Disneyland for their campaign headquarters.'

Tuttle made no comment on his superior's choice of office accommodation for herself. He wouldn't have chosen the Cinderella Coach; it was, for a start, too pink and too cramped - the right size for kids, maybe, but not for the Electoral Commission. No, given half the chance, he would have gone for the dazzlingly white Fairytale Castle, or - maybe - the Three Bears' Cottage, which had a sort of Wild West rustic look about it. Still, he reckoned that within an hour or two, they'd be moving out of the Coach into something more substantial, something with a bit more *gravitas*: Ashton would not want to be seen giving TV interviews to the Western World from a seat in a pink coach.

Over by the Gingerbread House, an ostrich wandered slowly past, clearly lost in deep consideration of its options. Tuttle and Ashton watched it in silence. All of a sudden, alarmed by a disturbance at the entrance to the car-park, the big bird turned smartly on one leg, and raced for cover with a certain elegance, concealing itself under the trees which bordered the great scar which marked the proposed track of the Peripheral Route.

The disturbance was the arrival of the first of the political parties. Ms. Ashton muttered something under her breath, adjusted her make-up in a tiny mirror and clambered out of the coach. The coachmen up above did not move, but gazed dutifully into the distance. The

New Warning About Climate Change

two police officers, whose pleasant duty it was to guard the independent Commissioner, dropped out of their brief day-dreams in fairyland, paid attention and looked with steely eyes at the cavalcade of cars and vans which now poured into the car-park. It was clear that the influx had also brought its own police protection.

For the next thirty minutes, there was chaos. The "Permitted Participants" and their authorised hangers-on clamoured for attention, eager as never before to get a first sight of their quarry, the unsuspecting and disenfranchised voters of Brigadoon. Ms. Ashton managed to prise the eight party-reps apart from their entourages, and take them to one side, to furnish them with a lucid update on the events of the morning. After seven nights which had been spent tossing between the opposite poles of elation and despair, these men and women were suddenly seized with redoubled enthusiasm.

For all of them, there was yet another battle to be fought. To all of them, in their sleepless nights, another realisation had been born. This was the realisation that, whether or not Scotland voted for independence, they would have to get back to party-politics, back-stabbing, and the ugly day-to-day business of fooling the country. To that end, they were busy re-aligning themselves. There were five flavours of "Yes", and three of "No", but all eight were prepared to state at the drop of a hat that they had naturally thought otherwise.

Meanwhile, the necessary entourages for each participant were organising accommodation. The first group to latch on to the possibilities was that of Jimmy Thompson, the main man of the Doric Country Alliance, aligned, perhaps only temporarily, with UKIP; this group had intimate local knowledge, which gave it something of an advantage. To the Doric Country Alliance therefore fell the greatest bastion of them all - the white and silver Fairytale Castle, with its many turrets and Disney-like façade. The small party that made up Jimmy Thompson's followers scurried up the hill, entered, slammed the main door and hung out a long banner from the ballroom windows signalling it as the possession of All Doric People. The banner read "Ay Fairly ! – Doric for 'Yes'".

Brigadoon Revisits

As soon as this daring act was witnessed and understood, the remaining parties took one quick look around and, throwing caution to the winds, took possession of the remaining accommodations. Ms. Ashton's briefing was broken up as the participants themselves spotted what was afoot, and went out to state their preferences and direct operations. The Tory made a bee-line for Snow White's Cottage, where, amongst the Seven Dwarves, she found herself most at home. The Labour man declared himself quite content with Pumpkin House, a rather basic orange shelter next to the car-park. The Scottish Green found herself strangely attracted to the Jack and the Beanstalk exhibit, disregarding her retinue's warnings that there was no shelter to be had. 'It'll never rain,' she scoffed, a remark which was picked up by a passing journalist from the *Sunday Telegraph* and re-worked at the weekend into a short article entitled 'Greens Issue New Warning About Climate Change.' Meanwhile, the SNP and the Liberal Democrats battled it out over possession of the Old Woman's Shoe, the SNP easily winning the day, leaving the LibDems to take possession of the Three Bears' Cottage. Eddie Quillan, of the People's Coalition, simply invaded the Fairytale Castle via the servants' wing, and claimed squatter's rights over the entire upper floor, disregarding the outrage of the Doric Alliance, who retreated in disarray and dudgeon to the ground floor, bearing with them their hopeful banner. Finally and trailing a bad last, the Independent, a lady who had shot to fame the previous year by reaching the finals of The X-Factor, and who now presented herself as "The No-Voters' Choice", found herself having to settle one of the Three Pigs' houses - two had already blown down and the third was in imminent danger from a wolf on the roof.

None of this, naturally, was to the taste of the manageress of Storybook Glen. She had been prepared, albeit unwillingly, to be brow-beaten by the American lady and the Basic Principles of Democracy; so she had conceded temporary usage of Cinderella's Coach. However, enough was enough.

'I have two coach-loads of school-children arriving at eleven,' she complained. 'They're expecting to enjoy all the attractions, get in and out of all the installations. I can't turn them away - they'll be devastated. And their parents will sue me for every last penny. They're like that round here, since The Oil !'

'Well,' said the Tory unsympathetically, 'they will just have to learn the hard way that Democracy comes first. If we were in Afghanistan or Iraq, they wouldn't be complaining, would they?' There was no answer to that view, although it seemed unlikely that al-Qaeda would have a Storybook Glen of their own. Or perhaps if they did, in the mountains of Afghanistan - it might explain a lot? The manageress retreated from Snow White's Cottage, and tried her luck with the Labour man, Barry Jones. 'Those kids,' said Mr. Jones, 'would do well to remember who paid for all their education.' Finally, she turned to Mrs. Kelly, SNP stalwart, but was rebuffed with a stiff lecture on the Importance to the Nation of the Coming Days, and a recommendation that the children be sent off to the west side of Peterculter, where they could feast their eyes upon a tartan-clad statue of Rob Roy Macgregor, and reflect on Braveheart and the Scottish Genius. The manageress, now close to tears, protested to the police, who shrugged their shoulders and talked inquisitively into their lapels.

The participants meanwhile, having secured their democratic right to campaign headquarters, demanded to be paraded before their new voters. Jane Ashton, feeling that she was in danger of becoming a de facto tour-guide for a bunch of rubber-neckers, arranged for Will Tuttle to take everyone down to Brigadoon.

'And try not to get it wrong, mister,' she hissed, 'or you'll be back in Holyrood shuffling paperclips before you can whistle.' She glanced at him through narrowed eyes. 'Or tweet,' she added, watching him very closely for a reaction.

Will Tuttle did not even blink. He was just so full of cool.

'Ladies, gentlemen,' he announced, 'follow me if you will and we shall take a tour of our new electoral ward.' Flanked by police-officers, he set off through the narrow band of the woods and emerged into the churned muddy field over which, still, Bob Tucker watched with all the patience and insouciance of a pit-bull terrier on crack. Trailing behind Tuttle, the politicians looked at the sea of mud in dismay, torn between the promise of electoral resurgence and irreparable damage to their footwear. Only the Doric Alliance man strode forwards, with confidence and pride born of the possession of a pair of Size 14 green wellies. The rest of them adopted various strategies for crossing to the village of Brigadoon - from ignoring the mud altogether (Greens), to removing shoes and socks and wading on gallantly (Labour and LibDem), to being carried piggy-back on a campaign-worker's back (both Tory and Peoples' Coalition). The *X-Factor* Independent's husband gallantly lifted his wife in his arms and carried her to the hump-backed bridge, a feat of which he remained inordinately proud for hours and which somewhat tempered the chagrin felt by his wife at receiving scarcely a mention in pre-Referendum media reports. A photo-gallery of the passage of the Permitted Participants made it to the front page of every newspaper the following morning; and a video-clip, uploaded an hour later from a mobile-phone which one might suppose to have been Tuttle's, received over eight million hits on YouTube in the following week.

When they finally reached the hump-backed bridge over the River Doon, Will Tuttle halted and called for attention. Reading from the tweet he had just composed and was about to send out to the world, he advised: 'One small stream, but this bridge crosses a huge gulf. This is where we reboot democracy. Welcome to Brigadoon!' So saying, he turned again and marched into the village. And surreptitiously tweeted.

As he did so, an ostrich came fleeing out of the village. Tuttle and the police officers threw themselves right and left, but several of the following party were bowled over like nine-pins, as the bird raced onwards up the hill. A mob of irate villagers arrived baying at the foot of the bridge, calling ancient Scottish curses down upon the head of their escaping prey. But when the hunting-pack saw the new arrivals, silence descended swiftly.

'And who,' demanded one of their number breathlessly - it was Harry Beaton himself, who had all but forgotten his gammy leg in the excitement of the Chase, and was now a veritable Nimrod and a Cuchullain among his people - 'and who are you?'

As luck would have it, the LibDem had positioned himself at the front of the posse.

'My name is Laing,' he announced loudly and clearly to his audience. 'Sir Hugh Laing. I recommend a "No" vote. We are better together.'

Some of the hunters nodded sagely, murmuring the name to each other. 'He seems like a fine gentleman,' observed some of the older fellows. But they did not have time to reflect on Sir Hugh's undoubtedly impeccable qualifications, for the SNP lady stepped in front of him.

'And I am Jean Kelly,' she said in an even louder voice, somewhat cracked by the stresses and strains of the past few weeks. 'Jean Kelly - remember that name if you remember no other. Jean Kelly says firmly, avidly, passionately – I am the one true Scottish voice. Without an Independent Scotland -'

A great roar of protest interrupted her, as each participant denounced this gross deception, and proclaimed him or herself to be more Scottish than all the rest. More Scottish and – depending on inclination – more forward-thinking than all the rest. The villagers - the band of hunters now rapidly joined by friends, neighbours and wives - looked on in wonder.

Jean Kelly continued, raising her voice above the hubbub. 'Without an Independent Scotland, you will suffer further injustice. I am here to relieve you of the weight of iniquity that has fallen upon you, and to seek massive compensation for your humiliation and suffering. I bring you the vote, and I advise you to use it wisely: you can, you should, you must vote "Yes" !'

Almost before the conclusion of these words, the dam was broken. All the politicians raced and slithered down the slope of the bridge, to begin the onerous task of shaking hands and slapping sweaty hunters on the back. Not far behind them came the campaign staff, handing out leaflets and pens and badges and rosettes.

Will Tuttle looked on for a few moments, smiled contentedly, and consulted his Rolex. It was half-past ten. Time to tweet.

~ 13 ~

Mr. Campbell Puts on His Best Waistcoat

'Mr. Douglas,' said Andrew Campbell, 'you are a man of this modern world. Tell me, who are these people? What do they want?'

Mr. Campbell sat in a fine old rocking-chair at the doorway of his cottage, gazing down in astonishment at a pile of leaflets which had been handed to him by all manner of impolite people in the preceding ten minutes, people who had even over-stepped the limits of human decency by demanding entrance to his home. A monstrous impertinence which he had flatly refused. In his desperation to comprehend the modern world that had all but broken down his door, he had turned to Jeff Douglas, a man whom he normally shunned.

Jeff took a contemplative drink from his flask; he offered the refreshment to Mr. Campbell, who shook his head disapprovingly. Then he sat for a moment, his large hands between his legs, leaning forward.

'Mr. Campbell,' said Jeff at length 'It's my opinion that the modern world is no better than the old world. No better, no worse. A man could give up on both of them. I know I have. It's all voodoo, Mr. Campbell, you can bet your life on that.'

'Voodoo, Mr. Douglas?'

Mr. Campbell Puts on His Best Waistcoat

'Mumbo-jumbo. Tosh. Gobbledegook. Hocus-pocus. They want your vote, Mr. Campbell, they'll take it, and then you'll never see them again.'

Andrew Campbell sighed and spent a while browsing reverentially through the leaflets. 'But they look so fine, all these people. Look at their honest faces in these pictures! Look at the grand, grand words they use! "Better Together." Who could gainsay that, I'm asking? And they talk so well of fine matters, matters to which a thinking man, in these enlightened times, ought perhaps to aspire. Justice, Fairness, Security. All they want is my vote - look, they say so in their wee books. A man should perhaps attend to their words, do you not think, Mr. Douglas?'

'No, I do not think, Mr. Campbell,' said Jeff wearily. 'Listen, you wanted my thoughts because I've seen the modern world? Well, it's fine talk, all of it. Fascinating. But it's bunkum. These guys - they make big promises, you give them your vote, and then they pay no attention to anything you might want in return. Not a damn thing, Mr. Campbell. You don't see them again - not until the next time they want your vote. Not a goddam thing.'

'Moderate your language, Mr. Douglas,' protested Mr. Campbell, lowering his voice and his brow simultaneously. 'My girls are in the house here and I do not like them to hear profane language.'

'I'm sorry, old man,' said Jeff easily. He took another swig from his flask. 'Don't you pay any attention to what I tell you. No one else does. Why don't you ask Tommy - he'll tell you quite different, I bet. He's a Republican, after all: he believes in Democracy. I'm a Democrat - I only believe in the Tooth-Fairy.'

Mr. Campbell's frown deepened even more. 'No,' he said decisively, 'I will not ask that man's opinion on this matter, nor on any other matter.'

Jeff shrugged. He looked about idly. 'If I had my way,' he said to no one in particular, 'I'd not let any of those politicians in here. Causes far too much excitement for this sleepy place. Look - there's Sandy Macmillan, running up to see us. That won't do him any good.'

Brigadoon Revisits

Mr. Macmillan arrived, red-faced and out of breath. He could not speak a word, although it was clear he had words to speak. He gesticulated wildly, pointing urgently back down to MacConnachy Square. At last, Jeff seized him by the shoulders and placed him on the bench outside Mr. Campbell's window.

'What's the matter, Sandy?' asked the owner of the bench. 'Has something frightful happened?' Is it,' his voice trembled, 'is it the witches? Speak, man, speak!'

'One of those -' gasped Sandy but could get no further.

'One of those - what?' demanded his friend. 'For Heavens' sake, man, what is it? Girls!' he shouted over his shoulder into the cottage, 'you stay inside for a while. There is something untoward going on in the village!'

Naturally, at these words, four or five girls came crowding to the door, fair screaming. They were all in their teens and Jeff Douglas considered them a pretty sight.

'One of those political people,' gasped Sandy with a supreme effort, 'he has bought Malcolm MacReekie's what-have-you!'

'His what-have-you?' echoed the father, confused. Jeff winked solemnly at the girls, who blushed and burst into giggles. 'Sandy, what are you talking about?'

'The great bird, the dead one that Malcolm has been trying to sell!' explained Sandy, gratefully accepting a small glass of spirits from one of Campbell's girls, Aphrodite.

'What? He paid ten shillings for it?' Mr. Campbell was astonished. 'Are these people princes or great lords, Mr. Douglas? What is that word I have heard you use - millionaires?' He turned to Jeff once more for an explanation of the modern ways.

'No, Andrew, not ten shillings,' gasped Sandy, overcome by the wonder. 'Not ten shillings at all.' He paused for effect. 'He paid ten guineas for it!'

There was a profound silence at this news. Both Sandy and Andrew breathed heavily, staring aghast at each other. The girls whispered urgently in a huddle, then ran back indoors to put on their Sunday shawls.

Mr. Campbell Puts on His Best Waistcoat

'Ten guineas, Alexander?' asked Mr. Campbell at length. 'That cannot be. Are you sure?'

Sandy Macmillan looked offended. 'Would I tell you a lie, Andrew?' he demanded.

'You would,' affirmed Mr. Campbell sternly.

'Aye, maybe I would,' conceded Sandy, 'but I would not invent such a story as this. The man, who goes by the name of Mr. Jones, took a fancy to Malcolm's what-have-you and -'

'It's an ostrich, Sandy,' interrupted Jeff. 'An ostrich.'

'Thank you, Mr, Douglas. The man Jones, I was saying, took a fancy to Malcolm's - ostrich - and says, "How much are you wanting for this fine bird?" he says. His very words. Malcolm looks him in the eye and replies: "Ten shillings, and not a penny less, sir". "Very good," says the fine gentleman, laughing. "Ten shillings is it? I'll tell you what," he says, "I'll give you ten pounds for it!" Malcolm MacReekie was so astonished that he fell silent.'

'That is a great wonder,' murmured Mr. Campbell, 'that is something I would have liked to have seen.'

'But that Catriona MacReekie,' continued Sandy, nodding at the propriety of his old friend's remark, 'she was not one to stay silent. "Make it ten guineas, sir, and the bird is yours!" she cries, the shameless besom. Mr. Jones smiles and shakes hands with Mrs. MacReekie. And she takes the man's money without further ado. A great big banknote it was, with the most beautiful pictures all over it, and a handful of silver pieces. "Now," says the man, still pleased with himself although it was clear to all that he had met his match, "now, here is what I think we should do," says he. "If Mrs. MacReekie here can arrange to have this great bird roasted, then anyone in the village who wants to eat of it may do so! We should have a celebration." There,' said Sandy, quite recovered now, 'what say you to that? A celebration.'

Mr. Campbell was moved beyond words. He gazed now at Sandy, now down the path that led to the centre of the village, now at the heavens.

Brigadoon Revisits

It was Jeff who broke the silence. 'Well, isn't that just a great thing!' he said sourly. 'This fellow is going to provide a feast at his own expense? Unbelievable.'

Sandy nodded gravely. 'He said that anyone in the village could come and eat, and that we were only to remember his name. "My name is Barry Jones," says he, "and I bring you the advice of the Labour Party. A "No" vote is a vote for a full stomach." he says loudly. So we all gave a cheer for Barry Jones and another one for the Labour Party, and I came up straight away to tell you, Andrew.'

Andrew Campbell rose from his chair and solemnly shook his friend Sandy by the hand. 'You did a fine thing there, Sandy Macmillan, and it will not be forgotten. Barry Jones, you said? Labour?' He stopped suddenly, struck by a thought. 'Sandy,' he said rubbing his chin, 'if all of those political people out there are as rich as this Mr. Jones, and as prodigal, perhaps…?'

He and Sandy looked at each other gravely. And then they both nodded.

'Well now,' he said cheerfully, 'if you will just give me a minute, I shall put on my best waistcoat, gather my girls, and we shall make our way down to this unexpected and generous feast.'

~ 14 ~

The Marrow of Modern Divinity

'It is Friday, sir, a school-day, and we see no evidence of the children in our care being given any education, do we?' The man looked sternly at Mr. Lundie. 'What is our explanation for this?'

Mr. Lundie sat down heavily on his garden bench and contemplated the blaze of daffodils which spread out before him. The impertinent man who had invited himself into his garden had disrupted the equanimity which had once again fallen on him after the upsets and doubts of recent hours.

The man persisted. 'Perhaps we do not understand, sir - what's your name? Lundie? Perhaps we do not understand the gravity of the position we are in and, more importantly, the seriousness of the position in which you, by your neglect, have placed these children. We are the school-teacher in this village, are we not?'

The dominie nodded. 'I have that privilege, sir,' he replied in a tone of weary defiance.

'And we have a schoolhouse, Mr. Lundie?'

'I have - it is but one room in my house yonder.'

The man did not even bother to glance at the house. He was busy jotting down some pithy notes about the neglectful schoolmaster.

'Good, and we must have a list of pupils, then, some kind of register?'

Brigadoon Revisits

'I did have, sir, I did have. Until two weeks ago. Now I have none.'

'What happened two weeks ago?'

'Mice,' said Mr. Lundie.

'Mice ate the school-register?' The man was unable to believe his ears. 'What are our standards of cleanliness, must we suppose?'

'But,' said Mr. Lundie, correctly guessing that he had best defend himself, 'I have all the names up here.' He tapped the side of his head and smiled encouragingly at the intruder.

'Well, let's start with what we have, then.' The man got out a pen and notebook and jotted down the names that Mr. Lundie rattled off; names, ages, addresses and names of parents. When the list was complete, the man examined it carefully.

'Thirty-eight children,' he stated. 'Would that be correct, Mr. Lundie?'

'Thirty-eight is correct, sir.'

'And not one of them over the age of ten. Are there,' the man, 'no children in this village over the age of ten? Or did the mice eat them?'

'No, not the mice,' Mr. Lundie was certain of that. 'Children in Brigadoon have never attended the school beyond the age of ten.'

'So they go off to secondary school somewhere else? Where would that be? Cults Academy?'

'No,' said Mr. Lundie simply. 'They will have had all their education.'

The man was dumbfounded. 'Had it all?' he asked, aghast. 'What about National 5s and Highers? Do we ever adhere to the provisions of the Curriculum for Excellence, for goodness' sake?'

Mr. Lundie looked at him blankly.

'Certificates, sir, certificates to prove what the children have learned. We have at least arranged the relevant National Assessment tests for the primary school?'

Mr. Lundie looked at him blankly.

'Mr. Lundie, you clearly do not understand anything. Let me put it to you simply. My name is Low. I'm from the Council, the Education Division. It is my job to ensure that all communities within Aberdeenshire are provided with a correct and sustainable level of education for all ages between two and eighteen. My office was alerted to your presence first thing this morning. I have therefore to report back at the earliest opportunity. And what I'm seeing, Mr. Lundie, does not come anywhere near complying with our minimum basic levels of provision. Are you even qualified, sir?' Mr. Low looked keenly at the schoolmaster.

The old gentleman looked Low squarely in the eye. 'Sir,' he said proudly, 'I spent three years at the University of St Andrews, before I returned to Brigadoon to take up my position. A position I have held with joy and with reverence for nigh on fifty years.'

Mr. Low noted this down. The man was well past retirement age, and had clearly not been inspected for decades. Possibly a little demented too, if he could announce that he held down a teaching post with feelings of "joy." This situation would have to be resolved immediately, for the good of the children. It was a scandal. His Director would blow a gasket. It was all that old fool Ames' fault, Preston Ames his immediate predecessor, who had taken early retirement last Christmas. How could he have missed something like this?

'Did you meet Mr. Ames from the Council?' asked Low, just to be sure.

'Ames?' Mr. Lundie paused for thought, then shook his head. 'I have not had that honour.' Then he remembered something. 'Charlie Dalrymple,' he announced with a smile, 'Charlie went off to Aberdeen, to the university there, to study law. Charlie received a certificate. And young Harry Beaton, too, he would have gone to Edinburgh, if it hadn't been for Jean.'

'Charles Dalrymple. When was this, Mr. Lundie?'

The dominie thought for a moment. 'That would have been 1752, sir.'

Mr. Low closed his notebook with conviction, and placed his pen firmly in his jacket pocket. 'I have no option,' he announced gravely, 'under the Education (Scotland) Acts of 1988, 2000, 2004 etc, but to close down your school with immediate effect.'

'Close it down?' asked Mr. Lundie astonished. 'By whose authority?'

'By the authority of the Scottish Government, Mr. Lundie, and ultimately the Queen,' replied Mr. Low testily.

'I recognise no Queen, nor yet any Scottish Government,' declared Mr. Lundie firmly. 'I recognise only the King in London, and his Government in Westminster. Any man who shall try to take away the right of the children of Brigadoon, to have a sound education, is a traitor to King and Country, sir, and I will have him know it!' The dominie stood and glared at Mr. Low. 'Sir,' he continued, 'come with me to my schoolroom and I will show you how I teach these children how to read, how to write, how to count, and, most importantly of all, how to respect their parents and fear the Lord God.' He gripped the man from the Council by the coat-sleeve and dragged him protesting down to the school-room. Reaching the door, he flung it open and pushed the man inside.

The room smelled vaguely of unwashed children and mice-droppings, but appeared otherwise clean and bright. Five rows of benches filled most of the room. At the front was a lectern and a large board on which some words had been written. Several nibbled maps and diagrams decorated the plain walls.

'This, sir, is my schoolroom,' announced the dominie angrily. 'In the course of fifty years, several hundred children have passed through my care, and not one of them - not one of them, sir - has disappointed, or remained in ignorance.' He paused for a moment, his brow clouded. 'Except of course young Archie Stewart. But Archie was never going to be anyone's but Satan's. And so it turned out. Never will I forgive him for leaving to march southwards with the Prince. We will not mention Archie Stewart again, if you please. Wait!' Mr. Lundie hastened to the open door. Two small boys were passing along the lane.

'Hamish Maclaren and James Macdonald!'

The two boys stopped and took off their hats. 'Good morning, Mr. Lundie, sir,' they chanted in unison.

'Could you two lads step inside here? I have a visitor.'

The innocent youths came in. Hamish was careful to leave Maggie the sheepdog at the door.

'Hamish Maclaren, will you recite your times-tables for this very important gentleman?'

Hamish did so, flawlessly, right up to twelve times twelve.

'And now James Macdonald, will you recite the 23rd Psalm?'

Again, the recitation was flawless.

'And now, lads, would you care to show our visitor the map of Brigadoon, and explain to him where we are?'

'One moment, sir, if you please!' Mr. Low pointed severely at another item on the wall. 'That map of the Island of Mull and surrounding districts,' he pointed out, 'is upside down.'

'It is indeed,' said Mr. Lundie placidly.

'Does that not send out the wrong message to our charges?' demanded Mr. Low.

'I could not agree more with you, sir,' replied the dominie. 'That map was given to me by our newly-resident gentlemen, Mr. Albright and Mr. Douglas. They insisted that it should remain upside down, since without it, they never would have found our village.' Mr. Lundie shook his head heavily. 'Sometimes, Mr. Low, I sincerely wish they had not discovered us.' He sighed. And then he turned his attention to his pupils.

'And now, lads, have the goodness to guide us around the map which Mr. Forsyth left to us.'

Hamish and James stepped up to one of the maps on the wall. Hamish cleared his throat and reeled off the names of the surrounding hills and rivers, while James assiduously placed his finger on each feature in turn.

'This is the village of Brigadoon, Mr. Lundie, and these are the boundaries beyond which we should not trespass: to the east, the bridge; to the west, the Old Kirk Road; to the north, the stone dyke that the edge of the forest; and to the south, Loch Arrol.'

Mr. Low was appalled. He turned to Mr. Lundie, and said in a low voice: 'Sir, this is madness. The bridge is to the south of here, and to the north is the River Dee. And there is no loch for miles around. What have you been teaching these children about their landscape?'

Brigadoon Revisits

Mr. Lundie smiled easily upon his critic. 'Mr. Low,' he replied, 'it matters not what is at the boundaries, nor what lies to the north, south, east or west. It matters only that the boundaries are there, and that these children know that they should not step beyond them, at risk of mortal peril. We wish simply to keep our children safe, Mr. Low. Do you not?'

Having himself been a leading committee-member on a panel of experts committed to the 2012 inter-service initiative '*Keeping Children Safe*', Fred Low could find not a word to say. He stared at the map and then he stared at the two boys.

The two boys stood politely and gazed back at Mr. Low. At length, the man smiled at them and congratulated them.

'Perhaps Mr. Lundie will allow me to ask you a few questions in my turn?' he said smoothly.

Mr. Lundie graciously agreed.

'Now, Hamish,' said Mr. Low kindly, 'how old are we?'

'Nine years old, sir,' replied Hamish politely.

'Well, well, nine years old! We're a fine big lad now. Now, I wonder what we know about computers?'

'Nothing, sir,' said Hamish instantly.

'Nothing at all?' asked the man.

'No, sir,' agreed Hamish, 'nothing. I've never heard of them.'

'Well, what about space-rockets? Do we like space-rockets?'

'I don't know anything about space-rockets,' said Hamish, eager to please.

Mr. Low raised his eyebrows in Mr. Lundie's direction. 'Well, then, perhaps we could say what our favourite activity is outside the school? Football, maybe, or fishing?'

'Watching over the sheep with my dog Maggie,' was Hamish's unequivocal reply.

'And do we do that often?'

'Six hours every day,' advised Hamish proudly.

'I see,' said Mr. Low drily, 'I see.' He turned his attention to the other boy. 'And you, James, can we perhaps recite for me one of Robert Burns' poems? I'm told every schoolboy knows at least one of the great man's verses.'

James was more nervous than Hamish. 'I don't know Mr. Burns, sir,' he stated, looking anxiously at Mr. Lundie.

'Wee cowering timorous beastie?' prompted the man from the Council.

James shook his head firmly.

'It's a poem about mice, James,' explained the inspector kindly.

'Ah, mice!' exclaimed James. 'I know all about mice, sir!' He darted around the edge of the schoolroom, stopping every so often to pick something up. He returned with an armful of primitive mouse-traps, each holding a small brown corpse. 'There,' he said proudly. 'Seven of them. We got fifteen yesterday and over two hundred last week!'

Mr. Low recoiled from the small Gehenna. 'Put them down at once, son!' he exclaimed. 'Go and wash your hands!'

Crestfallen, James placed the pile of dead mice on the dominie's table, and left the schoolhouse with Hamish. Maggie greeted them eagerly, and they ran off into the village, in hot pursuit of the good smell of roasting fowl. They did not stop to wash their hands.

'Mr. Lundie,' hissed Fred Low, 'we have never, in our entire career, come across such appalling conditions in a school! Have we never heard of basic hygiene?'

'A word, I suppose,' replied Mr. Lundie easily, 'that comes from the Greek *hugieineos*, meaning healthful. What could be more healthful, Mr. Low, if that is truly your name, than the fresh air of Brigadoon and the surrounding hills, and what could be more useful to young children than learning their times-tables, their psalms, and their alphabets, and enjoying each other's company in the safety of the schoolhouse?'

Mr. Low was struck dumb momentarily. Eventually, he found the strength to point accusingly at the pile of murine corpses.

'Mice,' acknowledged the schoolmaster. 'I told you that we have recently been visited with a plague of mice. It is the long nights, you know. An oversight of Mr. Forsyth, I have now concluded, rather than of the Good Lord.'

'Mr. Forsyth?' demanded Low. 'Who is this Mr. Forsyth?'

Brigadoon Revisits

Mr. Lundie took the time to explain patiently. His visitor grew steadily more nervous. But Mr. Lundie blocked the way to the door, and every move that Low made in that direction was opposed by an obstructive move by the dominie. The schoolchildren here were clearly in danger. He had to get word to the Director immediately. He took out his mobile-phone. Mr. Lundie whipped it out of his hands without further ado.

'I will not have you playing with toys in my schoolroom,' he said severely. 'It has always been a strict rule of mine, and one which I'll not have you breaking on a whim! Or do you wish me to take the tawse to you, sir?'

'But it's my mobile-phone,' argued Low.

'No mobile-phones in my classroom, sir!' repeated Mr. Lundie. 'I will lock it away in my desk until the end of the day. You may have it back then.'

Confused by the momentary illusion that Mr. Lundie was in fact quite sane, simply taking a professional and laudable stance on disruptive behaviour, Mr. Low yielded. But at that moment, the mobile-phone struck up with a couple of recognisable bars from the tune *School's Out For Summer*. Mr. Lundie, greatly startled, dropped the phone. Mr. Low darted to pick it up and answered it.

'Is that you, Hazel?' he said urgently. 'Listen, I've been taken prisoner by a lunatic. You've got to -'

Mr. Lundie clipped Fred around the back of the head and neatly relieved him of the phone. He spoke into it. 'Who is this?' he asked. He listened carefully to the answer. 'I fear that Mr. Low has been taken ill, and cannot speak to you. Yes, quite feverish, I'm afraid. It may have been something he drank, my dear. I saw him with a bottle of spirits just a few moments ago. I fear so, yes, indeed. And a good morning to you, young lady, and may the Good Lord watch over you.' He closed the phone and stowed it away with care in his desk.

'And so,' Mr. Lundie concluded his explanation of Mr. Forsyth's self-sacrifice, 'here we are, one week further on and, so it would appear, two hundred and sixty years have passed. From what I have seen of modern times, I cannot say that I am impressed.' He looked keenly at Low. 'Do you know Mr. Ebenezer Erskine, sir?'

Fred Low shook his head at length.

'No, I thought that you would be ignorant,' said Lundie, not at all surprised. 'For all that you claim to be an educator, you did not seem to have that demeanour about you. It is my fear that the teachings of Mr. Erskine have not survived into modern days, but are lost from sight amid the hurly-burly of the fashions of the years. We have followed, sir, the teachings and precepts of that eminent divine insofar as we have been able in these past few years. They have stood us, I firmly believe, in good stead. And especially here in the schoolhouse.' He looked defiantly at Mr. Low. 'A good grounding in fundamental Christian principles, sir, carries more weight in the souls of these children than a hundred lessons on numbers and letters. And now, sir,' he added, seeing that from the beads of sweat upon his brow that Mr. Low was so far out of his depth as to be drowning, 'I think it best that you take a rest here in the peace and tranquillity of my schoolroom, until you have recovered somewhat.'

The representative of the Education Division made haste to deny any feeling of tiredness, although, in truth, he would have been happy to sit quietly for a few moments. Just not in the company of this eccentric. But the dominie permitted no protest.

'Here you shall sit, sir, until your spirit has fully embraced the stern composure of a Christian schoolmaster, that quietude which comes upon the souls after a strict contemplation of their intrinsic sinfulness.'

At this proposal, Mr. Low made a dash for the door. But Mr. Lundie, despite his disadvantage of years, was too quick for him. Five decades of watching over small boys had honed his reactions to a keen edge. He stretched out a leg. Low tripped and went flying. Mr. Lundie then stepped easily to the door, secured it with a very heavy iron bolt that had withstood many assaults, and turned to look down upon Mr. Low.

'I have you now, sir, I have you now. You shall not move from here. Until the sun sets, you and I may profitably discourse upon Mr. Fisher's Marrow of Modern Divinity, for that is the food that nourishes The Bones of Modern Education.'

~ 15 ~

Catering Packs of Maltesers

At noon, Jane Ashton had been advised by her assistant that a Grand Referendum Barbecue was about to begin in the village and that the political parties were funding it. Accordingly, she made her way back across the muddy field to the hump-backed bridge. If there was the slightest whiff of undeclared donations or enticement, she had to be there - to observe, to investigate and, if necessary, to behead. Followed at a respectful distance by the two police-officers whom, curiously, she had begun to think of as her footmen, she set off at a smart pace. Just before the bridge, the little old woman popped up, as if from behind a gorse-bush.

'There you are, my dear,' she said, holding out a pair of smart Italian heels, 'I told you I'd have them done in no time at all!' She placed them in Jane's hands.

The Electoral Commissioner looked at them in astonishment. The shoes were perfect, just as good as the day she'd bought them. She turned them over and over, as the old woman watched placidly.

'Well, that's wonderful,' said Ms. Ashton. 'Thank you very much! How lovely!'

She slipped out of the glass slippers and put on the newly-repaired Italian ones. There was not, it had to be said, much to choose between them.

'That'll be sixpence,' advised the old woman, accepting back the glass footwear, 'if you please. As we agreed.'

Taken by surprise, Jane started fumbling around in her handbag. She only had credit-cards there. She doubted that the old woman would take American Express. And an Electoral Commissioner did not carry loose change about. That was one thing Will Tuttle was good for. As it happened, he did not carry loose change either, but it was not Ms. Ashton's business to know how he paid for taxis and newspapers: he just did. At length, realising that she would find no coins, she summoned the police-officers.

'Could one of you perhaps lend me some money?' she asked.

The taller of the two immediately produced a handful of coins and offered them to Jane. She picked out several silver coins and passed them to the old woman.

'Oh!' exclaimed the old woman. 'Oh! This is far too much!' She took them all the same, and tucked them away about her person. 'Bless you, ma'am, bless you, sir. May all your wishes come true!' She bowed to the Commissioner and the policeman, skipped round the back of the bush, and vanished.

Jane Ashton walked on, crossed the bridge and came shortly to MacConnachy Square. It seemed as if everyone in the village had gathered there, along with the media people and all the participants and their hangers-on. In the centre of the square, smoke rose from a fire and that is where the greatest press of people had gathered. There was the smell of roasting meat. She sought out Will Tuttle, found him and summoned him to her side with one raised eyebrow.

Breathless from fighting his way through the crowd, Tuttle arrived.

'Report,' commanded his boss.

'One roasted ostrich, paid for by the Labour Party, representative Barry Jones. Moneys in excess of ten pounds Sterling paid to a Mr. MacReekie, butcher. Invitations issued to every resident of the village.'

'And more,' commented Ms. Ashton critically, eyeing the milling crowd of outsiders. 'The media know a good thing when they smell it. OK, Tuttle, who knows that Mr. Jones paid for this?'

'Everyone,' he replied easily. 'He made no secret of it.' He might have added that the story had already reached London and New York, courtesy of a tweet sent out half an hour ago.

'Get those low-lifes over here,' said the Commissioner. 'All of them. Now, Tuttle!' She stood, arms folded, while she waited for Tuttle to gather in all the politicians. She watched the scene before her. This sort of thing had to be nipped in the bud; or, at the very least, managed.

The eight Permitted Participants soon arrived, accompanied by a distracted group of hangers-on, whose attention was focussed on the roast ostrich that was already being carved up. They cast anxious eyes over their shoulders. None of the media people chose to join them.

'So, Mr. Jones,' Ms. Ashton addressed Barry Jones, 'you represent the "No" campaign and have laid on a regular barbecue for the voters have you?'

'Guilty, ma'am, on both counts' said Jones easily. 'And you're welcome to join in, of course. Give you a taste of good Scottish hospitality before you leave these shores.'

The Commissioner looked at him steadily. 'The IIEC will always position itself at arm's length from such events, Mr. Jones. As you ought to know. You paid for this, did you?'

'Money well spent,' said Jones, winking cheerfully.

Ms. Ashton addressed the entire group. 'This is how it's going to be, people. You need to listen very carefully, because I'll be monitoring this and I'll be reporting back. Each and every one of you is going to contribute something to this barbecue, and each and every one of you is going to let the voters know that you've done so.'

A great muttering arose. 'My campaign funds won't stretch that far!' whined the Independent. 'This is unfair!' Everyone else agreed.

'Unfair it may be,' said Ms. Ashton, quite unmoved, 'but Mr. Jones here has signalled to a group of vulnerable voters -'

A cry of protest arose here, swiftly quelled.

Catering Packs of Maltesers

'- vulnerable, because they have no idea about the Referendum, or any voting-rights, or the democratic process. They are quite likely to vote "No" because Mr. Jones here gave them a free meal. I've been all over the world in the course of my duties and I've seen this sort of thing before, and I'll no doubt see it again. So, unless you all wish to see yet another procedural delay, I'd suggest you find the funds and you find the means of entertaining these people in like manner. Off you go.'

At the thought of more days and nights of waiting, the mood of the other parties soon changed. The "Yes" campaign briefly flirted with the idea of stitching up their opponents, by refusing to spend money on entertainments: that way, the "No" campaign would be hung out to dry. But then they fell to considering how that would look, come the next Election: the SNP refusing to fork out cash for a party for starving teuchters? Shame on them! They capitulated. There were furtive consultations and mobile-phones were whisked out in a fever of activity.

'One last thing, people,' said the Commissioner, interrupting the group muttering. 'I want all these gifts itemised and receipted and a full list passed to my assistant Mr. Tuttle. Anyone who omits to do so will find himself up against the full force of international law!'

And so it was that, by half-past twelve, the barbecue that had as its centrepiece a roast ostrich (Labour) had been turned into a feast of epic proportions with the addition of limitless beer (People's Coalition), bottles of cheap whisky (SNP), an endless supply of orange-juice (Green), a magnificent cheese-board hand-delivered from a delicatessen in Cults (Tory), a collection of cheesecakes and trifles (LibDem), pork sausages (Doric), and catering-sized packs of Maltesers (Independent). Ms. Ashton looked on in satisfaction as the villagers danced their way around the Square, consuming all of these delights, and individually shaking the hands of the donors. It was, she supposed, a triumph for the Democratic Process, even if it wasn't exactly by the book. All the participants also seemed pleased, with the possible exception of Barry Jones, who tried to put a brave face on things but was clearly disheartened at his wasted expense. And the media people were happy as well, because it was yet another free lunch.

Curiously, it was the Maltesers which found the most favour with the villagers of Brigadoon. The Independent, Elaine Stewart, could not believe her luck. In a clandestine move, which was never spotted by the Electoral Commission, her husband, Mr. Elaine Stewart, was dispatched to Sainsbury's at the Bridge of Dee in Aberdeen, to load up with other family-packs of confectionery. Over the course of the next few hours, these were surreptitiously handed in at every cottage in the village. When the packs were opened up, a mock voting-card fell out, with the "No" vote clearly marked with a large cross, and the *X-Factor* candidate's name in bold across the top. Even the schoolhouse was visited in this way and, although the door was not opened, a Monster Macaroon Munchies pack was handed in through the window. Its contents gave spiritual relief to Mr. Low of the Education Department, whose soul was full of the bitterness of contemplation and the Marrow of Modern Divinity.

Such regrettable subterfuge was not confined to the Independent. Realising that the bar had to be raised, Barry Jones decided that he would use his natural skills to entertain the villagers. An impromptu concert was arranged, a competition in the eisteddfod style, in which Barry delivered songs both comic and tragic in rich Welsh baritones. Several of the villagers were eager to participate in the competition, both young and old, male and female, some with the sweet voices of angels, and others without; there was also a dancing competition, a hard-fought one, since everyone in the village had quite astonishing natural ability and athleticism. Mr. Jones was very careful to avoid giving out large prizes, since that would only have got him into more hot water; however, a fortunate moment found him writing some notes on the back of a postcard depicting Crathes Castle. It immediately became clear that the villagers would greatly treasure picture postcards of the surrounding countryside. Accordingly, he sent a minion back to the Dingle Dell Gift Shop at Storybook Glen, there to acquire their entire stock of postcards; these small and precious items were then handed out to the winners in the various dancing and singing-competitions. Astonishment spread round the village when they saw what the modern world looked like.

Unfortunately for the "No" campaign, the postcard images of the various exhibits in the theme-park caused a deep division between those who thought the place was like the Promised Land, and those who suspected it to be the home of witches and wizards.

Virginia Bosler, for the Conservative and Unionist Party, observed some of these activities with disquiet. In particular, she frowned upon Quillan's cases of beer, rightly fearing a resurgence of support for "Yes". She sought to split his new-found following. She rounded up those whose view of Storybook Glen veered towards fearfulness and assured them of the "Better Together's" unwavering stance against fairy-tales. 'Would you have people like that living next door to you?' she asked rhetorically. 'How would you feel if your wives and your children and grandchildren encountered some of those people in the woods? These people should not be permitted to move into your neighbourhood! They have their own culture and we respect that, of course we do. We must always respect cultural diversity. But it need not be on our doorstep, here in beautiful Brigadoon. Let them pursue their lives somewhere away from here! This is no place for dwarves, nor for wolves and bears and witches!' There was general agreement on this principle, the words of the departed Mr. Forsyth being fresh in their minds. As the rumours spread through the village, people who were having a little sit-down with full stomachs and a few sweets to chew on, reflected uncomfortably on the presence next door of a community of fairies, dwarves and wild animals Mrs. Bosler's team capitalised on this uneasiness by producing a simple leaflet bearing the slogan "Keep Britain United - Keep Brigadoon Safe". Some words of Christian wisdom, purporting to be a personal endorsement of the policies of the "No" campaign by Mr. Forsyth, were printed at the end of the leaflet. Such was the persuasiveness of this leaflet that Archie Beaton proclaimed himself a fervent Unionist.

Harry Beaton did not take happily to his father's declaration of loyalty. 'If you had any sense at all,' he railed, in full view of their neighbours, 'you can, you should, you must vote "Yes", with Eddie Quillan! That man has been brought up in Edinburgh, I am told !'

So broke upon Brigadoon the Scottish Independence Referendum, that event which has spawned a controversy and a dissension capable of breaking apart families, sundering son from father, dividing daughter from mother, and splitting sister from brother. Not to mention severing friend from friend.

~ 16 ~

Bunnies and Sabbatarians

'Some pal you are,' groused Jeff. He applied his lips to the mouth of his flask and took another sip. 'In all the time we've known each other, have we ever argued?' He looked at Tommy Albright with a cocked eyebrow.

'Sure, plenty,' said Tommy. 'Every time we meet up we argue. So what?'

'So what?' asked Jeff. 'So what are we arguing for now, over some Dixie band of half-baked politicians? What's it to us whether they get a vote or which party gets in? It's not our country, is it? And anyway they're all the same.'

'Oh, put a cork in it, Jeff,' said Tommy, skipping a few dance-steps back and forth. 'How do you like this routine I'm putting together?' He did not wait for Jeff's answer to that one. 'Listen, if we all said we didn't care, like you do, then we'd never get anything. All these folks ought to get the vote and they should vote for someone reliable.'

'Oh yeah?' laughed Jeff. 'You show me a reliable politician! Just one, Tommy. I tell you, buddy, they're all the same, every last one of them. These folks shouldn't trust them any further than I can spit.' To illustrate, Jeff spat. 'Hey,' he said admiringly, 'that was some spit! See that, Tommy?'

'Lay off the booze, Jeff,' said Tommy wearily. 'You always said you were going to.'

Brigadoon Revisits

'Sure, I always said that,' said Jeff. 'And I meant it, too. But then I stopped one time, and the world didn't look too good, so I started again.'

Tommy stopped his tap-dancing and stood over Jeff. 'That's exactly your trouble, Jeff. You reckon the world is just a bad place, they're all out to get you. You're a victim, Jeff, a real loser sometimes. That's why you vote Democrat. Me, I reckon the world's a great place, full of opportunity, and go, and pizzazz - and that's why I'm a Republican. Hell, if they allowed it, I'd be out on the campaign-trail for this Referendum!'

'Why don't you, Tommy,' replied Jeff, a tone of mockery in his voice. 'Sure, go ahead, what've you got to lose? Tommy Albright, Republican, the Great American Hero - came back to Brigadoon to marry the girl and now he can't be bothered with her any more. That'll bring the votes in, won't it, Tommy?'

'You son of a bitch!' Tommy launched himself at Jeff, and the two of them fell to the ground, rolling over and over in the heather. No damage was done, except to Jeff's flask, which lost its contents. They fetched up at the foot of a short slope, entangled in the bracken, breathing heavily.

'You think I care?' asked Jeff after a while. 'You think I care about anything any more? About this place, this Referendum, about you, about Meg, anyone? No, sir,' he answered his own question, 'I do not. Why do I drink? I'll tell you why I drink. It's to get the voices out of my head, Tommy. Yes, you heard, I should put my Napoleon hat on. Sure, I got voices in my head, and they ain't saying nice things. You brought me back from New York, Tommy, you did it to me; and you had me holed up here with that mad-woman Meg and all her sheep. That's why I drink and that's why I'm not keen on voting. So stick that in your pipe, Tommy.'

'Meg's not my fault, Jeff. I never forced her on you - you know what she's like. The woman's crazy and so are you. Peas in a pod, made for each other, you are. Anyway, you've got nothing to complain of, Jeff Douglas: I've got real troubles of my own. Woman troubles.'

'And don't we know it, Tommy, don't we just know it?' Jeff shook his head at his long-time friend. 'You sure messed that one up, Tommy Albright. Big time. Bigger than the Republican Party, is my guess. Say,' he said in a lighter tone, nodding down the hill, 'that's those dames again. What do you say, Tommy, should we go and introduce ourselves?'

'What dames?' asked Tommy, dusting himself down and sitting up.

'Those ones - that one on the left, she's with some kind of Government Commission. Hey, I forgot to tell you - she's from New York, Tommy. How about that? The one on the right, she's a journalist. Real interesting lady, I'd say. Come on, let's go down and I'll introduce you.'

'Wait,' said Tommy, peering down the hill. 'Those girls look like they're having some kind of argument. We shouldn't -'

'Of course we should,' interrupted Jeff easily. 'That's exactly why we should. The little ladies shouldn't be arguing - smudges their make-up. Come on.' So saying, Jeff straightened his crumpled suit, brushed his hair with the comb he carried in his pocket, slid his battered flask out of sight and set off down the hill. Tommy followed him.

It was true. Ms. Ashton and Nana Visitor were locked in argument about the latter's access to certain privileged information.

'And I tell you, Ms. Journalist, that there is no way on God's earth that I can let you have that kind of access. It's way beyond your level.'

'*Scheisse !*' exclaimed Nana, turning quite red in the face. 'Excuse me, without me you would not be standing here now, in investigating this affair. You would be on an aeroplane back to America.'

'That is true,' conceded Ms. Ashton gracefully. 'And of course I am very grateful to you, lady, as is the Government and entire population of Scotland. But that doesn't change anything, with all due respect -'

'Dammit one more time! With all due respect, it completely changes everything! I deserve more than anyone to get to the story first. Or are you going to let those total pigs -' she jerked her head towards the press and TV teams who were following each other around in the village just over the dyke, '- have this story all to themselves? Is that actually your plan, Miss American Commissioner? Everything for the UK and the US, and nothing for Eastern Europe? Is that your completely imperialist plan? I will have an answer!'

'I,' said Ms. Ashton losing patience, 'treat all press and TV people in exactly the same way. As the roaches they are. I got where I am today by adhering to policy, Ms. Visitor, and I'm damned - damned, I say - if I'm going to start handing out favours, even to the most deserving. That, Ms. Visitor, is my answer, and if you don't like it, you can shove -'

At that precise moment, Jeff and Tommy turned up. Just as in the old days, they did a little tap-dance number - always got the ladies' attention. As indeed, it did in this instance. The two ladies stared in astonishment at the two young men tapping away in choreographed unison; incredibly, they wore tap-dancing shoes, and achieved a suitable clicking sound even on the boggy ground where they stood.

With a flourish and a bow, they stopped.

'This,' said Jeff, 'is my friend Tommy Albright, and I expect you'll remember me.'

'I remember you very well,' replied Ms. Ashton coldly. 'I just can't remember your name. And I can't quite remember why I should even bother to remember your name.'

'Jeff, Jeff Douglas,' replied that man, quite unperturbed, holding out his hand to shake.

'Ah yes, of course, Mr. Douglas,' she replied, quite ignoring the hand. 'Well, I've got work to do. I'm sure this lady,' indicating Ms. Visitor, 'will be very accommodating to you both.' She turned to leave.

'Hey, don't be like that, lady,' complained Jeff. 'I'm not the best catch in the world, sure, but I'm not a Republican or anything like that. Good Irish-American Democrat. Like yourself, I expect?'

'I have no political allegiance whatsoever,' replied Ms. Ashton, now extremely offended. 'And now, good day to you, sir.' She walked off as quickly as her Italian heels would allow.

Bunnies and Sabbatarians

Tommy looked after her retreating figure for some considerable time. His face showed a curious mixture of bewilderment and appreciation. While he observed the woman, Jeff observed him, a cynical smile on his lips. But neither man said anything.

'So, my friends,' said Nana, breaking into their respective male thoughts. 'How does it look out in Brigadoon? You approve the Referendum or you disapprove?'

'Hell, lady,' said Jeff easily, 'it's just a great game, hokum, that's my take on it. Just one big Easter Parade, with all the bunnies in full view, that's what I think.'

Nana looked at him carefully. 'So you do not approve of the democratic process? You think we might be as well in the bad days of Stalinism? Or in the Middle Ages? That is your view, is that correct?'

Jeff noted something in her voice that told him to change tack.

'Hey,' he said laughing, and boldly putting one hand against each of her shoulders. She measured up well. 'I'm not the sharpest knife in the drawer. Tommy here will tell you that. I'm a man of simple tastes. If I see corruption in high places - hell, I'm from New York, lady, I can't help but see corruption - then I get to thinking. I just can't see what anyone like me can do about it. But,' he added, giving a large slow wink, 'I'm a real fast learner.'

Nana Visitor was also a fast learner. There was an air about Jeff Douglas that attracted her. And since Sydney Guilaroff had been ignoring her all day, despite her journalistic coup - or was it because of it? - she wondered about trailing this man along. There might, in any case, be another story in him - one her shithead of an editor would like. For reasons that she had never understood, her editor had a soft spot for Americans abroad; perhaps it had something to do with black market dollars in the olden days. Herself, she agreed with her poor grandfather - she would happily round them all up and throw them into the salt-mines of Thuringia and take away the ladders. But not this one. Not yet at least.

'*Also*, Mr. Douglas,' she said, 'perhaps you and I will wander a little through the village. I will tell you about democracy and you will tell me about corruption in high places.'

Brigadoon Revisits

'It's a deal, lady,' replied Jeff enthusiastically. 'Just let me fetch a bottle from my cottage. I'm a bit thirsty.'

Arm in arm, the pair wandered off. Tommy Albright, meanwhile, stared and stared until he could see the Electoral Commissioner no longer. And then he gave a shrug and executed a few thoughtful dance-steps. He set off on a mission of his own.

~ 17 ~

Cheese-Boards or Social Housing

Cindy Charisse had had a brainwave. In the course of her campaigning since the morning, she had noticed that there was one thing about which her potential constituents seemed upset: and that was the damage done to the old hump-backed bridge. It was likely, although she knew she could never prove it, that the heavy plant on the construction of the by-pass had caused the damage. What a coup for the Green Party if she could somehow arrange its speedy repair! It would stand as a twin symbol - firstly, defiance in the teeth of the juggernaut of road-building; and secondly, as a bridge between the old world and the new.

Cindy knew just the man who could repair the bridge. Leaving her party to continue the distribution of leaflets and the gathering of intelligence regarding the needs of the electorate, she raced back up to Storybook Glen. As she came out of the woods, she looked around. All was quiet - the entire campaign-force of Permitted Participants, hangers-on and the media circus were still down at the village, as was the entire staff of the International Electoral Commission. Over by the shop, a forlorn figure - it was the manageress of the park - sat on a bench brooding. Furtively, Cindy made her way over to the Jack and the Beanstalk exhibit.

'Jack!' she whispered urgently, 'Jack!'

Brigadoon Revisits

Jack turned his attention briefly from gazing up through the leaves of the beanstalk. He kept his axe ready in his hand, should the Giant decide to start a descent.

'Jack,' continued Cindy in a low and urgent voice. 'I've got a job for you and - you know - him.' She jerked his chin upwards.

'You mean the big ugly Giant?' asked Jack.

There was a roar from above, and a loud angry voice said: 'I'm big, but I'm not ugly! And if you say that again, I'm going to come down the Beanstalk and eat you all up!'

Jack merely whistled and swung his axe ever so lightly against the Beanstalk. It quivered slightly. The voice roared again nervously and then fell silent.

'So what's the job, then, darling?' asked Jack.

Cindy explained.

'And you want him up there, old buggerlugs, to do the work?' Jack pursed his lips. 'I'm not keen on that,' he said. 'Not at all. Have you even seen him?'

Cindy admitted that she had not seen the Giant yet, but that she thought he would be open to suggestion. 'After all, how long has he been stuck up there at the top of the Beanstalk, waiting to come down?'

'Long enough,' replied Jack cheerfully. He shouted up the Beanstalk. 'Hey, dude, you want to come down and help out?'

The reply was a great growl that set the leaves swaying. Jack stepped back a step or two, the better to take a full swing with his axe.

Cindy intervened. 'Mr. Giant,' she called, 'I've got a proposal. Can you hear me?'

'Of course I can hear you,' grumbled the voice. 'I don't get any sleep up here with all your twittery little voices. What kind of deal's on the table, then?'

'We let you down, you repair a broken-down bridge. You do it well, you get to stay down, just as long as you don't come back here and frighten the kids or annoy Jack.'

'Hey, dude!' protested Jack. 'And what am I going to do then? No giant annoying me, no point in me hanging on down here. I'll be out of a job!'

Cheese-Boards or Social Housing

Cindy reassured him. 'Don't you worry, sweetheart. There's an opening coming up in one of the major banks. You'd do well there.'

'How come I'd do well there?' demanded Jack suspiciously. 'I don't know anything about banks.'

'You do deals with cows and beans, don't you?' asked Cindy, wide-eyed.

'Ye-es,' replied Jack, cautious and confused.

'That's all you need to know then,' said Cindy. 'Cows for beans. Big job at the bank, girls, money, fast cars. You'll be able to buy a mansion for your old widowed mother.'

The Giant shouted down. 'What's going on down there?' he wanted to know. 'Have we got a deal or not? I want to come down! It's no life for a Giant up here on my own.'

And so it was arranged. Jack lowered his axe and stepped back, and the Giant started clambering down the Beanstalk. It shook and it groaned and the leaves shivered as if electricity was passing through them. Every so often another branch of the stalk would break with a crack, there would be an ogreish curse from above, and Cindy would stand just a little further back. At last, Cindy and Jack could see a huge dirty bare foot appearing above them, and then another. Just then, Jack sprang forward and started whacking his axe into the Beanstalk.

'Stop! Stop!' roared the Giant in terror. 'I'll fall and kill myself!'

Jack jumped back again, laughing merrily. 'Just kidding, Giant! Got you there, didn't I? Come on, chop chop!'

At last, with a thump that shook the ground, the Giant came down to earth. He detached himself from the Beanstalk and turned round. He was, in fact, yes, quite ugly. And hairy and smelly. His clothes were stained with soup and tomato-seeds. Half-gnawed bones poked out of his pockets. But he had an oddly pathetic set to his mouth. Even when he scowled, as he now did at Jack, he seemed almost harmless.

'So, Giant,' said Cindy, 'I'll take you down to the bridge.'

'My friends call me Rory,' murmured the Giant shyly.

Jack burst out laughing and fell dramatically to the ground, clutching his ribs. 'That'll be no one, then!' he shouted cruelly.

Cindy ignored Jack. 'Come along, Rory,' she said, 'you follow me, my love.'

There was considerable consternation down at the village when Cindy, Jack and the Giant arrived at the far side of the bridge. Dogs barked and children screamed. Those with no sense at all crowded as near to the bridge as they could, while the rest stood at a respectful distance. Cindy announced that the Green Party would now, as a matter of priority, reconstruct the broken bridge, in defiance of any motorway-building project. Leaflets were handed out, exhorting everyone to vote "Yes" today and "Green" next time round.

It took the Giant a mere fifteen minutes to set the bridge to rights. None of the huge stones had gone astray, they had merely tumbled off into the river or the surrounding heather and trees. It was just a question of finding them, lifting them into position and standing back proudly. By the time the bridge was finished, it looked just as good as new and several people decided that Scotland should be Independent and that their political allegiance lay with a party that could so easily and so quickly repair the ravages of time.

Naturally, this sparked off an imaginative and unreasonable bout of wild promises by the rival parties. There were loud noises about social housing, about a sports centre, a community hall, even an Internet café. All of these, when explained carefully to the villagers, whose grip on reality was fast being eroded by this noisy invasion of people and ideas from the 21st century, found considerable acclaim. No one had the faintest idea what an Internet café might be, but all were agreed with the People's Coalition, that it was an awesome idea.

Jane Ashton kept a close eye on all of this, but could find no particular transgression. Will Tuttle cruised the crowds and the hustings, reporting back to his boss in the moments he could spare from tweeting.

But the plan to end all plans was that proposed by Jean Kelly of the SNP.

'Friends,' she announced at the newly-repaired bridge, thereby hijacking Ms. Charisse's event, 'it is more than your bridge that is threatened with destruction. Something far worse is on its way!'

Cheese-Boards or Social Housing

'Witches?' asked several troubled voices, 'are the witches on their way? Oh, Mr. Forsyth, Mr. Forsyth, you said they would not come!'

'No, my good friends,' Mrs. Kelly calmed the panic, 'it is not the witches. Your village is threatened by something far more visible and far more human.' She pointed up to the top of the hill, when the Portakabins of the construction company were clearly visible, where figures in hard hats stood idly and looked down the hill. 'Up there is a road, a mighty road, as wide as your village and as black as night.'

'Bigger even than General Wade's roads?' asked Harry Beaton. Harry was a young man who liked to keep up with the news of the moment.

'Far larger than even those roads,' announced Mrs. Kelly. 'This is a road such as you have never seen before. And unless we do something to stop it, that road will flatten your village, destroy your houses and turn your fields into deserts!'

A great groan went up. 'How can we stop this terrible thing?' asked Andrew Campbell. 'Oh, where is Mr. Lundie, that he might advise us?'

No one knew where Mr. Lundie might be, and Mrs. Kelly did not care.

'We can stop this, by working together. If you vote "Yes", the SNP will come to power and we promise - we promise here and now, before all you people, and before the newspapers and the TV, that this road will not damage one blade of grass, one stone, one tiny piece of the village of Brigadoon!'

A cheer went up and the crowd begged to know how this miracle of salvation would work. 'It is a pity,' remarked Harry Beaton in a low voice to Jeff Douglas, 'that this SNP was not around a week ago. It might have saved Mr. Forsyth a lot of trouble, don't you think?' Jeff made no polite comment.

'We will fight for a Brigadoon By-pass,' announced Mrs. Kelly triumphantly. 'A by-pass that, whatever it might cost, will divert the motorway around the village, and leave you all in peace, allowing you to get on with your lives in a dynamic, independent and secure Scotland. We will fight for it and, when we are a free country once more, we will make it happen!'

Brigadoon Revisits

The "No" parties, who had gathered round suspiciously, looked glum. Why had they not thought of that? It was so obvious! Rather than fooling around with cheese-boards or social housing, they should have gone for a by-pass. It was insane, of course - there was no chance of diverting the Peripheral Route now. How could you build a by-pass for a by-pass? It would cost millions - billions, possibly, if recent Scottish public works were anything to go by. It would set the motorway back months. No way would the motorway be diverted. But the Referendum would be done and dusted before the villagers realised that fundamental truth.

Virginia Bosler tried her best. 'That woman is a liar!' she heckled from the back of the crowd. 'She is promising you something she cannot deliver! Don't believe a word she says!'

Mrs. Kelly was unmoved. 'She calls me a liar? That woman represents a party that has lied to the Scottish Nation for decades. Her party closed down everything that made Scotland great. If you want cheese, vote "No". If you want a by-pass, vote "Yes"!'

There was much muttering among the villagers at this. It was a difficult choice. The cheeses had tasted quite wonderful.

'Behold,' continued Mrs. Kelly, pressing home her advantage. She pointed dramatically out beyond the River Doon and its little bridge, to the scarred and mutilated hillside which had already undergone clearance in advance of the motorway. 'That is how your village will look if the road comes down here. There will be no room for houses, and this beautiful glen will be polluted by noise and stench and filth. You will be cleared off your lands, like -' she was about to say "your ancestors", and then realised it should probably be "descendants", and so amended it to '- like your friends, and sent off to wastelands, far from your families and your loved ones. Do not permit yourself to be cleared from your lands! Vote "Yes" – with the SNP!'

'Remember Trump!' bellowed a voice from the crowd. It was of course Eddie Quillan, breaking ranks.

'Remember Trump!' The chant was taken up by several other ungrateful hecklers in the crowd.

'Trump had nothing to do with us!' proclaimed Mrs. Kelly brazenly. 'That was all down to the Liberal Democrats!'

At this, the scene broke up in chaos, as party shouted at party and occasionally fought hand to hand. All memory of campaign unity was obliterated. This was real. The police were obliged to pull apart the battling factions. The villagers stood back in astonishment. Some of them wondered whether it was wise to have one of these Referendums at all. Others feared that the Last Trump was about to sound, as Mr. Forsyth had long foretold, echoing the words of the divine Mr. Erskine. Others still considered it all to be mere trumpery. Nana Visitor was delighted and encouraged: all of human life was, at last, here. And Will Tuttle tweeted: 'We give them voters and they offer only insults.' It was one of his better tweets. He was very pleased with it. He repeated the words, orally, to Ms. Ashton, who had to admit that it looked that way.

At last order was restored. Mrs. Kelly, her blood now up, announced that she was going up the hill to dictate terms to the construction company. 'There will be,' she said in words that would haunt her for several hours, 'there will be a Brigadoon By-pass.' A good dozen party-activists, many with some domestic experience in dealing with builders, accompanied her. Anxious to witness history in the making, every single one of the newspaper and TV reporters tagged along behind. They all blundered through the mud and up the hill, slipping and sliding and cursing the unsustainable zealotry of the SNP.

The villagers stood around idly, awaiting the next wonder of this wondrous Friday.

~ 18 ~

They're Not in the Union

'It's effing one o'clock, Newcombe, and there's nothing effing moving!' Bob Tucker was out of sorts. There was the faintest hint of it in the way that he frothed at the mouth and lashed out with booted feet at anything that came within his compass. 'What are we? A construction company or social workers - that's what I want to know? No - don't bother: I'll tell you. Effing social workers, that's what! Look at us - we should have this road right down that hill by now and be starting to demolish those huts they've put up! And here we are, watching the politicians and the press and the police come and go, all nice and polite! And it's your effing fault, Newcombe!'

Warren Newcombe started to protest, even though he knew it would do no good. Tucker the Tearless was listening to nobody except himself.

'If I could do it, Newcombe, I'd take all this out of your wages! You'd be working for the next hundred years for free. Every day wasted here means another ten thousand in penalties. What the fuck were you doing, sniffing around down there at that time in the morning? Not enough for you to do up here, I suppose? You half-wit! When all this is over - oh shit!' Tucker interrupted himself to peer out of the Portakabin window. He slammed his mug of coffee down, shattering it into a hundred pieces, splashing coffee everywhere. 'What the fuck's this now? Is this your doing, Newcombe?'

They're Not in the Union

Warren gingerly took a couple of steps towards the window and peered out through the dust and grime. The window commanded the best view of the hillside and the village that lay peacefully in the September sunshine. At first he saw nothing unusual. He was about to ask Bob what was wrong when he noticed a file of children in colourful dress - hats, jackets and trousers in all possible combinations of red, green and blue. The children were marching in single file up the hill, directly towards them.

'I'd better go and see,' murmured Warren, and he stepped rapidly out of the hut. When the was out in the open air, he heard the sound of singing. It came from the children. There were seven of them. They seemed to be singing a song he knew from happier times - *'Heigh-ho! Heigh-ho! It's off to work we go!'* Yes, that was exactly it. A crowd of Warren's colleagues gathered to view the approaching band. Fifty yards off, and it became clear that these were no ordinary children out for a walk. Apart from anything else, they were unaccompanied by an adult. That never happened. Even this far north.

And most of these seven children had long grey beards.

They marched on merrily and came to a halt right in front of Warren. 'Company, halt!' bellowed the leader. With varying degrees of success, the six followers halted, some barging into others.

'Are you The Man?' the leader asked Warren.

Before he could answer, there was a muffled shout of rage from behind Warren. 'Get those effing children off this site! Now! Or I'll come out and kill them myself!'

'No,' said Warren to the leader of the little men. 'No, I'm not The Man.' He quietly signalled with his thumb over his shoulder. 'That's The Man.'

Without hesitation, the leader ordered *'Heigh-ho!'* and the small group marched neatly round Newcombe and up to the Portakabin. The leader stepped forward and rapped smartly on the door. Warren stayed where he was. He felt safer there.

The door flew open and Tucker stood there, face crimson, eyes bulging, momentarily rendered speechless with wrath.

'The Seven Dwarves at your service, sir,' said the leading dwarf. 'I'm Doc. And this is Happy and Sneezy and Grumpy and Dopey and Sleepy and -'

'I'm Bashful,' announced the last one, smiling winsomely and waving shyly to the company man.

Tucker the Tearless groped after breath. He could still find no words that would suffice. The dwarves continued to smile up at him. At last he gasped: 'What the fuck do you want?'

'We would like jobs here in this very fine open-cast mine, sir,' stated Doc boldly.

'Open-cast mine?' said Tucker, astonished, when he should really have been asking another question altogether. 'What mine?'

'Why, this one, sir.' Doc waved appreciatively at the panorama of rural devastation around them.

'This isn't a mine, retard, this is the construction-site of the Aberdeen Western Peripheral Route. Cleanhill.'

'Oh well,' said Doc, unconcerned. 'Don't you need good workmen? We've come to offer our services.'

Bob Tucker was about to carry out his threat to kill them himself when Doc added very seriously: 'We'll want a shilling a day, mind. We won't accept a penny less.'

The words hit Tucker like a douche of cold water. He found his blood pressure dropping back to normal as if on a silken parachute. A pleasant little tune played in his head, where previously there had been a strident clashing of drums and cymbals.

'Now, why didn't you say so? Come in, lads,' he said in a welcoming tone, 'we'll see what we can find for you. You boys wouldn't be in the union, now, would you?'

Doc denied all knowledge of any union; and in they trooped. The door closed behind them.

Before Warren had time to relax, an ostrich shot past, hotly pursued by a band of labourers. The bird was too quick for them - it had a turn of speed that could not be matched even by the dumper-truck which bucketed along in pursuit. The ostrich vanished down the hill and into the village. On its way, it ran through another small crowd of people.

They're Not in the Union

This one was led by a woman done up in a smart suit, closely followed by a couple of dozen reporters and cameramen.

'You there!' called the woman, in tones which demanded attention.

Warren looked to left and right. His colleagues had melted away all of a sudden. There was only himself, standing on the brow of the hill.

'Yes, you' she repeated, panting from the effort of the ascent. 'Are you in charge here?'

Warren stuttered a few words, which did not deny his status.

'Good,' said the woman, coming to a halt. 'My name is Jean Kelly. I represent the SNP. I have a proposal to make regarding this road you're building. We want it diverted around that village down there.'

Warren's heart fell. He thought of a solution. 'Perhaps you'd better talk to the representative from Head Office, madam,' he suggested. 'He's here on site.'

Mrs. Kelly nodded graciously. 'That will do admirably,' she said. 'Where is he?'

Warren led the way to the Portakabin. As the deputation arrived, the door opened, the Seven Dwarves marched out whistling, and went off to pick up spades and pick-axes. Bob Tucker stood watching them, rubbing his hands, a broad smile on his face. 'That'll cut costs quite dramatically,' he said. 'Do my Christmas Bonus no harm at all. I wonder if they've got any friends?' And then Bob saw that Warren was not alone. Another black cloud descended.

'What now, Newcombe?' he demanded. 'Is this the parish council, come to whine about the noise or the destruction of their buttercups?' He waved imperiously at Mrs. Kelly. 'Clear off, you bloody woman, and take all your lezzy friends with you. I've called security.'

Mrs. Kelly was not in the least perturbed. She turned round to the assembled reporters and TV crews. 'Are you getting all of this?' she asked cheerfully.

It was only then that Tucker noticed the cameras. He hesitated for barely a second.

'And you lot can get out as well - this is private land. You're trespassing! I'll be making a call to your papers - our company owns

Brigadoon Revisits

half of them, anyway. And you - Mr. Jay, yes, I recognise you - you can forget about your lah-di-dah investigative reporting here. It cuts no ice with me. So fuck off, the lot of you!'

Mrs. Kelly stood her ground. So did the press. Alan Jay, the famous investigative journalist, murmured something into his microphone.

'Clearly,' said the supporter of the "Yes" vote, 'you are not a man with whom I can, should or must negotiate.'

'Too effing right,' said Tucker, a shade brusquely.

'In that case, I'm staying here until you can produce someone with whom I can negotiate,' she retorted. In the traditional act of political defiance, she eased herself to the ground. 'I'm sitting here, sir, until your company talks to me. I owe at least that to the people of Scotland.'

Bob shrugged his shoulders. 'Sit there as long as you want, darling,' he said. He returned to the Portakabin to plan a recruitment drive down in Storybook Glen. If he could get another couple of dozen like those dwarves, he reckoned he could lay off a hundred men here. His bonus would skyrocket. Likely he'd get a seat on the board before too long. Sorted.

~ 19 ~

The Scarlet Woman, The Scoffer and The Succubus

'Now then, MacReekie,' asked Archie Beaton, 'what's TESCO?'

Mr. MacReekie did his best to look nonplussed. 'TESCO?' said he. 'Where?'

Archie pointed at the huge blue and red sign which was attached, a little precariously, above MacReekie's butchery. 'There,' he said, 'TESCO.'

'Ah,' said MacReekie, 'that'll be the name of the man who bought my business.'

'From over the seas, would it be, with a name like that?' asked Archie.

'Aye, something like, I expect. Now, you'll have to excuse me, Mr. Beaton, I must be getting along.' With which words, MacReekie the butcher hurried off.

Archie stood staring at the large sign, scratching his head. He was joined in moments by other worthies of the village.

'What's TESCO?' asked James Maclaren.

'Aye, well,' replied Archie cautiously. 'It seems a foreign gentleman has purchased the butchery from Malcolm MacReekie.'

'Is that so?' remarked James. He peered at the small building intently for a while. 'The new gentleman seems to sell all manner of things, does he not?'

Brigadoon Revisits

'He does, James, he does.'

A small crowd on onlookers had now gathered in front of the shed which MacReekie had until then used to slaughter birds and beasts, in darkness and secrecy. In the course of the past hour, unnoticed by all, it had undergone a transformation - the wall facing on to MacConnachy Square had been removed and replaced with large plate-glass windows, a door had been inserted round the side, and bright lights burned within. A small wind-turbine hummed busily beside it, capturing magical waves out of the ether and providing power for lighting and refrigeration. Foot by foot, the crowd moved forwards until noses were pressed up against the glass windows and wide eyes peered inside. It was now possible to see a number of shopkeepers scuttling around, loading merchandise on to serried ranks of shelves. All manner of goods could be seen - fruit, vegetables, bottles, packets, pots and pans, sandwiches. The whole place seemed far larger inside than it was out.

Prompted by his fellow-citizens, Archie Beaton cautiously pushed the door and went inside. What a sight! What a change! Instead of the putrid stench of dried blood and rotting offal, there was the enticing perfume of fruit, vegetables and plug-in air-fresheners. Archie blinked. Had he been transported to Paradise, perhaps? It seemed for the moment unlikely - Mr. Forsyth had rarely talked of Paradise, he was more your man for Hell. Archie took a deep breath. A shelf-stacker hastened past, clutching an armful of cheese. Archie took another deep breath and savoured the scent that eddied in the youth's wake. A manageress walked past and smiled at Archie.

'Triple points today, sir,' she said mysteriously. 'Double for the rest of the week.'

Archie nodded uncomprehendingly. It was all too much for him. He turned to leave the store. But a press of his fellow-villagers prevented egress and obliged him to go back in. For the next fifteen minutes, an astonished crowd made their way in a tight phalanx around the half-dozen aisles. They kept together and avoided the eyes of the staff. They whispered, pointed and muttered.

Finally, emboldened by the pressure of the friends at his back and by what he had seen, Archie accosted the manageress. She was a

The Scarlet Woman, The Scoffer and The Succubus

woman in her late thirties, smartly-dressed. 'Good lady,' he said, 'could I speak to Mr. Tesco?'

'I'm afraid that's not possible,' she replied, smiling all the while. 'Can I help?'

Archie was not disheartened. 'Are you perhaps Mrs. Tesco?' he enquired.

'No,' said she, 'I am Harriet Freed. I'm the general manager.'

Archie pondered this new word for a moment. 'The manager?' he asked.

'I look after the shop on behalf of Mr. Tesco,' she explained. 'Now, sir, how can I help you? Would you and your friends perhaps like to try some of our cocktail sausages? And perhaps sample some of the wines we have on special offer this week. We also have a whole range of nibbles and nuts.'

There was a loud murmuring of agreement to this proposal from behind Archie, so he dared not refuse. The woman seemed amiable enough, he thought, and perhaps might be persuaded to take up residency in his cottage: the place was sorely in need of a woman's touch since his wife Jeannie had died five years ago. Or whenever it was. He took the lady by the arm and together the little crowd headed off to Aisle 5.

One person who was not in this crowd was Sandy Macmillan. He stood firmly outside, deeply suspicious of such a sparkling hall of temptations. He gazed up at the sign in the sky. He, if no one else except perhaps Mr. Lundie, who remained mysteriously absent, remembered well the teachings of Mr. Forsyth: 'Let us not fall into the ways of evil, let us not feast upon the food of the profane, let us not be tempted by the cheesecake of luxury, nor yet swallow the wines of the wayward.' Mr. Macmillan wondered if the name TESCO could have significance: with the addition of a couple of letters, it could so easily be the name THE SCOURGE or THE SCARLET WOMAN, or, with some juggling, THE SCOFFER or THE SUCCUBUS ; how would it be with THE SORCERESS or THE SCARAB or - ? His black and ever blacker thoughts were interrupted as his eye caught Malcolm MacReekie slinking past.

'MacReekie!' said Sandy in a voice which could not be ignored. 'Stay thy step!'

MacReekie did so, nervously looking about for a route of escape.

'What have ye done, sinner?' demanded Sandy, indicating with a slow movement of his right hand the new Shrine of Moloch, with its bright red and blue sign. 'What have ye done?'

'The man,' muttered MacReekie, 'offered me a decent price for my outhouse, Mr. Macmillan, and I did not like to refuse him.'

Sandy Macmillan looked on the butcher with contempt. 'You would sell your soul for a few shillings?' he asked.

'Oh, you are very strong, Mr. Macmillan,' said MacReekie obsequiously, 'very strong, I think: I have not sold my soul to the man, merely a part of my business.'

'And how many pieces of silver did the man give to you? And was he cloven-hoofed perhaps?'

'No, not at all,' said MacReekie quickly. 'Just a man, you know, like so many others who have come here this day. He spoke to my wife -'

'Ah!' interrupted Sandy Macmillan, his brow furrowed. 'Your wife. That explains much.'

'Aye,' confirmed MacReekie cautiously.

'Your wife, who would sell not only the clothes you stand up in, but the roof over your head, for a silver sixpence? No, let us say that she would sell a silver sixpence for a golden guinea.'

'Aye, she would,' reflected MacReekie, suddenly struck with admiration at the most attractive quality in his wife. 'She would do just that. Anyway, the man spoke to my wife, and she agreed a fair price with him. What was I to do, but take his money? Am I to be faulted for that, Mr. Macmillan?'

'Yes, indeed, Mr. Macmillan,' chimed in another voice, 'are we to be faulted for that, I wonder?' Catriona MacReekie had emerged from TESCO carrying four bulging bags of shopping. 'No, I think not. We have to make our way in the world, Mr. Macmillan, I believe that Mr. Forsyth said that we must not hold back, nor languish in our own dung! No, Mr. Macmillan, we are not to be faulted for that. The man gave us an honest price, and now, like the lad in the Bible with his

The Scarlet Woman, The Scoffer and The Succubus

talents, we shall see our talents multiply and bring us great goodness, Mr. Macmillan.'

Sandy Macmillan eyed the proud woman for a minute and shook his head disapprovingly. 'You know not what you do,' he murmured prophetically, and, turning his back upon the new store, walked away to his sweetmeat stall.

'Aye well, old man,' Catriona called after his retreating figure, 'at least we will not rot in poverty any longer. Not like some I could mention!' She turned to her husband, her ostrich head-dress quivering with pride. 'Now, Mr. MacReekie, will you take a look at these chicken breasts - barely twenty shillings for the pair, and delicious, I think, with some lightly-steamed sugar-snap peas and a glass or two of Chardonnay.'

Her husband gaped at her. 'Twenty shillings, Catriona? We cannot afford twenty shillings! Have you lost your senses?'

'Of course we can,' she scoffed. 'Think, husband: how much did the man give for our bit outhouse? We can afford a wee treat now and again. Anyway, it's triple points today, and we'll get all our money back, I'm told. Now, I'm off to sauté these in some virgin olive oil and paprika, and we'll have a grand lunch. It is already one o'clock - my, how the time has flown, Mr. MacReekie! Twenty minutes, and you be home in time.' She hurried off, bags groaning and clinking with the weight of purchases. She had not told her husband of the family-size banoffee pie, which she intended as an afternoon snack in the privacy of her own scullery.

MacReekie stood for a good five minutes, feeling suddenly at a loss. No animals to slaughter, no knives to sharpen, no haggling, no cheating, nothing to do. He had lost his bearings in the world, and he felt very uneasy about it. At length, he opened the door to the new store and went in. Over in Aisle 5, there seemed to be some kind of ceilidh in progress, but he instinctively avoided it. He wandered up and down Aisle 2, in front of the chilled meats, astonished and appalled in equal measure by what his professional eye saw there. Were such cuts of meat even possible? Disheartened, he hurried back out into the fresh summer air and took a few deep breaths to calm himself down.

Brigadoon Revisits

The retired butcher heard the sound of an argument. He looked towards MacConnachy Square, where the market-stalls still stood. A number of the stall-holders stood around in a small group, talking heatedly to some strangers. MacReekie, ever attracted to an argument in the open air, strolled across to witness the excitement more nearly.

'I'm sorry, sir,' said one of the strangers, dressed in the modern style, 'I'm sorry but regulations are regulations. If you have not got a street-trader's licence, you cannot sell anything from a stall in the open air. That's clear enough, isn't it?'

'But -' said John Gilfillan, carpenter and trader in wooden spoons and chair-legs.

'I'm sorry, sir,' repeated the modern gentleman, 'but you will have to apply for a licence, in person, at the Council offices. It can take up to ten working days to process, and in the meantime, I must ask you to pack up and leave. As for you, sir,' he added menacingly, turning to Harry Beaton who stood minding his father's cloth stall, 'if you wish to avoid prosecution, get these imported Japanese tartans out of sight right away!'

Harry looked dazed. 'But these were woven by my own father,' he stammered.

The stranger merely looked Harry in the eye. 'You heard me, sir. There's no room for outlandish tartans like those in this county. Do you think I was born yesterday? I've never seen such loud colours and gaudy, shoddy stuff in my life before. I tell you, I've been twenty years in Trading Standards, and it takes a lot to shock me. But you've done it, you've done it! Now, I've given you a final warning. If I have to tell you again, you'll be up before the courts. And my colleague here from Environmental Health will have your friends up on charges as well. This place is an absolute disgrace!'

'Quite right, sir, quite right.' The second modern gentleman nodded agreeably and tapped Harry on the chest. 'Too much rogue trading going on these days. If we don't take a stand, the consumer will be ripped off - or worse, poisoned.' He eyed up Sandy Macmillan's sweetmeat stall, buzzing lightly with flies in the midday sunshine.

The Scarlet Woman, The Scoffer and The Succubus

Harry's face had slowly been turning redder. Now, without warning, his right fist pulled back and then rapidly forward. The blow hit the second stranger square on the chin, and he keeled over, moaning. The first stranger retreated hastily, pulling out his mobile-phone as he went. Harry was about to follow up his first assault with some closer contact between his feet and the man's stomach, but John Gilfillan held him back. 'Don't do it, Harry! He's not worth it! Anyway,' he added gloomily, 'look around you: there's no customers. The place is dead. We might as well pack up and go home.'

Harry struggled for a bit with Gilfillan, then caught sight of MacReekie.

'This is your fault!' he exclaimed.

'Mine?' said MacReekie, much astonished, but taking a few precautionary steps back. Harry was in another of his black fighting moods, it seemed.

'Aye, yours! Where are all our customers, then? I'll tell you where they are - they are in that fancy new shop that you've opened up in your outhouse, that's where!'

MacReekie put up both hands defensively. 'Not my outhouse, Harry, not any more. Not at all.'

'No, because you sold it for thirty pieces of silver. Judas!' Harry hurled the word at the butcher. 'You sold it, and now that man Tesco has got all our customers in his shop there, leaving us with nothing! Nothing, Judas - you've ruined us!'

'It was considerably more than thirty pieces,' protested MacReekie. 'I would never sell out for so little as that.' At that moment, his wife called him from their cottage and he retreated to feast on chicken breasts and sip cool Chardonnay.

'Judas MacReekie! May God turn your food to ashes in your mouth!' The curse flew like a burning spear from the echoing market-place and smote MacReekie between the shoulder-blades. He moved all the faster, and was much relieved to shut the door behind him. He sat down with his wife and gabbled a grace in favour of TESCO.

Back at MacConnachy Square, the three stall-holders sat, heads in hands.

Brigadoon Revisits

'It's all over,' said Gilfillan. 'Look at us: since Mr. Forsyth called down the protection of the Good Lord upon us, we have not been able to trade with anyone. No one comes to the village, except those who wish to gape at us, or torment us. We set up our stalls and sell only to each other, simply for old times' sake.'

'Ah, haste ye back, Mr. Forsyth,' said Sandy fervently, his eyes raised heavenwards, 'haste ye back, for we have lost our way.'

Harry Beaton looked darkly upon Sandy Macmillan. 'Forsyth,' he muttered darkly to himself, 'I trust you have received your reward for what you have done to us.'

The unpleasant episode with Trading Standards and Environmental Health had attracted the attentions of Eddie Quillan, representative of the People's Coalition, and his inseparable comrade-in-arms, Ivan Johnson.

'Met your match, then?' asked Eddie coolly of the two Council employees. They glared at him and retreated to lick their wounds. Trading Standards had already submitted a verbal report back to his office and had set in motion the due process of law. Eddie ignored them and turned his attention to the downcast market-traders.

'Problems, my friends?' he asked solicitously.

'Oh, sir,' replied John Gilfillan, 'how can we tell you? Troubles? We have not seen the like in many a long year. Had the witches that Mr. Forsyth foretold come down upon us, I doubt we could be more troubled!'

'Aye,' interjected Mr. Macmillan, 'first these gentlemen who threaten us with the full force of the law, and then that Mr. Tesco whose grand new shop appears to sell everything that we do, but more cheaply and elegantly than we could ever hope. Aye, and a temptress in Aisle Five forbye! Oh, but the flesh is weak! Sir,' he continued in a lower voice, 'if I come before the judge, will I be hanged or will I be sent to the colonies, do you think?'

'Oh, it will not come to that, my friend,' laughed Eddie Quillan easily. 'And if it does,' he shook a fist at the oblivious Council officials, 'the People's Coalition will defend you to the hilt. To the hilt, regardless of what is put up against you. Eddie Quillan, People's

The Scarlet Woman, The Scoffer and The Succubus

Coalition,' he added, shaking hands all round. 'To the hilt: you have my word on that.'

Looking much relieved, the tradesmen relaxed. 'Well, then,' said John, 'that is a fine thing to know. The People's Collation, you say?'

'None of the other parties can offer you what The People's Coalition offer,' pursued Eddie. 'Not one of them - they are too busy propping up the corpse of a rotten system, kow-towing to a corrupt judiciary, and fawning before the hyenas of late Capitalism. After the Referendum, when the dust has settled and Scotland is Free once more, you vote for Eddie Quillan, my friends, and we will represent you in every court in the land. And we will win!'

Everyone nodded enthusiastically. A few other villagers had arrived, seeking a new curiosity. All economic life had subsided in the village - sheep wandered aimlessly in the barley-fields, school-children ran wild, men and women gather in groups to gossip or peer through the windows of the new TESCO. What was it to be? The daily drudge? Or the excitement of yet another day in a century to which they had barely had time to accustom themselves? There was no contest. A small crowd had therefore gathered to listen to Eddie's pitch and were greatly impressed.

'Now,' said The People's Coalition, rubbing his hands. 'My comrade here, Mr. Johnson, is my economic adviser, he has some experience in the ways of market-trading. Van, what strategy can we develop for this situation?'

Ivan 'the Van-Man' Johnson had indeed had much experience in market-trading, graduating from car-boot sales, through a stall in The Barras in Glasgow, to a "new and used" CD empire that stretched over most of North-East Scotland. But at heart, he was no petty capitalist - he was bringing the small luxuries of life to the ordinary people, at affordable prices. A vocation which frequently attracted the unwelcome attention of bureaucrats.

'I think,' began Van, 'that you should concentrate on that segment of the market which the monopoly capitalists can't see.'

His audience looked at each other, puzzled and ever so slightly disappointed.

'Look,' explained the Van-Man, 'what does TESCO sell?'

His audience shrugged. 'Everything,' they replied, in one voice. 'And today we get triple points, too,' added someone from the back of the crowd, a remark greeted by mutterings of disbelief and sudden interest.

'No!' shouted Van. The muttering stopped. 'They don't sell everything. Look,' he said patiently, 'you're sitting on a goldmine here.' The crowd looked at the earth beneath their feet. 'A real goldmine. Your village has the potential to be the greatest tourist attraction in Scotland, in Europe even. So, what do tourists want?' There was a profound silence. Everyone - including Eddie Quillan - looked at Van Johnson, waiting for the answer to a question that was incomprehensible. 'I'll tell you what they want. They want Nessies. Jimmy Hats. Tartan rugs. Sticks of rock. Small and large Saltires and Lions Rampant. Teaspoons with pictures of castles. Egg-cups in the shape of Robbie Burns. Whisky miniatures. Soft-toy haggises. Dolls dressed in kilts. That's what tourists want. That's what TESCO doesn't do. Ever.'

The silence continued for a while after this exposition. Then Eddie slapped his comrade on the shoulder. 'Brilliant, Van, brilliant. That's exactly what's needed here. Local crafts and local industry. Something TESCO don't understand at all with all their centralised purchasing. And we supply what the people really want. That's the game, eh, my friends?' He appealed to the crowd. A few of them nodded, convinced by Eddie's enthusiasm alone.

'But what about them?' asked John Gilfillan doubtfully, nodding his head towards the Council officials who glowered in the background.

'Them?' replied Van contemptuously. 'Listen, my friend, are you going to let some jumped-up clerks take away your right to a decent living? Are you? I think not! Are the people of Brigadoon going to lie down and take injustice?'

Gilfillan shook his head.

'Well, then!' said Van.

'Nessies for the People!' shouted Eddie.

'Tartan rugs for the People!' answered the crowd cautiously.

'Soft-toys for the People, by the People!' shouted Eddie.

The Scarlet Woman, The Scoffer and The Succubus

'Haggises for the People, by the People!' answered the crowd more confidently.

'Power to the People!' shouted Eddie.

'Power to the People!' echoed the crowd. 'Power to the People!'

Over by TESCO, a handful of Participants, queuing for their lunchtime baguettes, Tortilla wraps and cans of Diet Coke, looked on contemptuously.

'Rabble-rouser,' said Barry Jones and Virginia Bosler. 'Where's that woman from the Commission, anyway? Shouldn't she be keeping an eye on all this?'

Young Will Tuttle was just behind them in the queue, advising his followers that he was just buying his lunch - a panini filled with feta and pine-nuts, a packet of Fair Trade cashews and a bottle of locally-sourced fizzy water: he liked to eat healthily. He looked up from his mobile at the mention of the Commission.

'Miss Ashton is talking to London and New York,' he announced, almost certain that she was not. The last he had seen of her, she was taking a power-nap in Cinderella's coach. She had sent him out for some lunch, which he had omitted to mention on his most recent Tweet - a man going places did not admit to buying his boss's lunch at TESCO. 'But in -' he looked theatrically at his Rolex, 'in twenty minutes she will be overseeing the registration of the voters. There's a party expected from Aberdeen shortly. I'm sure all you folks will be interested in getting the numbers?'

They would not admit to it - it's not about numbers, it's about principles: but, yes, they might be interested. The numbers meant everything at this point in the Referendum: surely the numbers would tip the result one way or the other? The eyes of the world were on Brigadoon.

A rhythmic chant reached their ears from outside, as they shuffled towards the tills behind a gaggle of confused shoppers: 'What do we want? Jimmy Hats! When do we want them? Now!'

~ 20 ~

He Came From a Long Line of Giants

'Now,' said the Chief Executive of the Council in a loud and authoritative voice, as befitted a man at the centre of a media feeding-frenzy, 'the people of Brigadoon should form an orderly queue. We will note down names, dates of birth and so forth, and - um - whatnot.' He turned to the Electoral Registration Officer for confirmation. The latter gentleman nodded politely, hands crossed in front of him. His name was Vince McAnnelly, and he had already expressed his delight to the Press at being able to gather up these lost voters into the system. Beside Vince sat two of his staff, pens and forms at the ready, a camping table in front of them. Slightly to one side and behind stood the two representatives of the International Independent Electoral Commission, eagle-eyed and watching for the slightest discrepancy, oversight or flaw in the proceedings. Despite his tone, the Chief Executive felt exceedingly nervous.

'So,' he continued, forgetting all the good points he was going to make before the Press, 'without further ado, let us proceed with the act of registration. Ah,' he said cheerfully, 'these look like out first customers of the day. Welcome.'

Sure enough, three people had forced their way to the front of what was still only a very short queue, clearly anxious to sign up to the electoral process. The Chief Executive and Vince motioned them to step forward, vying with each other to make the first and ceremonial registration. Vince won out, by dint of having concealed about his person a bunch of forms and a pen. With a lift of his eyebrows, he secured one of the two seats behind the camping table.

'Now, if I might take the lady first?' he said urbanely, smiling the while. 'Your name, madam?'

The old woman hesitated. One of her male companions jostled her roughly. 'Come on, grannie, we haven't got all day!' He raised his voice and bawled in her ear. 'He wants your name!'

'Well, sir,' she said in a little voice, 'I'm Grandmother.'

Vince stroked his chin and hesitated with his pen. This was going to be difficult - perhaps he should have let the Chief Executive do it after all. 'Quite right, madam, quite right. But do you have a surname, your husband's name perhaps?'

The old woman looked around anxiously. 'No,' she said, 'nothing like that, I'm just Grandmother.'

'She's my grandmother, sir,' piped up a small voice. A small girl dressed in a red cloak with a hood stepped forward and curtseyed politely.

'Oh,' said Vince clutching at the straw thus offered, 'and your name, young lady, is?'

'Little Red Riding Hood,' she answered. 'And that's my grandmother'

There was a long pause. At last Vince asked: 'And do you live in this village - Brigadoon?'

'Oh no, sir,' said the little girl seriously. 'I live on the other side of the forest, with my father, the woodcutter. I'm just visiting Grandmother at her cottage - up there.' She pointed up the hill to Storybook Glen.

'So,' said Vince carefully, 'your grandmother doesn't live in this village either?'

The little girl shook her head firmly.

'Good, well, in that case,' replied Vince, nervously looking over his shoulder at Jane Ashton who sat smiling benignly, but saying nothing, 'in that case, I'm afraid she can't register for voting here. Next person please!'

Brigadoon Revisits

Jack and Rory the Giant stepped forward confidently. But no sooner had Vince opened his mouth to ask for the relevant personal details than they were denounced by young Hamish Maclaren.

'That's two wizards from the witches' village up on the hill!' he shouted. 'They don't belong here neither!'

'Is this true?' demanded Vince. 'You're from the same place as - as - as Grandmother there?'

The Giant lowered his head and nodded shamefacedly. 'All true, sir'

Jack was less submissive. 'So what if we are, mister?' he wanted to know. 'We may not live in this village, but we've got rights like anyone else. Haven't we, Rory?'

Jack kicked the Giant's shin and the Giant growled horribly and rolled his eyes. All who could, fell back several paces. Rory looked very fierce indeed

'Well, sir,' said Vince unhappily, but very anxious to avoid trouble. 'What we'll do is take your details and when we've processed all the registration forms, we'll let you know of our decision. Your name?'

'Jack Nipper.'

'Occupation?'

'Farmer's son.'

'Age?'

'Eighteen last week.'

'Address?'

'Poor Widow's Cottage, Storybook Glen.'

'How long have you lived at that address?'

'Quite long enough, thanks. All my life, I expect. Time for me to move along.' Jack laughed merrily and executed a little dance on the spot.

'And your friend here?' asked Vince, putting Jack's completed form to one side.

'Rory, sir.'

'Occupation?'

'Giant, sir.'

'Age?'

'Three hundred and forty-three, sir.'

He Came From a Long Line of Giants

'Address?'

'Ogre's Castle, Beyond the Sky, sir.'

'How long have you lived at that address?'

'Oh, all my life, sir,' the Giant assured him. 'Like my father the Giant and his father the Giant before him. And his father was also a Giant, I think. I come from a long line of giants, sir.'

Wearily, Vince passed the form to his assistant for stamping and filing. Then he stood and freed up his seat again for the other assistant. 'We'd better get that old lady back,' he muttered unhappily. 'Take her details - whatever you can. And then the rest of them' He wandered off, looking for a drink: the sparkle had suddenly gone out of the day. Meeting the people was not his forte, he should have remembered that; he was an office-man, an organiser.

Behind him the villagers, anxious to sign up to Democracy, formed a patient queue. Jane Ashton never faltered in her gaze, never let one single name go by. She captured every little detail, and would be going through the forms when the process was complete. She had grave doubts about Jack, the Giant and the Grandmother - there was something not quite right about them, something weird.

Will Tuttle had already sent a tweet announcing the start of the whole tedious process. An extra one had gone out when Red Riding Hood's Grandmother was recalled for registration. But then he had to struggle to keep his eyes open. Those four beers last night were catching up on him. A man going places should not have to mingle with the great unwashed - it was certainly not doing his career any good. And he certainly wasn't about to announce to the world that he was stuck here for the next two hours. He considered twibbing, but then remembered that the Press were barely ten feet away and would frown upon any economy with the truth passed out on Twitter. He was shafted. He sighed. Jane Ashton turned her head very slightly. He fell silent.

Grandmother, having had her details recorded at the second attempt, was led away by her fair grand-daughter. She felt quite exhausted by the long walk, and the necessity of running quite hard to evade the wolf which was always lurking about near her cottage.

'I'd like to sit down for a minute,' she said breathlessly. Red Riding Hood led her to a small bench neatly placed under a broad beech tree. An elderly gentleman was already in possession of the bench.

'Might my grandmother sit here, sir? asked the small girl politely.

'Why, of course,' said Andrew Campbell, for it was he. 'There's plenty of room for all of us.' He half-stood and bowed slightly to the old lady. She sat down with thump, and proceeded to talk to Mr. Campbell about everything under the sun. He sat entranced, hearing her voice, but not listening to the words, which were mostly nonsense anyway. The little girl played with beech-nuts on the ground before them. So engrossed were they, all three, that they did not notice Mr. Lundie the dominie passing by, proceeding from the school-house to register himself for the voting.

Mr. Lundie had been apprised of the arrival of the Registration Officers by Sandy Macmillan, who had toiled up the brae and rapped on the door.

'Mr. Lundie, Mr. Lundie!' yelled Sandy.

There was a pause, and then Mr. Lundie began to unlock the door. The door opened an inch, and the dominie's eye appeared in the crack.

'Well, it's you then, Sandy,' said the dominie. 'What a noise and hubbub! Whatever is the matter?'

Sandy explained the procedure for Registration.

Mr. Lundie considered this for a moment. 'I expect it is my duty, then, Sandy, in the absence of our dear Mr. Forsyth, to set an example to our fellow-citizens?'

Sandy nodded enthusiastically. 'It would be the Will of God, I expect?' he suggested.

The door opened another couple of inches. There was sudden disturbance inside, a roar, and then a yelp as if a dog had been kicked. Mr. Lundie's face re-appeared, smiling. 'Will you not come in, Sandy Macmillan? If I am to appear before the magistrates, then I have to ask you to do something for me.'

Sandy stepped inside. If he was surprised to see a modern gentleman sitting on the dusty floor of the schoolroom, massaging his knee, he did not show it.

'The gentleman,' explained Mr. Lundie, 'is Mr. Low. He is a teacher, he tells me. I do not believe him. We have been debating Mr. Fisher's *Marrow of Modern Divinity*.'

'Oh delight!' exclaimed Sandy in deep and heartfelt approval. 'Most praiseworthy.' *The Marrow* was indeed one of Sandy's favourite subjects for serious debate, although he rarely understood any of it. Just to sit, on a winter's evening, listening to the dominie and - in his day - the minister talk of Divinity, every now and again detecting amidst the cloud of unknowing a little luminous shaft of understanding - that was nourishment indeed.

'So, Sandy,' continued Mr. Lundie, 'if you will just keep Mr. Low company awhile, and perhaps explain to him why we are all unworthy, I will go down and talk to the magistrates about their Referendum.'

Sandy bolted the door carefully behind the dominie when he left, and turned to Fred Low. 'So, sir, you are keen to debate theology?'

Fred groaned and closed his eyes. Sandy took the groan for the submissive utterance of a sinner who recognised his own Fall from Grace, and proceeded to wax lyrical on Mr. Ebenezer Erskine's famous sermon "The Wind of the Holy Ghost Blowing Upon the Dry Bones in the Valley of Vision."

Mr. Lundie made his way to MacConnachy Square, where the queue of registering villagers had not diminished at all in thirty minutes of feverish activity by Vince McAnnelly's staff. As one person registered and vanished from the head of the queue, it seemed that two more would join the end of the queue. Jane Ashton was keeping a tally in her head. Seventy-six so far.

It was not for Mr. Lundie to languish in the unusual heat of the September day. Willing hands propelled him forward, despite his humble protestations, to the front of the queue. On arrival there, he smiled kindly upon the American woman he had met before, and then stepped forward to announce his name, his profession, his age and his willingness to cast a vote in the Referendum.

'Oh yes,' he said modestly, 'it is not for a poor sinner such as I to turn aside from my responsibilities in the matter of A Referendum.' These words met with enthusiastic approval from those now at the head of the queue, and he walked away sedately, very satisfied. He looked around him as he went. Some changes had been wrought in the village, he saw. Not for the better, he supposed, but he was resigned to that now. If the witches had come, let them do their worst. He felt no rancour, only awaited the final mercies of God. If the Good Lord chose to send down a mighty scarlet sign upon Mr. MacReekie's outhouse, then so be it. It was clear that the Lord was displeased with the butcher - why else would the sign be indicating that he was THE SCOUNDREL? Ah, but here were some more of the modern gentlemen, sitting on the steps of the market-cross, looking hot and bothered. He must bring them succour.

'Good day to you, gentlemen,' he greeted them, and approached wearing his most welcoming smile. 'It is a very warm day, is it not?'

One of them nodded and muttered that it was.

'I am Mr. Lundie,' he continued, introducing himself, holding out his hand to shake. They could not refuse.

'Vince McAnnelly,' said one of them, 'I'm the Electoral Registration Officer.'

'Oh, delighted to meet you, Mr. McAnnelly,' said Mr. Lundie animatedly, 'I was just there myself, letting your assistants know of my interest in your Referendum. How nice it is to have you here. And these are your friends?'

'These are gentlemen from the Council,' replied McAnnelly, suddenly finding himself in a slightly awkward social situation. He had no idea of the names of these Council officers. 'This chap is from Environmental Health and this one from Trading Standards. I believe they have been very busy here this morning.'

'Oh yes, I can believe that,' replied Mr. Lundie, smiling and shaking their hands. 'So much to do, so many of the old ways, perhaps, to sweep away. So much to overturn and cast down. Thirsty work.' He paused and studied them, in a friendly manner, of course. 'From the Council, you say? Now, I have a colleague of yours taking his ease up at my schoolhouse. And I have some cool drinks up there. Would you perhaps care to -?'

The three found it difficult to turn down such a kind invitation from a courteous old man, and, slinging jackets casually over shoulders, followed him up the brae to the schoolhouse. It was indeed a very mild day, and a cold drink of some sort would be more than welcome. There was little enough that any of them could do for the moment.

'And here we are, gentlemen,' announced Mr. Lundie cheerfully, when they reached the door of the schoolhouse. 'My friend Mr. Macmillan will let us in.' He rapped on the door, two short knocks and then a third. The door opened an inch.

'It is myself, Sandy,' said Mr. Lundie. 'And I have brought some more guests.'

Sandy opened the door wide and the dominie led in his party. Sandy carefully shut the door behind them, and pushed the bolt home again.

It was a little gloomy inside, musty. When Vince's eyes adjusted to the dimmer light, he was a little surprised to see a man sitting bound and gagged at a child's school-desk. But even more surprised to see an ostrich pacing up and down in front of the blackboard, its eyes fixed in a glare upon the new arrivals.

~ 21 ~

The Pumpherston Chipper

'Newcombe!' shouted Tucker the Tearless. 'Get over here! Now!'

Warren's nerves were in shreds since Tucker's arrival. He had no idea what was happening, what was about to happen and what, if it ever did happen, would happen after that. The aborted attack on the village had given him cause for hope, but the arrival of the press and the woman from the SNP, and their subsequent departure in the face of corporate disregard, gave Newcombe the feeling that Tucker was planning something else, something they'd all regret, something he'd get sucked into against his better judgement.

'See that?'

Warren followed Tucker's outraged finger. Half-way down the hill, he saw a cloud of dust. On looking more closely, the cloud was preceded by an ostrich, hotly pursued by a number of men in yellow hats.

'What are those fuckers doing down there?' demanded Bob.

'I've no idea,' replied Newcombe incautiously.

Bob rounded on him, spraying him with saliva. 'I know you've no idea! Christ! Effing find out, you pillock! What do I keep you for? Am I some kind of arse-hole, that you think you can pussy around with me? Am I, Newcombe? Tell me, Newcombe, tell me what you really think! Go on!'

Warren thought it wisest not to tell him. Instead he asked whether he should go and find out.

The Pumpherston Chipper

Bob paused for three seconds. 'And what do you think, Newcombe?' he asked in a quiet voice. 'Do I want you to go,' he said quietly, 'or do I want you to get down on your knees and tug my effing tadger?'

Warren wisely and urgently chose the first option and left Bob Tucker raging at the gods. He ran down the hill as fast as he could. The small group had already crossed the bridge and into the village of Brigadoon. However, the cloud of dust that zigzagged through the village like a miniature tornado showed him where they had gone. He caught up with the men outside a building that was clearly marked as the schoolhouse.

There was no sign of the ostrich.

'Hullo, Mr. Newcombe,' one of the men greeted him. 'Hope you don't mind us getting a bit of exercise?' The man smiled, showing a large number of white teeth in a ruddy face framed by a red beard.

Newcombe recognised him - it was one of the five brothers from Pumpherston who had come up specially "at their mam's request" to build the Aberdeen Western Peripheral Route: it had long been a dream of hers that such a road should be built. The other men now standing outside the schoolhouse were his four brothers. They nodded to Newcombe, and kicked the toes of their massive boots in the dust.

'Where's the bird?' asked Warren, looking around.

'Went inside, didn't it?' said the eldest Burnturk brother, indicating the schoolhouse. 'The wee buggar.'

'In there?' said Warren, a little surprised. 'Went in and closed the door behind it?'

'So it would seem, Mr. Newcombe,' said Burnturk calmly.

Warren paused for thought. If there was an ostrich loose in the schoolhouse, perhaps he ought to get it out? The villagers would most likely not be very pleased at all. He walked up to the door and turned the handle. It turned, but the door did not give. A few seconds later he was greatly astonished to find the door opening a crack and an eye, a human one, appear.

'Aye?' said the eye.

'Oh,' said Newcombe, falling back. 'I didn't realise there was someone in there.'

'Well, sir,' said Sandy Macmillan, 'there is.'

A long pause followed.

'Can I help you gentlemen further?' said Sandy at length.

'We were chasing the ostrich,' said Burnturk by way of explanation. His four brothers nodded their heads in synchronicity. It was an impressive sight and a credit to Pumpherston.

'Ah, so it was you that chased the poor helpless creature,' said Sandy. 'God's Doves Flying to His Windows, as Mr. Erskine said many a time. Well, you can go away now, the bird is safe enough from you in here.' The door closed and the six men outside heard the sound of a bolt being shot home.

'Oh well, lads,' sighed the eldest Burnturk. 'And mam was so looking forward to us bringing something special from Aberdeen this weekend. We'll have to try something else now.' With those words of resignation, the five brothers headed slowly down into the village. Newcombe thought it best to accompany them.

When they arrived at MacConnachy Square, the place was swarming with villagers who had finished registering for the voting and who once more found themselves waiting for a new experience. It had become like a drug to them now: if ten minutes went by without some surprise or shock of the future, then they were cast into Despondency. There was no point in settling down to any tasks, since they would be sure to be interrupted by another earth-shattering event.

Warren felt his arm grabbed. He turned, startled.

'If it's not himself!' exclaimed Meg Brockie. 'Couldn't keep yourself away from me, could you, Warren Newcombe? Oh, but you're a winning lad, to be sure!'

Warren did his best to disentangle himself, and denied - but not forcefully enough - that he had come looking for her. The woman was attractive enough in a ruddy, healthy sort of way, but she was perhaps a little forward.

'Here,' she said laughing, 'come and sit down with me in the shade of this tree. There now,' she said, when the two of them had fallen,

The Pumpherston Chipper

rather than seated themselves, on the mossy ground, 'is that not better?' She stroked his thigh and pinched his cheek. 'Oh, but you're a fine figure of a man! You and I should get married, I think. You're not married, are you?'

Foolishly, Warren admitted that he was not.

'Well,' laughed Meg, 'that's settled then. You and I will get married, like you said we should, and then you'll come and keep me warm in bed. You can do that any time you want.'

The woman had one leg thrown over his, and she was half-lying on his chest. He could not move without actually hurting her. Desperately, he tried to ease her off.. She only gripped him the tighter, giggling. 'Oh, but you're a strong, strong lad!' she said appreciatively. 'I like that in a man. You know,' she added, 'there are not enough men in Brigadoon.'

Warren expressed the view that he had seen lots of men, and most of them were surely far more suitable than himself?

'Oh no,' said Meg, 'I'm not saying there's no men - just that there's not enough of them. And anyway, I'm looking for a different sort of man now. A man like yourself, a real winning lad, with a bit of get-up-and-go!'

Warren looked round for help. There was none forthcoming. The five Burnturk brothers from Pumpherston were not far distant, but were at present surrounded by a bunch of girls and so temporarily distracted.

Meg toyed with Warren's hair, and breathed improper suggestions in his ear. He blushed. She smothered him with kisses, and gripped his buttocks tightly.

Then she said: 'If Jeff finds us lying together like this, he will surely murder you. Such a pity for a fine lad like yourself. He's a very strong man, you know, is Jeff. And when he's murdered you, he'll beat me black and blue.'

Warren did not find this at all comforting. 'Perhaps we should get up and go our separate ways, then?' he suggested.

Meg shook her head energetically. 'Oh no, my darling. We mustn't do that! You said you'd marry me. And once we're married, Jeff won't be able to do a thing, now will he?'

Brigadoon Revisits

Warren doubted that strongly, and was about to make one last physical effort to get free of Meg when the Burnturk lads came over, accompanied by five giggling girls. The brothers made some well-meant, but inappropriate, comments to Warren about his present position, and then sat down right beside him and Meg.

'These are the Campbell sisters,' said the eldest brother, introducing them. 'This is Mary, and this is Margaret, and Catherine, and Jenny, and this very pretty one here is Aphrodite. And this is -?' He indicated Meg questioningly.

'I'm Meg,' said that woman, turning her attention to the five brothers. 'My, what a fine set of winning lads you are, to be sure! Will you sit with me, perhaps?'

'Meg Brockie,' said one of the young girls tartly, 'you leave these fine young men to us. They were just telling us of the grand town of Pumpherston, where they live. All its shops, and the - what was it? - the Chipper, and the Chinese and the Indian - oh, it all sounds so exotic! The Pumpherston Chipper! I think I'd like to go and live in Pumpherston!'

Her sisters all giggled and whispered to each other. The five brothers blushed. Meg laughed in a way that Warren could tell had little of amusement in it. And when she turned her attention to the eldest Burnturk, she released her grip on Warren. He managed to slip away quietly. Meg did not even notice.

~ 22 ~

Fleeing the Close Company of Fornicators

'That dame's name,' said Jeff in a low voice, 'is Jane Ashton.'

Tommy Albright stopped in his tracks, astounded. 'Are you kidding me, Jeff?' he whispered.

Jeff shook his head. 'No kidding, Tommy. Say, we've seen some strange things in our time, but that dame takes the prize, huh?'

Tommy said nothing. He looked over the heads of the dozen or so villagers who were queuing patiently to be registered, and fixed his eyes on the tall middle-aged woman who presided over the entire affair. Beside her stood the arrogant young man, clearly not interested in what was happening in front of him.

'Dead ringer, eh, Tommy?' asked Jeff, clearly highly delighted with his discovery.

'What do you mean?' asked Tommy, averting his eyes from the woman ahead and fixing them on his friend.

'For your Jane Ashton, back in New York, who do you think!'

'She's not my Jane, Jeff,' objected Tommy. 'Not any more.'

Jeff shrugged. 'Tommy, I don't care if you think she is or not. But we both know who I mean. You were engaged to her once, would have married her if we hadn't come back here. You were sweet on her, she had you well and truly hooked. What a dame! Same nose, same eyes, same grating voice, same sharp dress-sense.

Could be the same woman. Hell, even the same way of ignoring me or brushing me off whenever she sees me.'

Tommy said nothing. The thought that it was the same woman whom he had once loved, and whom he had abandoned barely a week ago, to take the transatlantic flight back here to marry Fiona - that thought gnawed away at his heart. What had happened to his marriage? He couldn't tell - the years had gone by in a flash and he could no longer remember much about that furious, irresistible blaze that had driven him back across the wide ocean to Scotland. Sometime, someplace, the fire had just run out of fuel, the last spark had been extinguished. There was no big drama. Just a flicker one morning, after one of those long restless nights that were beginning to really take it out of him; then the flame went out. And now here was some kind of ghost back to haunt him.

'It couldn't be, could it?' he asked in a low voice. 'She looks fifty if she's a day, and my Jane - that Jane Ashton back in New York - she was only twenty-six. Can't be!'

Jeff yawned. He was already regretting having pointed out the similarity in looks. 'Well,' he said, 'if it's not her, then it must be her mother. What's her mother look like, Tommy?'

Tommy considered. 'Not much like that,' he admitted. 'Hang on, Jeff, how about this! It's two weeks since we arrived here.'

'Sure,' said Jeff, taking a sip of whisky to ease the pain in his gut.

'But the world has moved on - what? - fifty, sixty years?'

'Whatever you say, Tommy,' conceded Jeff.

'So it can't be the same Jane. Or her mother.'

Jeff said nothing. He had caught sight of Nana Visitor over by the market-cross, talking to some of the locals. He reckoned he might slip over there after Tommy had registered for voting, maybe take her for a walk. He knew some good walks. Just as long as Meg didn't come across them.

'But - think about it, Jeff!' said Tommy, excitedly grabbing his friend's sleeve. 'It could just about be her daughter!'

Jeff blinked. He hadn't followed the logic. 'Her daughter? What the hell, Tommy, you losing your marbles or what? She hasn't got a daughter.'

'Sure, Jeff, her daughter. Let's say my Jane gets over being stood up at the altar. Say, a year or two, she gets married.'

'I'd give her about three months,' muttered Jeff. His opinion of the original Jane Ashton was not high. Him and her, they had never hit it off. Why should they? - he was only Tommy's oldest pal, knew all his secrets.

Tommy was oblivious to the jibe. 'Say she marries - oh, I don't know - say she marries Harry, that guy from Sales who seemed to be going places. Buck teeth, thick glasses, smokes a pipe. Dependable. A good catch for someone like Jane. She marries in two years time, let's say. 1956. She has a son. A son would be good to have.' Tommy Albright paused for a moment's introspection and regret. Then he went on. 'And maybe a daughter in 1960. That would make the daughter about fifty.' He paused and stared again at the Electoral Commissioner, who sat, oblivious to this genealogical speculation.

'Well,' said Jeff, 'why don't you ask her?'

Tommy shook his head very firmly.

'Well, if you ain't going to ask her, then I will,' stated Jeff. 'I'll find out what you need to know.'

'I don't need to know anything, Jeff,' said Tommy, a look in his eyes of sheer panic. 'Listen: if she is Jane's daughter - hell, that's all screwed up! She can't be anyway - she wouldn't be called Ashton! No way - unless there was a divorce. Sure - that's one way it could happen. Hell, Jeff! A man meets the daughter of the woman he used to love, and she's old enough almost to be his mom! I can't handle that, buddy - leave it alone!'

'Pretty sweet looking mom, though,' said Jeff appreciatively. 'I've seen a lot worse. Listen, Tommy, I'll be discreet.'

'You? Discreet?' Tommy burst out laughing. 'How long have I known you, Jeff?'

'Oh, about twenty years,' said Jeff wearily. 'Give or take two hundred fifty.'

'Not once have you ever been discreet, Jeff.'

Their argument was interrupted. 'Next!' came a voice. They had reached the front of the queue. A very harassed clerk was waving them up to the desk. They stepped up together.

'One at a time, please, sir,' warned the clerk.

'Oh,' said Jeff, 'I'm not registering, I'm just his friend.'

'Nevertheless,' stated the clerk, 'I must ask you to respect the client's privacy and stay out of earshot.'

'Sure, sure, whatever,' said Jeff. He stepped sideways and ogled Jane Ashton, while Tommy sat down to announce his name and age and to argue his qualifications as a citizen of the United Kingdom, by virtue of marriage.

'Say, lady,' whispered Jeff, once he had edged closer to Jane. 'You're from New York, right?'

Jane Ashton looked up briefly at Jeff and made no reply. Will Tuttle began to frown - it was, he supposed, his job to protect his boss from nutters. And this place was full of nutters. A lengthy tweet sent out barely twenty minutes ago had confirmed this irrefutable fact to the Referendum Nation. He slid his mobile into his pocket for a well-earned rest and buttoned up his jacket.

'See my friend there,' continued Jeff, ignoring Will's preparatory movements, 'that's Tommy Albright.'

The Commissioner glanced at Jeff for a moment, then switched her eyes back to the registration process. 'Will,' she said simply.

Will took a step towards Jeff. Jeff turned slowly and held Will in a lengthy and challenging stare. Will coughed discreetly and stepped back again.

'Tommy Albright was once engaged to a beautiful dame named Jane Ashton, in New York. Manhattan.'

At last, Jane Ashton stood up. She was a good couple of inches taller than Jeff, even without her Italian heels. She towered over him. A policeman who had been standing in attendance looked on in alarm and mumbled into his radio.

'Listen very closely to me, buddy,' she said in a strained voice, the pressure of the day finally getting to her, 'if you don't take your sicko fantasies somewhere else, right now, I'll have you castrated and your balls hung up to dry on that pillar over there.' She nodded in the direction of the market-cross. 'You hear me? Tuttle!'

'She's done Afghanistan and Iraq,' said Will Tuttle supportively, from a safe distance.

Fleeing the Close Company of Fornicators

'What's that supposed to mean?' asked Jeff, momentarily diverted from his goal.

'It means,' said Will a little nervously, 'that Miss Ashton has seen a lot worse than you.'

'Vamoose,' said Jane very quietly. 'And stay well away from me. Go.'

Jeff grinned. 'OK, lady,' he conceded, 'you win. But don't forget what I said. Tommy Albright, Jane Ashton, New York 1954. If that rings any bells with you, you know where to find me.' He sauntered off towards Nana and the crowd of people around the market-cross which stood in the centre of MacConnachy Square.

Tommy, who had completed the registration process, caught up with him. 'They wanted to see my marriage certificate,' he told Jeff. 'I haven't got one.'

'What happened to it?' said Jeff.

'Mice got it,' replied Tommy. 'Looks like they've got my vote as well.'

'Who cares?' said Jeff, thereby showing himself to be a true voter. 'Nana!' he cried more enthusiastically.

The journalist looked up and waved back. She was seated on the low stone steps of the market-cross, looking rather fetching in her military clothes. A number of the locals sat around her. There was Hamish the young shepherd, with his dog Maggie; the boy had apparently forgotten all about his shepherding, and even the dog had lost all interest in sheep for the moment. The dog had found someone to worship - it was Little Red Riding Hood, who was sitting there with her Grandmother and with Mr. Campbell, who was as taken with the old lady as the dog with the small girl.

'Tommy,' acknowledged Mr. Campbell to his errant son-in-law, with more than a hint of coldness in his voice.

'Mr. Campbell, sir' replied Tommy.

'You have been registering for the voting, then?' asked Mr. Campbell after a pause.

'I have, sir,' replied Tommy. 'although there may be a difficulty. I have no marriage-certificate, and without it I cannot prove that I am a citizen of this country.'

165

'Tsk, tsk, Tommy,' said Mr. Campbell, in a very poor imitation of sympathy. 'No marriage-certificate? And is that so? What have you done with that very important piece of paper, then, that you have not had the goodness to look after?'

'The mice got it,' explained Tommy.

Mr. Campbell ignored the answer completely. He turned to Grandmother and said, in a loud voice. 'This son-in-law treats his wife as he treats his pieces of paper, madam. His wife and all her family. With neglect. He pays no attention to them, and is surprised to find them missing.'

'Say!' protested Tommy. 'That's not fair, sir!'

But his father-in-law continued to ignore him and remarked instead on the good quality of the provisions which Little Red Riding Hood had brought as a picnic. 'And did you bake these cakes yourself?' he enquired of Red Riding Hood, who was pleased to announce that, no, she had bought them with her pocket-money in the Visitors' Café at Storybook Glen.

'They are nevertheless delicious,' judged Mr. Campbell. 'You have a very clever grand-daughter there,' he bellowed at Grandmother, who smiled sweetly and adjusted her bonnet.

'Phew!' said Jeff, mopping his brow. 'It sure is hot out here. Why don't we all move into the shade of that tree over there?' He pointed over to a stand of beech-tress at the edge of the Square.

'Mr. Douglas,' said Andrew Campbell loudly, 'we shall not go back there. We were there earlier, but were obliged to flee the close company of fornicators.' He glared in the direction of the shady spot.

'Is that so?' said Jeff, looking interested. 'And who would they be?' he wanted to know.

Mr. Campbell merely, and wisely, raised his eyebrows and bit into another double chocolate muffin.

'*Also*, Mr. Douglas,' said Nana conversationally.

'Call me Jeff, won't you?' interrupted Jeff.

'*Also*, Jeff,' said Nana easily, 'have you registered to vote?'

Jeff laughed shortly. 'Me? Hell, no! That kind of hocus-pocus isn't for me. They're all the same, Nana - I tell you. No, I leave all that to my buddy Tommy here. He does the voting for the two of us, don't you, Tommy? When he's allowed to, that is.'

This idle chit-chat on the democratic process were interrupted by a commotion on the far side of the market-place, where the notice-board stood. In the middle of the disturbance was the representative of the Doric Country Alliance, Mr. Thompson, and a tech-savvy camp-follower, Albert Sharpe. Nana, with a keen nose for a story, was up on her feet immediately. Jeff followed her at close quarters, anxious not to lose sight of this good woman.

'The telephone,' Jimmy Thompson was saying proudly, grandly sweeping his arm towards a phone-box which had appeared out of nowhere. It was no mere rustic phone-box, this one: emblazoned on its glass-doors were the words "Internet Access."

'Ah,' said Thompson further, 'the reporter.' He had noticed Nana's arrival. 'Here's a story for you, my dear. Come over here.' He swung a familiar arm around Nana's broad shoulders, much to Jeff's annoyance. 'Now, as we know, there is no Broadband here yet, far less any wifi. But this phone will give this deprived rural community access to the wide world web. It will - um - what's that word, Bert?'

'Empower, Jimmy,' replied Sharpe obligingly.

'That's right, it will empower them. At the press of a button. All courtesy of the Doric Alliance. Bert here set it all up - I can't take any of the credit, of course. Bert works for BT, and he pulled a few strings. But - my dear!' He patted Nana's hand in intimate manner - 'don't go telling that harridan down there, will you now?' He indicated the distant presence of Jane Ashton. 'Don't want her spoiling the fun, do we? Now, Bert,' he said, 'are we set up yet?'

'Just a couple of adjustments to make,' said Bert, who was round the back of the phone-booth, fiddling with some kind of control-box. The Internet phone-booth was something of a technical rarity, almost a museum-piece now. But it should still work. 'Just tweaking the signal.'

'Radio-signal,' said Jimmy knowledgeably. 'From that mast over there.' He pointed vaguely in a northerly direction. 'Bert knows about signals, don't you, Bert?'

'That and power-supply,' winked Bert. He had sneaked a cable from TESCO's wind-turbine and trailed it across the grass to power the phone-booth. 'OK,' he said, 'that should be it. Who's going to make the first call?'

The Doric Country Alliance looked around benignly. His gaze settled upon Andrew Campbell, who had wandered over to see what new unnatural horror had sprung up in the village. 'Mr. Macdonald, is it not?'

'Campbell, sir,' said the old gentleman stiffly.

'Of course, Mr. Campbell. Foolish of me. Would you like to make the first call from this public phone-box? It will cost you nothing - all services provided free-of-charge by BT, I believe. Isn't that right, Bert?'

Bert nodded, looking around rather shiftily.

'So, Mr. Campbell, would you like to do the honours?'

At that moment, however, the phone rang. Mr. Campbell fell back, startled. He stared at the machine that so insistently shrilled at him.

'Go ahead, sir,' encouraged Jimmy Thompson. 'Pick it up!'

Mr. Campbell lifted the receiver and looked at it.

'Put it to your ear, sir!' advised Jimmy strongly, as one who knew technology inside out.

Mr. Campbell did so, and listened carefully. He listened for quite some time. Then he shook his head determinedly, muttered 'No, no, no, no,' and put the receiver away from him again.

'Well?' asked Jimmy.

'Who was it on the apparatus, Mr. Campbell?' asked Nana.

Andrew Campbell stroked his chin. 'It was,' he said at last, 'a young woman. With an American accent to her voice, much like that of my daughter's husband.'

'And she wanted actually what?' asked Nana further.

'The young lady wished to congratulate me on having been selected for a competition that would allow me to have a life-time of holidays in the sun. There would be no charge for any of these, as I would own the property that she had in mind. All I had to do was phone her back and my name would automatically be selected as the

Fleeing the Close Company of Fornicators

winner.' He looked round at the assembled company. 'I believe,' he added, 'that she may have been a sorceress.'

There was a sharp intake of breath among the nearby villagers.

'Aye,' continued Mr. Campbell, 'a witch. For who else would offer me such vast wealth, who else would tempt me to a life of idleness and sloth, and offer me a prize which I had done nothing to earn?'

'Who else indeed,' came the echo from the villagers. There was much shaking of heads and a general move away from the phone-box.

'Damn and blast!' hissed Jimmy Thompson, slamming his fist into the side of the phone-box. 'Bert, you and your bloody ideas! We're the party supporting witches now! You're fired! Damn you!'

'Fascist,' declared Nana contemptuously.

But there was little time to debate the unwelcome outcome of the experiment in telecommunications. Another gaggle of strangers had arrived in Brigadoon, a group of about half a dozen men and women, wearing suits and carrying briefcases and clipboards. One bore a camcorder and wore a hoodie. No sooner were they over the bridge than they split up and headed in different directions. Soon, most of them were knocking on doors. One made a bee-line straight towards Jeff, Nana and the group at the phone-box.

'Good afternoon,' he said, smiling gaily. 'Am I talking to a –' he consulted his clipboard, 'Mr. Andrew Campbell?' He looked round the group expectantly.

'I am he,' said the old man, stepping forward. 'And what do you want with me?'

'Mr. Campbell, sir,' exclaimed the young man, gripping the widower by the hand and shaking it firmly. 'I am pleased to have found you here, because I think you and I have much to talk about!'

'Is it about Mr. Forsyth?' demanded Andrew Campbell.

The young man faltered, but recovered quickly. 'No, it's not, not this time, Mr. Campbell. It's about something else altogether. Now, sir,' he asked, 'are you aware that you may be paying too much for your electricity and gas?'

Mr. Campbell stared at the man, utterly baffled.

'Gas?' he asked. 'Electricity?'

'Yes, sir, and what you pay for them.'

'I've no idea,' began the old man.

'Well, that's not uncommon,' chirped the salesman cheerfully, 'not at all unusual. But I do think it's time for you and me to take a look at some figures and maybe see if we can come up with a better deal for you.' So saying, he took Mr. Campbell by the elbow and steered him off to a quieter spot where he was soon to be seen energetically waving brochures and a calculator. Red Riding Hood's Grandmother was listening in carefully, deeply interested.

Nana, in the meantime, was watching something else, very closely. It was the man with the camcorder and the hoodie. He was not at all like the others - he was dressed very casually, and appeared to be filming every alley, lane and house in the village.

'Jeff,' she said, nudging her new friend, 'I am completely suspicious of that type. I am going to follow him and see what is his game.'

'Sure thing, Nana,' said Jeff pleasantly. 'I'm with you all the way.' He had to struggle to hide his eagerness. It was not a feeling he had experienced for several days.

The pair set off after the walking man. He talked to no one, simply pointed his camcorder in the direction he was walking. When he reached one dead end, he turned slowly, walked back at an even pace. Every so often he halted and tapped something into an iPad. At length, he set off up the lane that led to the schoolhouse. Nana and Jeff followed him at a safe distance.

Outside Mr. Lundie's schoolhouse door, a minor disturbance was in progress. At first glance, it appeared to stem directly from the fact that two rival sales reps had arrived there at the same time. But, as Nana and Jeff came closer, it grew evident that they were together on one side in the argument and that Mr. Lundie was on the other.

'And you are selling,' said Mr. Lundie, who stood half-concealed by the door, 'what exactly?'

'Gas and electricity,' said the pair. 'Now, if you'd only let us come in, sir,' said one, 'we could sit down and explain it all to you.'

Mr. Lundie smiled benevolently. 'Well, maybe I will at that. But first let me consider. "Gas" - what would that be now? Perhaps a word derived from the Greek *chaos*, or air? And "Electricity". There is of course the Greek word for amber, *elektron*. Would that be it perhaps? Air and amber, that's what you're trying to sell me, now?'

'No, sir, not at all,' said the reps desperately. 'It's all explained here in these brochures, if you'll - '

'So you say, so you say,' said the dominie silkily. 'And you'd like to come in and talk to me about it. Well, you're never to old to learn, I suppose.' Just then, Mr. Lundie noticed the dubious character in the hoodie. 'You, lad, what are you doing here?'

The casually-dressed person shut off his camcorder and strolled up to the door. 'Nothing for you to worry about, pops,' he announced. 'Just taking some views of the village.'

'Oh, just some views, I see. And for what purpose?' demanded the schoolmaster in his most terrible soft voice.

'Well, you've probably heard about us, gramps,' said the young man nonchalantly, unable to pick up on the tenor of the old man's voice. This was in part due to the earphones he had plugged into his iPad. 'This is for Google's Streetview, you see. All perfectly safe and legal.'

Mr. Lundie recoiled at the mention of the name. He paused.

'Gog and Magog,' he muttered. 'Heathendom is come at last. The final struggle is about to commence.'

'No, no,' said the viewer of streets impatiently, 'Google, Google - has the old geezer not even heard of it?' He sought sympathy with the sales reps, who, fearing for their commission, looked elsewhere.

'Oh, fear not, youth, I have heard of Gog and I have heard of Magog. It is written in Revelations.'

Rolling his eyes heavenward, the young man turned on his heel and continued his slow parade through the village, recording every building and every bend in the road.

Mr. Lundie watched him closely, until the follower of Gog had left the scene; then he opened the door and the two sales reps disappeared inside the schoolhouse. The door slammed behind them. Nana and Jeff heard a startled shout and a brief scuffle. Something hit the schoolroom window inside and a face appeared briefly there, before vanishing again.

Brigadoon Revisits

Outside, Nana looked on, worried. 'You think, Jeff, we should - ?'

Jeff shrugged and kept an eye on the window. Nothing else showed there. All of a sudden the door was wrenched open and one of the sales reps appeared, very briefly.

'Fetch the police!' he shouted, 'there's a -' He got no further. The head of an ostrich appeared in the air beside him, like an evil spirit in a nightmare. There was a scream. The sales rep collapsed to the floor, then vanished back inside. The door slammed shut.

'It's only Mr. Lundie,' Jeff told Nana reassuringly. 'Got a screw loose. Always has done. He's wacko.'

~ 23 ~

Double-Glazing and a New Conservatory

A guilty queue had formed beside Mr. Thompson's phone-box. Word had spread amongst the villagers that, if the bell sounded and you picked up the receiver, you would be certain to hear be the voice of a comely maiden, offering exotic revelations and sinful pleasures. All for free, not a penny need be spent. Double-glazing, new kitchens, luxury bathrooms, sundry home improvements, a new conservatory. Men, mostly married, both old and young, hovered around the booth, avoiding each other's eyes and praying that the women in their lives would not find them there. Sometimes, the charming girl at the end of the line would ask questions about lifestyle: the first person to take such a call was John Gilfillan and he later regaled an avid audience with the questions. Questions to which he had had no answers. James Maclaren, distiller of spirits, had the extraordinary good fortune to receive a congratulatory call from a lady who advised him that he had won a free cruise to the Caribbean. He emerged from the phone-box, dazed, confused and utterly enchanted. Andrew Mackintosh, the most venerable man in the village, stirred himself from his hearth and took a courtesy-call from a polite lady in inconceivably distant India: he said not a word to his fellows afterwards, but went straight home and stared for hours into the peat fire.

Brigadoon Revisits

'Aye,' observed Malcolm MacReekie, patiently waiting his turn at the Box of Forbidden Delights, 'it is a grand thing this telephone.'

Albert Sharpe who was at that moment passing in a black mood, considering several different vengeful plans against his erstwhile political colleague James Thompson, was encouraged to divert his thoughts down a new road. He should take up a parliamentary career himself. Given his political leanings, he would have to set up a new party - perhaps "New Doric Solidarity"? He smiled to himself at the power of technology, and walked on, head held high and full of new ideas. He made straight for TESCO to acquire a banana as brain-food for the further development of his plans for fame and fortune.

The manageress of TESCO, Mrs. Freed, stood at the Customer Service desk, busy registering a formal complaint with one of the policemen who had come into Brigadoon with Ms. Ashton.

'Comes in,' she said, 'rushes round knocking things over, and then grabs whatever it fancies and rushes out again.'

The policeman eyed her carefully. 'Without paying, then?' he summarised.

'No intention of paying, is my view,' said Harriet Freed. 'Doesn't seem to have any money on it at all.'

'And can you describe the suspect?' asked the policeman, taking some notes.

'About eight feet high, big brown eyes, long thin neck, spindly legs.'

'Ah, that would be one of the ostriches, then?' asked the policeman politely.

'I suppose it could be,' agreed Mrs. Freed cautiously.

'Been having a bit of trouble with them all over, today,' advised the policeman.

'Don't get me wrong, officer,' said Mrs. Freed anxiously. 'I've nothing against ostriches, nothing at all. Some of them are probably quite honest. I'm sure TESCO has many of them in its customer base. But this one is taking liberties, you know what I mean? And company policy is always to prosecute, so my hands are tied. Head Office - oh!' she exclaimed, 'here it is again!'

Double-Glazing and a New Conservatory

Sure enough, an ostrich came belting up the short path that led to the main door, paused with one foot raised to wait for the doors to open automatically, then rushed in. It shouldered aside the policeman and the manageress, knocked over the political leader of New Doric Solidarity, and headed unerringly for Aisle Four. Before anyone had a chance to recover their composure or balance, the bird came hurtling back out of Aisle Four, two bags of Werther's Originals in its beak, made for the door and disappeared in a cloud of dust.

The policeman was neither slow-witted nor slow. He raced after the vanishing bird.

It led him straight to Mr. Lundie's schoolhouse. Panting and puffing as he came up the brae, the policeman saw the tail-feathers of the bird vanish inside the door, and the door slamming shut. He strode up to the door and hammered loudly.

'Police!' he said very loudly indeed. 'Open up!'

As with all things in this village where everything was a novelty, a crowd was gathering behind him, commenting volubly on the action as it unfolded. He wished it was not. He banged on the door again, and demanded entry.

At length, the crowd heard the bolt sliding back inside. There was a pause, and then the door opened a crack. The unmistakable white hair of Mr. Lundie poked out.

'Ah, an agent of the Law. Excellent. We are in safe hands, I must suppose. Can I help you, young man?' asked the dominie politely.

The police officer kept his voice low. 'Do you have an ostrich in there, sir?'

'An ostrich?' Mr. Lundie gave every appearance of being astonished. 'And what is that - an ostrich?'

'A large bird, sir - very large.' He was not to be put off. 'I saw it entering your premises, just a minute ago.'

'Is that so?' said Mr. Lundie. His head turned, as if he was scanning the premises. He turned back again, smiling nicely, but saying nothing.

'The bird was in possession of stolen property,' said the policeman.

Brigadoon Revisits

'Oh, shocking, shocking,' murmured Mr. Lundie in a disappointed tone. 'There is so much sinfulness in this modern world. But I suppose we cannot expect the fowls of the air and the beasts of the field to have the same high moral standards as Man, can we? Before you go, young man, would you like one of these sweetmeats?' He held out a newly-opened bag of Werther's Originals.

The policeman ignored the offer. 'I need to inspect the premises,' he said firmly.

'No,' said the schoolmaster equally firmly, 'no, that would not be possible, I fear. I have visitors you see.' He began to close the door. The police officer, with great presence of mind, stuck his boot in the rapidly-closing gap. The door opened very slightly again and Mr. Lundie's voice drifted out: 'You appear to have caught your foot in the door, young man. If you will just remove it, that would be best for both of us, I think.'

'I have to come in, sir,' warned the officer in a more determined tone than heretofore. Behind him, the crowd grew restless. The villagers were deeply critical of this outrage upon their elderly dominie, and the press and media were champing at the bit to record another example of police brutality. There was a suggestion made by several hotheads - Jeff Douglas being one - that the crowd surround the officer and "take him down."

There was no need. The door was wrenched open from inside and in a flurry of feathers and flashing eye, the ostrich flew out, bowled over the policeman, turned, gave him a sharp tap in the groin with a foot and rushed back inside. The door slammed shut and the bolt was pushed home. It was all over in five seconds. The policeman lay groaning on the ground before being raised to his feet by the reporter from *The Press and Journal*.

'What's this?' said Cindy Charisse for the Greens. During the commotion at the door, a small ball of paper had been flung out of the gap and it had rolled to her feet. She picked it up and flattened it out.

'Help!' it said, in rather shaky writing. 'Help! We taken hostage. Fetch Police. (Signed) officers of Aberdeenshire Council.'

Double-Glazing and a New Conservatory

Alan Jay from the TV show was on the story right away. He had not made a name for himself by ignoring big stories that fell at the feet of others. 'Let me have a look at that.' he said. He examined the note. 'Not much point fetching the police, I'd say,' he muttered, nodding over at the maimed policeman. 'Something more effective might be required.'

'Oh no,' said Charisse, snatching back the paper, 'I am not going to permit any heavy-handed response, not until we know what's going on in that school-room. We don't know the rights and wrongs here. I,' she said, and immediately regretted it, 'am going in there to negotiate a peaceful solution.' She paused for a moment, appalled at her own words. But it was too late now - all the cameras were already on her, and an interview was taking place.

'Do you have any message for the people of Scotland before you go in?' Sky News wanted to know.

'Only this,' said Cindy, 'that I am prepared to sacrifice myself for the greater good of an independent Scotland. I cannot evade my responsibilities. Should I not return from this mission, then I trust that my successor will carry on my work.' With these proud words, Charisse stepped up to the door. Before the eyes of a nation who were by now watching events in real-time, on TV and on the Internet, she knocked firmly three times on the door.

'Who is there?' came Mr. Lundie's voice.

'Cindy Charisse, from the Green Party,' replied that lady, her voice only slightly shaky.

The door opened. 'That would be the Party which rebuilt our bridge?'

'Indeed, sir,' confirmed Cindy. 'Might I have a word with you concerning your guests?'

'My guests?' asked Mr. Lundie. 'Now what would you want with them, I wonder? We are having such a fine discussion in here, you see, on the works of Ebenezer Erskine, and would not wish an interruption.'

It seems astonishing to tell, but Cindy Charisse knew one or two things about Ebenezer Erskine. It was one fruit - almost the only one - of a wasted university education. 'A favourite of mine,' she stated, although not entirely truthfully, 'is *"God's Little Remnant Keeping Their Garments Clean in an Evil Day."* There is,' she went on, 'so much for the modern world to learn from that sermon.'

With that, the door was flung wide open and Mr. Lundie grabbed Charisse by both hands. 'You are most welcome, sister, into our company. There are friends in here who can only dream of discussing *"God's Little Remnant"* in these evil days. Is that not the way of it, Sandy?'

'That is correct,' agreed a voice from within. 'Although one of our guests here professes a desire to talk at length about *"The Wind of the Holy Ghost"*'

'Sandy Macmillan, we shall find the time,' exclaimed Mr. Lundie generously, 'to discuss both of these in the greatest detail, and perhaps to examine *"The Backslider Characterized"* as well.

Groans of despair arose within.

'Ah,' smiled Mr. Lundie, *'"The Groans of Believers Under Their Burdens!"* Come away in, Mistress Charisse, come away in!'

The middle afternoon hours slowly ticked away. People engaged in languorous pursuits. The police officer, still white, but beginning to recover, had already contacted HQ who in turn had called in a specialist siege negotiation team - this would have to be flown in from Yorkshire, the Scottish people rarely having the patience to be besieged - and was preparing to take a well-earned rest outside the schoolhouse door, observing and gathering intelligence. A call to TESCO would complete his recovery, if the grateful manageress could perhaps be persuaded to send up some refreshments?

In that same local convenience-store, an idle queue had formed at the self-service till, now much in demand since Harry Beaton had discovered the amusement that could be had from provoking it into announcing that there was an unexpected item in the bagging area.

Their innocent amusement was interrupted by an ostrich. When Mr. Lundie realised that he was now committed to an hour or so of Erskinite rapture, he opened the door and his ostrich stepped out. It took a moment to get its bearings and then headed off down the lane at thirty mph, its legs pumping like pistons, its feet thumping on the ground. It headed straight for TESCO, stepped smartly in through the door, trotted easily up and down the aisles, and then departed with a party-pack of Buckfast. Religious Debate surely requires a Religious Cordial

In a small copse of trees, Meg and a Burnturk were discussing the merits of Brigadoon as against Pumpherston. Further up the brae, the X-Factor woman, Elaine Stewart, lay in the heather on a gentle slope. On top of her, in the heather, was Tommy Albright. Both were recovering from a strenuous dance-routine. Tommy had accidentally come across Elaine who was practising some dance-steps as a means of relieving the boredom. She failed to see the point of hanging around this God-forsaken dump, and had told her husband so in a few short words. Her husband had taken it badly and gone off to sulk in the car up at Storybook Glen, barely promising to come back and fetch her later.

'Say, you're one helluva dancer!' said Tommy admiringly, when Elaine had finished the routine which had got her through the preliminary rounds for the TV show. Startled, she turned round and saw Tommy, who was at that moment executing a few neat steps of his own.

'Oh,' said she, enchanted. 'And you're a dancer too!'

And so it had begun. Within minutes, the two of them were leaping gracefully, and swinging each other in that small clear space in the heather, laughing and singing. Time flew past. Tommy held Elaine in his arms and she was lost in paradise. Elaine followed Tommy's every light footstep and he was hers forever.

Neither of them noticed that Will Tuttle, anxious to get away from the dictatorial gaze of his boss, had come up the hill for a few moments of peace and quiet, and to compose a few tweets for his following: he'd barely been able to get one off since two o'clock and it was getting on for four now - they'd be desperate out there, he reckoned. He was composing one now on his mobile, about the goings-on at the schoolhouse, with his eyes fixed on the tiny rectangle of the screen. Accordingly, his feet caught on the entwined bodies of Elaine Stewart and Tommy Albright. He fell over.

'My God!' he exclaimed, sitting up. 'Can't you find somewhere else to screw? I've lost that tweet now - must have pressed Send before I'd finished. What are they going to think?'

'You, buddy, need to watch where you're going,' replied Tommy, getting to his feet rapidly. 'Now, you just apologise to this lady for your foul mouth.'

Will looked angrily at Tommy. The American was a good deal shorter than Will, but seemed to make up for it with a bright fire of anger in his eyes. He muttered an apology to Elaine, who kept her face averted, and then he went on his way.

'Just caught an Independent in the arms of an American. Better together? Both married but not to each other.' The tweet went out.

'Hell!' he muttered to himself. The fall into the heather had scratched the screen on his Blackberry. He was livid now: no one damaged his Blackberry and lived to tell the tale. 'They broke my phone - so let's name names - Elaine Stewart in the arms of Tommy Albright. "No" team canvassing hard for votes? Better Together!' The tweet went out.

Down in the village of Brigadoon, Fiona Campbell was being chatted up by one of the TV crew.

'See this?' said the young man. 'It's my i-Phone.'

'Eye-phone?' asked Fiona, troubled. 'You look into it, then?'

'No, no, that's just what it's called. No idea why. But I can do anything on it - texts, blogs, the web, pics, movies, tweets, the lot.'

'Tweets? What are those?'

'Well, they're kind of - look, here's a couple come in now! They're from -' The technician lowered his voice and looked around, using this an excuse to get closer to Fiona. 'They're from that guy who goes around with Miss Ashton, the commissioner over there. Does them in secret, I reckon.'

'Oh,' said Fiona, little enlightened.

'Let's see what they say - some nonsense probably, but you never know. Do you want to read them?' He handed his phone to Fiona.

She took it and read the screen. Her face turned red and then it turned white. She said nothing. She handed the phone back.

'Cool, huh?' said the young man. He had not noticed the changes in Fiona's demeanour and prepared to launch into a killer demo of all the other things he could do on his i-Phone. 'Look - here's all the apps I've got. Fifty-seven and counting. Awesome!'

But Fiona had slipped away quietly.

~ 24 ~

Americans, Nothing But Trouble

'It was a tweet!' sobbed Fiona, hanging on to her sister for dear life.

'What's a tweet?' asked Bonnie Jean, fearing the worst..

'I don't know,' confessed Fiona, 'but I read it on an eye-phone and it must be true!' She renewed her crying, fit to burst.

'And what did you read? Not everything you read must be true, now, don't you think?' Such was the dislocation of the residents of Brigadoon that she could make such a statement and not be struck down. Had Mr. Lundie not been otherwise occupied with a bottle of Buckfast, several chocolate doughnuts and a captive audience, he would have had words to say.

It was some minutes before Fiona could get the words out. They came out like drops from a pail carried from well to hearth. But Jean finally understood.

'Tommy is sweet on another, is he?' she asked quietly, trying hard to dry Fiona's eyes, and keep her long black hair from turning to rat's tails. 'On one of those Referendum people?'

Fiona nodded, then renewed her sobbing, which was gradually robbing her of all strength. Where had things gone wrong? This wasn't what she'd waited all those years for, this mockery of a marriage. Oh, when Tommy had first arrived and how they had danced, danced together on the braes and in the heather, she was lifted to heaven; and when he had gone - she thought she would die. But he had come back almost, it seemed, on the very next day, and

Americans, Nothing But Trouble

she had been so happy. And then one morning the light had gone out of Tommy's eyes, and she had watched him slipping away, like a leaf birling on the current of the burn, away and away and away round the corner. No matter how fast she ran, he drifted further away. Her heart shrank within her and she clung grimly to her younger sister.

Bonnie Jean made up her mind. 'Charlie!' she called, 'Charlie!'

Charlie Dalrymple, never far from Jean day and night, came running up.

'Bonnie Jean,' he said ardently, 'what can I do for you?'

'Charlie, is it true what they say about Tommy Albright and the woman called Elaine Stewart? It seems that a tweet has exposed him.'

'Jean, I cannot say. What's a tweet?"

'Cannot say, Charlie, or will not say?' demanded Jean, looking hard at him. 'Or must not?'

'Cannot, Jean, cannot,' said Charlie quickly. 'But I will find out.'

'Do so, Charlie,' said Jean. 'Can't you see that our sister is crying fit to die? Quick, make haste.'

Charlie sped off, yellow jacket and tartan trews a mere blur against the hillside. He had a fair idea where Tommy might be. He had no idea who or what was a tweet. It seemed not to matter.

Meanwhile Jean continued to listen to her sister's lamentations.

'I knew it would come to this, Jean. He has been cool on me for almost a week now. And then the other day, in Edinburgh, with those American women - ah! It is too awful! I shall die, I shall die of grief!'

'There, there, Fiona, you shall not die. You have me and you have father and you have all of our dear sisters.'

'But I shall not have Tommy!' she wailed. 'Another woman has him already in her arms!'

'Let us just wait and see what Charlie tells us - now, see, he's running back to us now. Perhaps it will be good news, perhaps it's all a big mistake.' She was not hopeful.

Charlie came running up and skidded to a halt in front of the two sisters. 'It's all true, Jean - I saw it with my own eyes. He was in her arms, and she in his. Are you pleased with me?' In his joy at having

Brigadoon Revisits

been helpful, at last, he did not choose his manner of delivery carefully.

Jean glared at him and waved him away angrily. Devastated, Charlie made his way to the hovel in which James Maclaren sold sour ale from time to time: the Brigadoon Inn. He had not been there since his marriage, never thought to see the inside of it again. It had been a den of insobriety in his bachelor years, now it was a haven of comfort in the crisis of his marriage.

Behind him, Fiona's anguished shrieks rent the air. They soon attracted the attention of all the womenfolk of Brigadoon, and they congregated around the sisters. First among them was Meg Brockie.

'Fiona, my dear,' said Meg helpfully, 'men are all the same. Every last one of them. They are oh-so sweet to you, then, when they have taken what they want, they toss you away like - like some filthy rag!'

There was considerable agreement with this judgement among the assembled audience, but Fiona was having none of it.

'Not my Tommy,' she protested, between sobs, 'not my Tommy. He's not like all the rest!'

'Well, my Jeff is,' muttered Meg, 'and he's American like Tommy, isn't he? And Tommy's a man, isn't he? At least, that other woman seems to think so.'

This touched off a landslide in Jean's mind. Americans, she thought, nothing but trouble. They come over here and stir up trouble and - and poor Harry Beaton gets almost killed, and her poor sister dies almost from heartbreak. Brigadoon had never heard of tweets or infidelity before the Americans came. It was all such a huge shame. If only she could turn back time, reverse the passing of the days. If only. She looked up and saw, beyond the crowd of women, Harry Beaton go limping past. As she saw him, he glanced at her, for the first time, it seemed, in over a week. Something clicked. Jean made a decision. She kept it to herself for the moment. She would be silent, but strong - silent for Charlie, strong for her sister. She would be bold enough for the two of them, and all of her other five sisters, too, if need be. She would turn back the tide and do battle against Mr. Forsyth's unforgivable foresight.

Americans, Nothing But Trouble

In the Brigadoon Inn, Charlie sat in almost total darkness and warmed his can of ale between his hands. The darkness suited him. He sat with his back to the door and stared into the dampest, darkest corner of the inn. James Maclaren chased some mice around in a corner while his cat looked on regally, blinking slowly. The air smelled thick and sour, the dregs of days and nights coiled rank in the nostrils. But Charlie did not notice: his world had fallen in around him. Bonnie Jean had returned to Harry Beaton, he knew it well, just from that one angry gesture a few minutes previously. What was he to do? He could leave the village, like Harry had once wanted to do. But if he left, Mr. Forsyth's curse would take effect - yes, indeed, it was a curse, nothing more and nothing less; Brigadoon and all those within would vanish forever, into a long, dream-filled sleep that would last for Eternity. He could not do that. Or could he? He could go back to Aberdeen, take up his studies again, maybe. Or head for the Indies and make his fortune or die of fever, whichever God preferred: it made no difference. Or he could stay here, watching Jean pine for another man, and do nothing to win her back. Harry Beaton's misfortune would always stand between man and wife.

Americans, he thought, nothing but trouble

He got up mechanically and went to pour himself a sufficiency of beer from the jug that stood on the table, next to the cat. Maclaren had vanished somewhere and could be heard out the back, swearing at the mice.

As he returned to his seat, a scrum of people entered through the low doorway, stooping to avoid hitting their heads on the lintel. He peered at them, but did not recognise anyone. He put down his can carefully.

'Can I help you?' he asked.

One of the group stepped forward.

'Ah, good day to you,' said the man cautiously. 'Is this the Brigadoon Inn?'

Charlie confirmed that it was.

'Excellent, excellent' The man seemed pleased by this news, as did his two companions.

'Excellent, excellent,' they echoed.

'And can we get a couple of rooms for tonight?' continued the first man.

Charlie was a man much given to gaping. So he gaped. Fortunately, it was so gloomy that the visitors could make nothing of his expression at all. At last he composed himself.

'A room?' he asked. 'Here in the inn?'

'That's right,' said the man. "At least two are required, of course, but three by preference. One for the lady here, the other for myself and my colleague.'

Charlie began to laugh. Slowly and with some effort at first. But he found the heaving of his chest did him good and he let it out. In a few moments he was laughing out loud, his stomach-muscles aching. He began to hiccough. Tears sprang from his eyes, which, he found, immediately recalled his sorrow, so that in a few moments more, he was sobbing hysterically.

The visitors looked on appalled. At last, since the scene gave no appearance of changing, the woman in the party approached, patted him on the back, and offered him a pack of tiny paper hankies. 'There, there,' she murmured. 'It's not that bad, is it?'

Charlie shook his head violently. 'Oh yes,' he wept in denial of his head movements, 'it is worse than that. Far, far worse!'

'There, there,' repeated the woman. 'Here, have a drink of your -' She paused, having picked up the can of ale. She sniffed at it and recoiled sharply. She put it down. 'Maybe a glass of water would be better?' John,' she said to one of her colleagues, 'could you perhaps find a glass of water behind the – the bar?' She gestured vaguely into the gloom. Her colleague, the man who had made the enquiries, walked gingerly into the darkness. He stood on the cat and knocked over a pile of empty bottles. The squeal and clatter attracted the attention of James Maclaren, who stepped back inside.

'And what do you think you're up to?' he demanded to know, seizing the searcher by the elbow.

'Ah, just looking for a glass of water to help the landlord here,' replied John nervously.

'I,' said Maclaren proudly and with a hint of bottled-up wrath, 'am the landlord of the Brigadoon Inn. Mr. James Maclaren is my name. I do not sell water. For why would a man sell water? You're a fool.' He looked sideways into the gloom. 'And that man who is in the arms of some loose woman, whom I have never seen before, is my customer.'

Charlie and his nurse, on hearing these words, jerked apart. No further proof could be demanded for their guilt.

'My apologies, sir,' said John recovering himself, and managing to prise his arm out of Maclaren's grip. 'If you are the landlord, Mr. Maclaren, then I am pleased to meet you. We are from *VisitScotland*, you see.' He paused to let this news sink in. To his distress, it appeared to bounce off Maclaren like an empty bottle off a table on a Saturday night, causing no dent and no ill-effects.

'Aye?' said Maclaren with equanimity. 'And that, I suppose, gives you leave to poke around in my establishment, does it so?'

'Well, not entirely,' replied John. 'But I think you'll appreciate that we do have to inspect the premises before making our report. And now, since I have your attention: we'll be wanting rooms for tonight.'

There was a clear danger that Maclaren would go the same way as Charlie before him. First, he gaped, in a manner which was easy to interpret. Then he began to laugh, silently, and then more loudly. He had to sit down. But he veered away from outright hysteria by dint of seizing the jug of stale warm ale from the table and unloading the contents down his throat. He choked and spluttered, and then regained his composure.

'So you'll be wanting some rooms, sir? How many would that be?'

'One for each of us, by preference,' said the gentleman, somewhat nervously now. He was already composing the site-visit report in his mind. It would not be a particularly good one. 'On a B&B footing only, of course.'

Maclaren looked around at the visitors, curling up his fingers one by one. Then he counted his fingers. 'That would be three rooms, then?' he wanted to know.

'Three, yes,' said the man from *VisitScotland*, who was growing a little annoyed by this very low standard of hospitality. 'And then we'd like to inspect the premises in detail, for our report.'

'The report,' repeated Maclaren slowly, 'the report. You said that before, I recollect, so you did. And this report would be for whom, exactly, sir?'

'Well, for Head Office, of course. And, depend upon it, Mr. Maclaren, it is a report which will not go unnoticed. Improvements will be required, dramatic ones. You may be sure that we will be following this up with further inspections.'

'Reports and inspections and cups of water, is it?' asked Maclaren, whose blood was beginning to boil. After a day such as today, he felt he could easily dispense with the modern world. Them and their TESCO and their cheap drinks – their BOGOF deals or whatever - and their reports and their inspections! Was a man to see his livelihood just slip away, day after day, as the world danced off down some road to Hell? 'Well, sir - and madam, if I may call you that - let me show you the premises. Step this way, if you would. Charlie,' he said, turning back, 'keep an eye on things, like the good old days, won't you?'

Charlie was more than willing to continue the customs of the good old days, and nodded eagerly. He dabbed his eyes and sat down to enjoy the dregs of his beer.

Maclaren heaved open the rotten door to his back-yard and ushered the party of visitors outside. He would give them the guided tour, if that was what they wanted: of the wood-shed, of the cess-pit discreetly screened by a few upright branches, and finally of the small turf and stone bothy in which he distilled spirits from various unlikely roots and bits of tree. That was three rooms he could offer them for the night, and he would be pleased to take their money. He did not forget that he owned the only inn in Brigadoon, and so was at some advantage in the matter of travellers seeking hospitality. But he never completed the tour. As he proudly hauled aside the wooden planks that covered up the cess-pit, there was a great commotion, howling and repeated screams, from somewhere outside. Startled, Maclaren dropped the plank, splashing effluvia upon the suits of the visitors, and ran off as quickly as he could, wiping his hands on his apron. Some further excitement had been smitten Brigadoon and the reporting deadlines of *VisitScotland* would have to wait awhile.

Some damage had already been done to the frontage of TESCO: the sign had been torn away from its moorings, as if by a high wind, and one of the glass doors had folded in backwards. A crowd of shoppers and shop-staff cowered inside, next to a giant stack of Pringles which was swaying dangerously in a breeze. Outside, a small but vocal crowd had gathered, urging on the main perpetrator of the violence. It was, of course, the Big Bad Wolf, fresh from his exploits with the Little Pigs' houses up at Storybook Glen.

'Come on, Wolfie!' exclaimed Jack, 'blow harder! You already blew down two of the pigs' houses, this one should be a doddle!'

'Harder, man, harder!' exclaimed James Maclaren. 'Bring down the Halls of Monotony!'

'Monopoly,' whispered Jack.

'Come on, Wolfie!' encouraged the rest of the small crowd, radicals all, anxious to see destruction brought down upon the doors of the usurping grocery.

The Big Bad Wolf blew and blew and blew. The remaining door trembled in its frame, the wide glass windows vibrated, the sign above the door gave one last squeal and crashed down. A huge cheer went up from outside, screaming from inside redoubled. The Wolf blew again, but he was beginning to lose his puff. He stopped.

'I need a rest',' he wheezed, and hunkered down, drawing air into his lungs. 'This is as bad as the third pig's house.'

'Yeah,' said Jack, unsympathetically, 'you never have managed that one yet, have you? Some people are beginning to say you're not up to it any more, Wolfie.'

The Big Bad Wolf looked up, aghast. 'They're saying that about me?' he gasped.

'Some people, yeah - I think you can probably guess who they are. But now's your chance to prove them wrong! Go on, crush the Citadel of the Capitalists!'

The Wolf stood up straight and tall, flushed a little around the muzzle. 'I'll show 'em,' he muttered. He drew a deep, deep breath, held it for a moment and then brought out a hurricane. Those around him reeled back. A wolf's breath does not smell very sweet. Those within the shop found the stacks of Pringles falling about their ears and boxes full of crisps (three-for-two offer) sliding hither and thither over the floor. The wolf blasted and gusted, and he huffed and he puffed; but he could not blow TESCO's down.

At last, broken, weak and defeated, the animal sank down to the ground. There was a cheer from inside and a huge groan from outside.

'Call yourself a wolf?' demanded James Maclaren, the disillusionment with petty-bourgeois terrorism beginning to set in. 'My dear departed mother could raise more wind than that!'

'Seems they were right, then,' murmured Jack into the Big Bad Wolf's furry ear. 'Wimp. Has-been.'

Only the Giant, who had had the idea of recruiting the wolf's specialist skills in the first place, was at all sympathetic to the poor predator. 'Never mind, Wolfie,' he rumbled, 'just think of this as a practice for the third pig's house. Now you know which bits of a stone building are the most vulnerable, don't you?'

The wolf said nothing, just slunk away, over the bridge, up the hill and back to his hunting ground. He did not bother the three pigs for several days, much to the chagrin of a generation of small children.

Meanwhile, a squad of policemen had arrived. Some of their number were from the local force, diverted down from Storybook Glen. For the past hour, cars and motor-bikes and vans had been converging from all directions, intent on attending a huge free concert they'd heard about from a tweet. Now that the roads had finally clogged up and no vehicle could move a yard in any direction, the police were of no further use up there, and found it expedient to be out of sight, on 'security duty'. The balance was made up by the siege negotiation team from Yorkshire, whose helicopter had landed in the fields of the now-abandoned ostrich-farm, allowing the marksmen to jog down professionally to the scene of the crisis.

Americans, Nothing But Trouble

On seeing the approach of the men in uniform, the small crowd outside drifted apart gently, like peat-smoke on a summer's breeze. By the time the law was on the spot, only the evidence of the wolf's abortive attack could be seen. A trembling crowd of shoppers inside peered out into the open air.

'Where did they go?' demanded the commander of the police task-force.

The shoppers shrugged, and pointed in several different directions. The manageress of the shop was too busy directing operations within, knowing that an untidy store was a badly-run store and that the monthly regional review would centre upon certain CCTV footage of crisps scattered in the aisles.

Exasperated, the policeman asked for his fellow-officer, the one who had raised the call about the siege.

'Oh, you want the siege?' asked Catriona MacReekie, who had been trapped in the store while looking for a jar of artichoke hearts in extra virgin olive oil. 'You're in the wrong place for that. This isn't the siege,' she said scornfully, 'that's up the hill at the schoolhouse!'

The police commander blinked, but said nothing. He knew the Scots did things differently, and the secret of success in siege negotiation was to blend in with the locals. He led his team at a half-run, up the hill to the schoolhouse.

In the interim, Jack and the Giant had accosted Will Tuttle down at MacConnachy Square. Over the course of the past hour, Jack had decided that he wanted to form a political party and stand for election in Brigadoon and the surrounding constituency. Any Election would do – Scottish, British, whatever. He had no doubts as to his chances. 'You've seen how popular I am with the kids,' he told Rory. 'I'm that archetypal figure, the giant-killer.' Rory flinched at this. 'Sorry, dude: you know it's all show - but the kids love to see that - the small people against the big people. And so do their parents. Strikes a chord. If I stand for election against all these fakers, then it'll be a walk-over. And,' he added, 'if you just keep in the background, I'll let you be my campaign-manager and right-hand man.' The Giant brightened up at this thought.

However, to form a party and stand for election, Jack needed to be eligible to vote.

Tuttle now had the unenviable task of explaining to them that their application for a vote had been turned down. It was not his job, not his at all, as he had explained in several daisy-chained tweets in the course of the past hour. It was the job of Vince McAnnelly, the Electoral Registration Officer or, if not him, then his two clerical officers. But the latter had explained at considerable length that their job was not commonly customer-facing, and that they would have to seek the personal authorisation of Mr. McAnnelly before undertaking any such interface. And that gentleman seemed to have vanished from the face of the earth, much to Ms. Ashton's annoyance and Tuttle's wrath.

'You'll have to do it,' said Jane Ashton to her personal assistant. 'Get on with it, then we can tidy up here and get back to our hotel. I'm wiped out.' Her Italian shoes hurt like hell, and she longed for the glass-slippers that the old lady had lent her. That and a cold, dry Martini.

Tuttle clenched his teeth and went out to explain matters to Jack and - more worryingly - the Giant. In the dozen steps that were required to reach the pair, he sent out a tweet: 'Could be a dead man walking here. Thanks for following me.'

Fortunately for Referendum Nation and the rest of the world, it was not Tuttle's last tweet.

The Giant just looked glum; but Jack laughed. 'So much for democracy, then,' he said. 'See this, Rory? We work for years and years, day in and day out, all kinds of weather, to keep the kids happy. We pay our taxes, don't we? And do we get to vote? No, dude, we don't. We're second-class citizens. Come on, Rory, we'll do this another way!'

With these dark and possibly threatening words, Jack walked off with the Giant, back towards the hump-backed bridge. Will breathed a sigh of relief and carefully wiped the sweat from his brow.

'Sorted,' he advised the International Electoral Commissioner.

~ 25 ~

The Oil of Gladness and the Tappan Presbyterian Association

'Green, Johnny Green,' announced the police-commander. He and his squad had come up to the school-house casually, so as not to provoke fear and dangerous excitement. He had tapped on the door, quite patently just making a social call - no weapons, no provocative badges of power. The door had opened an inch and Mr. Lundie had peered forth, annoyed.

'What do you want with us, Mr. Green?' asked the dominie. 'We are very busy in here just now, considering the words of Mr. Erskine in his great sermon "*Worthless Man, Much regarded by the Mighty God.*" Can your matter not wait?'

'I'm afraid it can't, sir. It is police business. May I ask your name?'

'You may,' replied Mr. Lundie.

There was a long pause.

'And your name is?' asked Johnny Green.

'Thessalonius Lundie,' replied the old man proudly. 'You have doubtless heard of me? Your colleague will have told you about me, I expect?'

Green nodded and smiled pleasantly to gain time. 'And how many people do you have in there?' he asked.

'Let me see, now.' The schoolmaster considered for a moment. 'I have seven eager pupils in all, I believe. A very propitious number for a theological debate, I think you'll agree. Oh, and Sandy and God's Dove, of course.'

'Is anyone hurt?'

'Hurt?' Mr. Lundie was astonished by the question. 'Not in body, not at all. Why, if anyone had been hurt, I would of course have sought out old Mrs. Mackintosh, who is very good with remedies. Perhaps,' he smiled conspiratorially, 'perhaps one or two of my guests are hurting in spirit, though: it has been a long and rewarding debate that we have had. Oh, we are very worthless, sir, very worthless indeed!' He rubbed his hands in glee. 'Would you like to come in and join us, Mr. Green?'

'No, not at the moment, Mr. Lundie,' said Green.

'In that case, sir, I'll beg leave to shut the door.' He did so, leaving Johnny Green to consider the wood an inch from his nose, and to ponder the logistics.

When he turned round, he was a little surprised to find himself all but surrounded by a crowd of villagers and others. They had broken through the cordon established, following procedure, by Commander Green's team. A man stepped forward.

'My name is Sharpe, Albert Sharpe, of New Doric Solidarity,' he announced. 'On behalf of the people of Brigadoon, I demand that you withdraw your men and let us sort out this situation for ourselves!'

There were mumblings of agreement from those who surrounded Albert, much to his own satisfaction. Somewhere in the background, his former comrade-in-arms, Jimmy Thompson, was heard to cry 'Treacherous loon!' Albert acknowledged the epithet with a simple clenched fist punched in the air and shouted back: 'New Doric Solidarity!'

'I must ask you to move along,' began Johnny Green - but he got no further.

'Police brutality - out!' shouted Albert. The cry was taken up by several of his new followers. These included many of the villagers and - in a cunning strategic move - Jack and the Giant. 'Out! Out! Out!'

The Oil of Gladness and the Tappan Presbyterian Association

Mr. Lundie banged on the window, and put his finger to his lips. He frowned impressively.

Johnny Green remained unflustered. With a single gesture, he ordered his team to re-group and to push back the protestors. They did so with great efficiency, provoking further outrage. 'Pigs! Hired Thugs of the State! Fascist Pigs! Fascist Pigs! Fascist Pigs!' shouted Jack, the shout taken up by not a few of Sharpe's followers. At the top of the hill, the Big Bad Wolf, hearing the words "Fattish Pigs", pricked up his ears and wondered whether to retrace his sad steps. Perhaps fortunately for everyone concerned, he was so depressed that he simply lay down in the shade, curled up and dreamed of times of glory past.

Inside the schoolhouse, the discussion of Mr. Erskine's divine teachings proceeded apace, despite the hubbub from outside. That is to say, Mr. Lundie quoted the Sermons from memory, now that the mice had digested the books, and interrupted himself every so often with a commentary. The three officers of Aberdeenshire Council, the two salesmen, Cindy and the Electoral Registration Officer listened glumly. Indeed, the Education Officer and one of the sales reps had fallen asleep. At the front of the class, the ostrich paced up and down, keeping a close eye on them. Every now and then, Mr. Lundie took an appreciative sip of Buckfast, smacking his lips and growing a little more excitable with each swallow. He moved on from the sermon concerning The Worthless, and launched into a new one - the divine's Second Sermon on the topic of "*A Lamp Ordained for God's Anointed.*"

The salesman representing Scottish Hydro to the benighted people of Brigadoon had struck up a low conversation with Sandy Macmillan, over a glass or two of the same cordial. His words could barely be heard above the long recitation of Ebenezer Erskine's wisdom.

'Who is this that cometh up from Edom, with dyed garments from Bozrah? Wherefore art thou red in thine apparel, and thy garments like him that treadeth in the wine vat?'

'See this, pal,' he advised Sandy, 'you want to get into The Oil.'

Brigadoon Revisits

'The Oil?' asked Sandy, astonished. 'The oil of the anointed?'

'Aye, ken, that's where a' the money is. This village, staying here - that's a mug's game, I tell you. If you got into The Oil, you'd be a rich man in no time at all. The rigs is where to start. Two weeks on, two weeks off, and then you're made.'

'But what is it, The Oil?' asked Sandy in a low voice, the sneaking, creeping, snagging Brambles of Allurement beginning to ensnare him.

There was a short pause, while Mr. Lundie refreshed himself with a Werther's Original. This required some adjustment of the sweetie in his mouth before he could continue. The heavy breathing of Mr. Low was the only sound inside the stuffy, sunny, mote-filled room. Invigorated by the rush of sugar, Mr. Lundie continued. 'Has ever the lamp of the gospel dropped some of the oil of God's Anointed upon your souls?'

'The Oil - see, it's where the money is,' the man from Scottish Hydro quietly took up the thread of his argument. 'Look, oil is what drives the world around. They need it for a'thing - cars, planes, ships, plastics - you name it. It's not going to run out any time soon. You just go out to the North Sea and you bring it up from the depths. And they pay you over the odds. You can't fail! See this - in six months, you'll have a fine bungalow, a smart car, maybe a wee girl-friend? Or if you want, you can donate loads of money to the church or whatever.' The Sales Rep was well-versed in human psychology.

'Oil,' revealed Mr. Lundie, 'maketh the face to shine. Hence the spouse cries out, "His countenance is as Lebanon, excellent as the cedars." Oh, my disciples, such is the oil of gladness!'

Sandy Macmillan was sorely tempted. Money for the Good Lord? He could become a big man in Brigadoon if he came home every month with a bag of gold; he could build up the chapel again and hand out money for the school - aye, maybe he could buy the works of Mr. Erskine bound up in leather and embossed, as they should be, in gold, and set up a wee library: the Macmillan Library. That would sound good. But no! - therein lay the Sin of Pride. He would make an anonymous donation, that would be better. "The Forsyth Library, Erected by the Kind Gift of a Son of Brigadoon." But was it not

The Oil of Gladness and the Tappan Presbyterian Association

astonishing what the Modern World could do with the fruit of the olive tree that is so praised by the Prophets?

At that moment, there was a further rapping upon the schoolhouse door. Mr. Lundie groaned and continued his reading in a louder voice. The knocking resumed, even louder. At last, the dominie decided that he could not continue. With a flick of his finger at the ostrich, commanding the bird to accompany him closely, he strode to the door and flung it open.

Johnny Green stood there once more.

'What do you want, importunate beggar?' demanded Mr. Lundie. 'Did I not say to you that I have no time for idle conversation? I have yet to finish Mr. Erskine's second sermon on the matter of the Oil of the Anointed, and have his third, and most sublime, yet to begin.'

'I am sorry to disturb you once more,' said Green with a crass pretence at humility and regret. 'But I have been informed that a deputation from Holyrood and another from Westminster has arrived and that they wish to talk to you.'

The school-master laughed long and loud, Buckfast coursing in his veins. 'A deputation, you say, a "deputation" - or do you, sir, really mean a *"depuration?"'* Much overcome by his own wit, which he could only attribute to the divine power of wisdom in Mr. Erskine's words, Mr. Lundie reached out and tapped Green playfully on the cheek. The policeman recoiled. 'Do not, sir,' he growled in a low voice, 'lay hands on an officer of the law.'

In reply, Mr. Lundie smiled and then closed the door again. Almost immediately, it re-opened to allow the ostrich to head off on another mission to collect spiritual sustenance from TESCO.

Commander Green sighed. This was not going to be an easy one. He had recently had a run of short-lived sieges, which were resolved within minutes or a couple of hours - most notably, the infamous Subo Siege, during which five disappointed fans of Susan Boyle, who had been denied tickets for a sell-out concert at the Leeds Playhouse, barricaded themselves into the ticket-office with a hapless parking-warden: that one was easily resolved by the promise of a clutch of tickets for the final of the next series of *Dancing on Ice*. So he was due a tricky one, he supposed. He'd rather it wasn't in the full glare of the TV and - of all things – under the close scrutiny of the national leaders of all the major political parties. It had been made quite clear to him that any letting of blood, in the full view of the watching world, would not be an attractive addition to his CV when, as would surely be the case, he was looking for another job.

He need not have worried. The people from Holyrood, who had finally arrived by fast car from Edinburgh, had no time for sideshows. They were more concerned with taking the political temperature around MacConnachy Square, believing that they could detect voting intentions in the wide-eyed looks of the people of Brigadoon. For her part, the Westminster Minister for Community Engagement, who had arrived on the first afternoon flight into Dyce, had found her way to the Internet phone-booth, following her nose for easy political pickings. Here she came across Andrew Campbell, arm in arm with Red Riding Hood's Grandmother.

'Good-day to you, sir,' said the Minister in her best campaigning manner, 'I expect that you speak for the older generation in this delightful community. Can you tell me, then, what is your view of DirectGov? Do you," she smirked, "'*like*" it?'

Mr. Campbell had to admit that he had no knowledge on the matter

The Minister was appalled. 'What has Holyrood been doing all these years?' she asked the surrounding Press phalanx. 'This is the fate which awaits an independent Scotland! Parochial ignorance. The Dark Ages.' Turning back to Mr. Campbell, she said: 'Have you not heard of Facebook, Mr. Campbell?'

'No, madam,' he replied sadly. 'There is much that seems to have passed us by, here in Brigadoon, over the past few days. And much sorrow has come into our lives.'

'I am sorry to hear that, Mr. Campbell. But I am sure my colleagues in the United Kingdom Government will help you in the difficult times to come. Increased funding for Community Engagement in Scotland will, of course, be made available next year.' She cut to a more pressing issue. 'But what are your voting intentions, if I may ask? I expect a man of your standing in the community would be a "No"?'

'Oh,' replied Mr. Campbell, 'I have not yet decided. There is so much to commend on either side. Some encouraging me to vote "Yes" are most generous, that they are, and some of the "Noes" have been very kind. I would not like to upset either side. What,' he wondered, 'would you recommend, madam?'

'Well, Mr. Campbell,' answered the Minister, trying to look thoughtful. 'I've met many of the "Yes" group, of course,' she fibbed brazenly, 'and found them very enthusiastic. Sadly, enthusiasm is not always enough. In my experience, security lies in unity." She paused to let the Press write that one down. "But what are your interests, Mr. Campbell?'

'I am very interested,' he said, 'in books.'

'Books?' asked the Minister. 'Any particular kind? Dan Brown, maybe, or - ' she struggled to think of another author. She failed. 'Or maybe political autobiographies?'

Mr. Campbell looked a little confused. 'Is there more than one kind of book?' he asked, feeling wearier now than he had felt all day. Surely the modern world was a tangled web. He should go home and rest, while his daughters cooked his supper. 'Surely a book is a book, and if it is printed by God-fearing men in, say, Edinburgh or London, perhaps, then it is worthy of my attention?'

The Ministerial aide looked askance at this entertaining idea. He pondered for a moment, as his Minister floundered. Then he was struck by a brainwave. He muttered the mysterious words "Google Books" in the Ministerial ear. The Ministerial eye brightened. She decided that a demonstration was in order. The idlers at the curious phone-booth awaiting the next call from a young lady were pushed to one side. The Minister watched patronisingly as her aide called up the Internet, asked Mr. Campbell a question regarding his favourite author, and - wonder of wonders - found the Reverend Ebenezer Erskine's *Whole Works* (Third Volume) published in 1836 and presented to the Tappan Presbyterian Association by the Hon. D. Bethune Duffield from his late father's collection. Soon, Mr. Campbell was in seventh heaven, scrolling his way through the 600 pages that had been carefully scanned in by Gog and Magog's slaves. In minutes, the idle few were peering over his shoulder, finding that the words of Mr. Erskine, preserved for posterity, gave them far more of a shiver than the honeyed promises of young ladies: the words were like a drink from a cool mountain stream after a night of sickly-sweet osculations at the mouths of cold-callers.

'Tarquin,' said the Minister to her aide, 'find me this Mr. Sharpe. The man's clearly an organisational genius.'

Sharpe was soon tracked down outside the schoolhouse, denouncing with great energy.

'Down with the ruling parties!' he was shouting. 'What have they done for the common man? Nothing. What have they done for the North-East? Nothing. They've taken our oil, taken our beef, taken our sand-dunes even. What have we had in return? Nothing! Does even one of those lackeys of monopoly capitalism dare come here and show his face? I think not! The old parties are dead. They are buried. That is why, brothers and sisters, we need a whole new party! Join New Doric Solidarity and I promise you this: you will never see me shirk my responsibilities to you, nor ever pander to the whims of big business! New Doric Solidarity'

There was a burst of enthusiasm at these heady words, applause led largely by Jack and the Giant. After a defiant clenched fist punched in the air, Albert Sharpe stepped down and began to shake hands. He shook hands with the Ministerial aide.

'The Minister wishes to congratulate you on your fine work here,' murmured the latter, 'and to discuss possible opportunities in London.'

'Indeed?' whispered Sharpe. 'But discreetly, mind?'

'It goes without saying,' said the Ministerial aide, very discreetly.

~ 26 ~

Four Doctors and an NHS Dentist

The five junior Campbell sisters, instead of being at home making Mr. Campbell's supper, were out on the hillside gathering heather with the five brothers Burnturk. All the Permitted Participants, with the sole exception of Albert Sharpe, who was deliberately being excluded from that select company, had arranged for a grand ceilidh to be held that evening in the re-emergent village of Brigadoon. It was to start at six o'clock, and go on all night if necessary: in the words of Barry Jones, Scotland would celebrate the saving of two hundred-odd votes from perdition, and celebrate - big time !

 Blooming heather was traditionally the decoration of choice for such grand events. The gathering of blooming heather was traditionally the excuse of choice of young folks going a-wooing. Such an activity had cemented the relationship of Tommy Albright and Fiona Campbell. It would probably work for the rest of them, the Campbell sisters calculated. The Burnturk brothers innocently went along with the plan.

 Meg Brockie watched the five happy pairs dance off to the hill. 'Aye,' she shouted after them bitterly, 'take away all the fine winning lads, you do that, why not? There'll not be a fine lad left for any of the rest of us! Go on, away with you!' To vanquish her disappointment, she went off to the Brigadoon Inn, and boxed Charlie Dalrymple into a corner.

The girls took Meg's advice to heart. The eldest Burnturk thanked his lucky stars that that he had been able to escape the traps set by the shepherdess, interrupted as they had been by the vulpine onslaught on the shop.

When they reached the brae above Brigadoon, the party split up into couples, each to their own little patch of purple and white heather. Each girl asked her beau for more information about Pumpherston.

'Well, there's Subarus, lots of them,' said the youngest Burnturk, whose own Subaru was sitting back in his mam's lock-up, gleaming. He only got to drive it now once or twice a month, racing his pals up and down the country roads of West Lothian. 'Mine's the best, though,' he added. 'The biggest spoiler. And the fastest.'

'Is it that?' sighed Aphrodite, and loaded her beau with an armful of blooming heather.

'And I do kick-boxing twice a week, down at the sports-centre in Kirkliston,' he added.

'And then my mam goes to LIDL a lot - you'd like that,' said the second-youngest brother. 'Foods good, and there's always great deals – satellite-dishes, bicycle-pumps, blankets, nice clothes and things like that. My mam loves all that. You would too.'

'I think I would,' sighed Catherine, imagining the life of a princess, where she was dressed in the finest furs and dripping with diamonds. Truly, Pumpherston was a fine, fine place for a girl to be. LIDL sounded better than TESCO.

'There's cable TV,' said the third brother, suddenly filled with a yearning for home-comforts. 'Cable's got everything - films, rock-concerts, football. I watch Sky Sports a lot, you know,' he admitted, 'when I'm not working out and that. You can get anything you want. It's just great!'

'It sounds wonderful,' sighed Jenny, idly rotating a small sprig of heather under her nose and making huge eyes at the middle brother. He was smitten, and blushed.

'We've got some grand recycling facilities in Pumpherston now,' boasted the second-eldest brother, who was of a more serious mind altogether. 'The Council put them in last winter - paper, cans, plastic bottles, cardboard, you name it. Even for old clothes and that. It's as green as you could hope for now. And I think that's what we should be doing, don't you?'

'Oh,' said Margaret eagerly, 'I love green places. It'll be like Brigadoon, then?'

'Aye, I suppose,' said the young man doubtfully, not looking directly at the pretty young woman, 'it'll be just like here. Perhaps a little more modern - but I suppose you can't hold back two hundred years of progress, can you?'

'It's not in Pumpherston itself, mind, but we've a new Health Clinic in Broxburn, which is just down the road,' said the eldest Burnturk, who was reaching that age where all his pals were getting married and settling down. He ought to do the same, his mam thought. Maybe she was right. He was earning a good wage. And he'd heard his pals' wives say that the Clinic was fair posh. 'Four doctors and an NHS dentist, would you believe?,' he advised his sweet Campbell. 'And a special mother and baby clinic every second Wednesday.'

Mary Campbell said nothing. She simply swooned into her Burnturk's arms. Bunches of heather cascaded to the ground, fortuitously providing a soft landing for Pumpherston Man and Brigadoon Woman.

~ 27 ~

Petrol-Heads With Powdered Wigs

Bob Tucker had not relaxed for one minute. Throughout that long day, he had paced back and forth at the top of the hill, keeping an eye on all the movement down below, awaiting his chance. Newcombe was dispatched at regular intervals to scout out the land: 'They think you're one of theirs, Newcombe,' scorned Tucker. 'So do I. Make yourself useful, and then I might review some of my options.'

Warren Newcombe did not ask what Tucker considered his options to be. He had a good idea, however, that they did not include Warren's rapid advancement through the management-structure. He made his little trips down into the village, some more perilous than others, and returned bearing his reports. Each piece of news was slightly worse than the one before.

'Shit lot of use you are, Newcombe,' advised Tucker. He jabbed him on the chest. 'These hippy bastards are not, repeat not, going to get away with this. I'll have that effing camp cleared before nightfall.' Tucker stormed off, to calm his soul with the sight of the Seven Dwarves labouring away at a rate which was quite astounding, for a rate of pay that was quite astounding. At least something was going right.

It was while he stood in smug contemplation of the seven new hands that he noticed a woman arrive in a car, bouncing over the rough ground from the country road that led to Stonehaven. She

Petrol-Heads With Powdered Wigs

pulled up in a cloud of dust, and clambered out. Some idling fools pointed him out to her. 'What does this bitch want?' he muttered to himself.

'Are you in charge here?' asked the lady, looking rather annoyed.

'Certainly am,' answered Bob easily. 'What of it?'

'You've stolen some of my employees,' she replied.

'I very much doubt that,' laughed Bob in an unpleasant way. 'I don't steal anything from anyone. Least of all employees.'

'Well, that's them over there,', she said, pointing at Doc and Happy and Sneezy and so forth.

'Excellent workers, thanks,' said Bob. 'Now eff off.'

She stood her ground. 'They're under contract to me,' she said angrily, 'and I resent your tone.'

'You can resent my tone as much as you want. It's a free labour-market. Now, you get off this land - you're trespassing, and accidents can happen to people who stray onto this property without permission.'

'Are you threatening me?' demanded the manageress of Storybook Glen.

'I certainly am,' replied Bob, staring at her contemptuously. 'Oh look,' he added, nodding over her shoulder, 'I think your car's had an accident.'

She whirled round. Her car still stood where she had parked it, shimmering in the hot late afternoon sunshine; there was no sign of any damage. 'No, it hasn't,' she said.

'Not yet,' said Bob. With a brief gesture, he waved to a dumper-truck driver, who fired up his machine and revved the engine noisily.

Defeated, the manageress warned that Bob would hear from her lawyers and then she ran back to her car. The truck followed her, dumper to bumper, at high speed all the way down to the road.

'Bloody lezzie,' muttered Bob. 'Hey!' he shouted angrily at the Seven Dwarves, who had stopped for a brief rendition of *Heigh-ho!*, 'get back to work, you lazy short-arsed bastards! I don't pay you to have a sing-song, do I? Are you tugging my tadger, or what?'

Doc touched his forelock, had a sharp word with his brothers, and Bob's cheapest labourers - ever - got back to shovelling and digging.

Brigadoon Revisits

Tucker the Tearless smirked and went back to his Portakabin to grab a cup of coffee and make his last report of the day to Head Office. He glossed over certain unwelcome facts and assured his Director that work would be proceeding as normal from oh-six-hundred hours on Saturday, and no, George, there was no chance of overtime being paid even if it was a Saturday. 'Effing wanker,' he shouted at his phone, once the connection was safely broken. He turned round and glowered at the obstruction in the path of his grand new road. That camp would be gone by morning, he knew that for a fact.

'What the fuck!?' he exclaimed suddenly, spilling his coffee. 'Newcombe! Newcombe! Get your arse in here! What's that lot doing? Walking their dogs or what?'

Newcombe peered down the slope. A group of figures had emerged from the trees that bordered the theme-park. 'Not dogs,' he said confidently, 'pigs.'

'Pigs? Pigs? Get down there and tell them to eff off out of here, you hear me? I've just found out what I keep you for. Get your finger out!'

Newcombe sighed and headed off downhill again.

Taking advantage of the manageress's absence, a larger party of her employees had sneaked out of their compound. The party comprised: the Troll who lived under the rickety bridge, preying on passing goats; the Three Little Pigs who were now on the Council's accommodation waiting-list after years of harassment by a certain furry-eared anti-social bully; and the Three Bears who were fed up of being bested by a small girl who, it seemed to them, could never do any wrong in the eyes of their employer. A passing bluebird had advised them of the successful application by the Seven Dwarves for work elsewhere. So now they all made their way up the hill to seek employment.

They were making good speed and Newcombe met them barely a hundred yards from the ridge.

'Sorry,' he said politely, 'private property.'

The pigs halted. But the very big and ugly Troll growled menacingly and the Bears snarled in harmony. Warren thought it best to let them through. He tagged along behind and was thus able to accept all of Tucker's compliments when he employed the Troll and the Bears at the same rate as the Dwarves. 'You finally got one bloody thing right, Newcombe - take five minutes, why don't you, have a cup of tea. And then get these effing pigs out of here.'

The Three Little Pigs looked glum. The largest began to snivel and weep. It did no good. Tucker was having no pigs on his workforce. 'Nor no billy-goats neither,' bawled the Troll triumphantly after them, as the rejected swine made their way back down the hill.

Some five minutes after the pigs had left, another party of job-seekers arrived. The four coachmen, abandoning Cinderella's coach, walked in with their powdered wigs and long blue coats frilled with lace. At the sight of the massive bulldozers and dumper-trucks and the heavy plant that perpetually criss-crossed the building-site, they hugged each other with glee. 'A real set of wheels, at last,' breathed one of them, his eyes shining. 'This is what I've been waiting for all my life. Oh - smell that diesel! Mr. Tucker, Your Excellency,' he begged, holding out his driving-licence, 'I'll drive those for nothing. Any one at all. Please, oh please, my lord!'

'Are you in the union?' demanded Tucker.

'No, Your Majesty, never!' said the coachmen, in the voice of solidarity.

Without further delay, Bob signed up all four of the bewigged and powdered petrol-heads, unable to believe his luck. Extraordinary, he thought to himself, effing extraordinary. Once things got moving again, he would have a workforce that would out-perform any he had had in the past. This road would be finished well before its contracted completion-date, and would come in under budget. It was a first in the construction industry. He was effing made! He even felt a momentary twinge of satisfaction at Newcombe's actions.

'Newcombe, put that bloody mug of tea down! Did I say you could take a siesta? You tugging my tadger, or what? Are we any further forward? No, we're not any further forward, like I told the Project Director - said to him, Newcombe's not lifted a bloody finger, I said. So, get down there now and see what's happening.'

Brigadoon Revisits

Newcombe, glad of any excuse to get down there, made haste. For some reason, he wanted to see Meg again. The woman appalled him, but, if his career on the Peripheral Route was finished, she was a refuge for a while. If her man Jeff turned up and beat the living daylights out of him - well, so be it. That would be a vast improvement on working in the close company of Tucker the Tearless.

~ 28 ~

The Macy Deming Memorial Library

As Newcombe crossed the hump-backed bridge, he greeted the two boys, Hamish and his friend James. But the greeting was not returned: the two were immersed in some game on a mobile-phone. The engineer walked past the pair, wondering how they had got hold of the phone, and sighed for the lost innocence of youth. He turned onto MacConnachy Square, and bumped into Will Tuttle.

'You,' said Will, grabbing him desperately by the arm, 'have you seen my mobile?'

'Have you lost it?' asked Warren.

'Someone's stolen it, I'm sure,' said Tuttle bitterly. 'Can't trust any of these locals. What am I supposed to do without it?' he demanded. 'Tell me that!'

Warren shrugged helplessly.

'I'm shafted,' said Warren. 'I've got everything on there. Ashton's going to kill me if I can't contact anyone! And what's worse - I'm due to tweet in the next ten minutes - I can't suddenly go off-air, can I? The Nation cannot wait. This is a disaster. Oh God, what's this?' He pointed back to the bridge.

Warren turned round. To his surprise, a long and noisy procession of people was coming across the bridge. They seemed intent on festivity - they were laughing and singing, many of them were dressed in garish tartans, or carried banners. *'Me Encanta Brigadoon!'* stated one

Brigadoon Revisits

Hispanically; '*Es lebe Brigadoon!*' urged another. 'Surrey Brigadoon!' yet another. At the head of the procession danced a number of people dressed as witches. Warren saw Hamish look up from his game, very briefly examine the witches, and then return his attention to the game.

The new arrivals halted when they reached Warren and Will.

'Where's the party, bro?' demanded one of the witches.

'Party, party, where's the party?' chanted the rest of the crowd in cheerful unison.

'We got a tweet from that Electoral Commission guy, saying there was some kind of a party here,' explained the first witch. 'Thought we'd better come along and join in - you know, like, solidarity with the people of Brigadoon.'

Will waved them in distractedly. All around the Square, preparations for the ceilidh were in full swing. The Burnturks and the Campbells had even managed to bring back a few sprigs of heather, albeit broken and crushed. The manageress of TESCO had donated several crates of beer and some barbecue starter-packs. The political camps, taking as authority their exertions of earlier in the day, excelled themselves in the matter of crisps and nibbles. Some of the local men were practising their dance-steps. Notable by his absence was Charlie Dalrymple; but Tommy Albright was out there, dancing like a dervish with Elaine Stewart. Some men in orange-jackets were erecting stakes around the perimeter of the Square, and linking the stakes up with red-and-white striped tape.

With a whoop of glee, the new arrivals raced past. A band unpacked its instruments under a banner that stated 'Brig-Aid-Doon'. A local DJ announced that all proceeds from the ceilidh would go to help the poor people of Brigadoon find their way to Democracy. A great cheer went up. The DJ made especial mention of all the Brigadoon Fan-Clubs who had made extraordinary efforts to get here, 'from all parts of the globe - Spain, Germany and Guildford!' More unrestrained cheering. 'And now,' announced the DJ, 'let's give a great welcome to a local band who are really going places: fae Inverurie let's welcome – Rat-Arsed Beaver!' Wild enthusiasm, which soon gave way, alas, to deaf ears and apathy.

Harry Beaton walked hand-in-hand with Jean Campbell. It was brazen, it was adulterous, it was assuredly a sin, but neither Harry nor Jean cared a whit. Had Mr. Lundie not been otherwise occupied with the disciplining of Modern Man in his schoolhouse, he would certainly have had a stern word with the pair. But in his absence, no one attempted to express a judgement: Jean's father was totally absorbed in paging through the on-line resources of the Tappan Presbyterian Association; Jean's elder sister Fiona sat indoors, crying her eyes out and distractedly pulling apart the still-fresh bouquet of flowers which she had carried at her wedding, all those years ago. Harry's father Archie smiled grimly at the sight of his son reconciled to his childhood sweetheart, and assured himself that, if he ever tracked down Mr. Forsyth, he would rub the late departed minister's nose in sights such as this. All that Mr. Forsyth had succeeded in doing was destroying the people of Brigadoon, and that misguided fool Lundie was no better. Archie shook his head sadly and then accepted the offer of a dance from a vision in pink tartan, who had come all the way from Marbella that very day to see him.

The Campbell sisters, arm in arm each with a brother from Pumpherston, found their progress halted as they tried to join in the dancing. Two young men, with Borg-like attachments in their ears and wrap-round shades concealing their eyes, stepped in front of them and held up a forbidding hand.

'Tickets,' they said.

'Tickets?' asked the youngest Aphrodite.

'Tickets?' echoed the eldest Burnturk.

'Tickets,' repeated the two men in shades. 'No entrance without tickets.'

'But we live here,' complained Margaret Campbell.

'No exceptions, miss,' said one of the bouncers. 'No ticket, no entrance. We want no trouble now, ladies, gents. If you'd just like to move aside and -'

He got no further. The youngest Burnturk, carefully placing Aphrodite behind him, executed a remarkable flying kick upon one bouncer, while his next brother felled the other. A tussle ensued, and the Campbell sisters screamed in harmony. Site security, in orange jackets and proclaiming themselves to be 'Rock Steady', waded in carefully but irresistibly.

Meanwhile, on the small stage, Rat-Arsed Beaver came to the end of their set and departed amidst general relief. 'And now,' cried the DJ over the sound of the brawl, 'our next band told me just a few minutes ago that they're donating their entire appearance fee to the "Brigadoon Solidarity Fund" - thanks, guys - awesome! So let's hear it for our very own Jimmy Shand Tribute Band!'

Those residents of Brigadoon who had been lucky enough to gain entrance to the concert were enjoying themselves, at least a little. There was dancing to be had, and much singing, and it reminded the benighted villagers of happier times, when day and night they jigged and reeled and leaped with never a care in the world. Brigadoon, old and young, shrugged off care and trouble, clasped each other by the hand, and launched into such a virtuoso display of The Dancing as would have perhaps given Mr. Forsyth pause for thought before he ascended the mountain.

Up at the Schoolhouse, Mr. Lundie refused to be drowned out by the music and the noise. He simply smiled at the challenge, turned to a new topic in the memorised canon of Mr. Erskine, and started in earnest on the sermon *"The Standard of Heaven Lifted Up Against The Powers of Hell and Their Auxiliaries."* His hostages were slumped in piles around the schoolroom, overcome by a heady mixture of Buckfast, Werther's Originals and the Reverend Ebenezer Erskine's words of relentless comfort.

Caught up in the carefree Saturnalia, Jeff Douglas swept Nana Visitor off her feet. In a dazzling display, where North American East Coast Tap met Eastern German Hoedown, the pair carved a swathe through the gathering crowds of festival-goers, exciting dismay and applause in equal measure. On the sidelines, Sydney Guilaroff, journalist and one-time admirer of Nana, was struck dumb and reminded himself that, the next time he was abandoned in a magic coach with a tall red-haired German woman, he should make the most of it. Jane Ashton had consented, against her better judgement, to stay on a little and participate in the celebrations. Alan

Jay, the creepy TV anchorman, advised her that her presence would send out a good message to viewers worldwide. In any case, that fool Tuttle had vanished on some unlikely errand - said he had lost his phone. Not a moment too soon, in her view. It was with a little trepidation that she consented to a leisurely, and remarkably smooth, dance with Andrew Campbell, who had been lured away from his phone-box by the siren sound of the music.

'And have you completed your duty here, Miss Ashton?' asked Mr. Campbell politely, still in some doubt as to the nature of the lady's mission.

'I have indeed, thank you for asking,' she replied, relaxing just a little. The man was surely a very fine dancer. She swayed into the rhythms. 'And can I ask you if matters have gone satisfactorily?'

Andrew Campbell handed his partner back and forth between left and right and left again, before replying. 'Oh, very satisfactory indeed. I have decided, you see,' he added in a lowered voice, 'that I will go and visit America.'

'America?' repeated Ms. Ashton, a little surprised. 'Well, I can only say that you have made a wise choice. Did you have somewhere in particular in mind, might I ask?'

Mr. Campbell nodded. 'I have it in my mind to go and visit a grand library there, in a place named Tappan.'

Ms. Ashton stopped dead and stared at the old man. 'Tappan?' she repeated.

Mr. Campbell looked around nervously. 'Tappan,' he confirmed and attempted to lead his partner back into the dance: they were getting in everyone's way when they stood still.

'You know, Mr. Campbell,' replied Ms. Ashton, refusing to budge, 'that is my home town: Tappan, New York. My parents moved there when they married in 1956, and that is where I was born and grew up. Tappan.'

'It must be a fine, big place,' remarked Mr. Campbell, whose knowledge of fine, big places was perforce restricted. 'It has a most learned library - do you know it?'

'The Macy Deming Memorial Library?' she replied. 'Sure. Spent many happy days there when I was young.'

Brigadoon Revisits

'No, that was not the name,' said Mr. Campbell, frowning. 'I was thinking more of the Tappan Presbyterian Association's library.'

'Ah yes,' said Ms. Ashton diplomatically, 'of course.' She resumed her dancing, remembering with a little regret now the long-lost days of her youth, growing up with her parents, her older brother, and two much-maligned cats named Tommy and Jeff. Tommy and Jeff...? Now *there* was a helluva coincidence.

'Jeff,' said Nana as they cavorted around the Square 'you live here already for a long time?'

'A week maybe, call it fifty years,' gasped Jeff, who was finding that the German pace of life was way beyond what he was used to.

'Have you ever met Mr. Forsyth?'

'I tell you, Nana,' answered Jeff, twirling, his view of heaven and earth dizzily switching, 'I tell you: if I had met that man, I'd have punched his nose. The man was nuts. Lost his marbles. A screwball. OK, witches might be scary, but more scary is when you lock up an entire village for a hundred years at a time. That's psycho, in my book, and I'd like to tell him that. Say, Nana, can we stop a minute? I'm getting a pain in my side.'

'Dammit again, Jeff!' exclaimed Nana, 'we have just only started! Have you no balls?'

For answer, Jeff slumped to the ground, moaning. His face turned ashen. In a second, Nana was down beside him. 'Jeff!' she screamed at him, 'Jeff!'

'Just give me a drink, honey,' said Jeff weakly. 'Left-hand pocket.'

In a trice, she had the flask out and applied to his lips. The cure was instantaneous. He flushed from white to red again, then sprang up and began to dance.

'You are one serious dipsomaniac,' said Nana admiringly. '*Herrgott noch mal*, Jeff, I thought you had completely died on me!'

'Nana,' said Jeff easily, 'who cares? No one cares about Jeff Douglas. Tommy doesn't care and he's my best friend. Mad Meg doesn't care and she wants to marry me. Harry Beaton doesn't care and I even shot him. And I don't care, Nana, because I'm stuck in this nut-house for ever, no chance of parole. What's the point?

Nineteen thousand years, Nana - I worked it out - nineteen thousand years in Sing-Sing. You got that?'

Nana stopped the dance suddenly. She grabbed the American by the chin and peered into his eyes. 'Yes, I care, Jeff! I care, *Du Arschloch!* And if you try dying on me again, I will actually suck every last drop of blood out from your sorry body, Carpathian-style, you can just watch me. I am mad for you, Jeff.'

Jeff stood astonished at this display of affection. Then he shrugged. 'Whatever you say, lady, whatever you say. Makes no difference to me.'

And they danced on into the evening.

~ 29 ~

Lustful Looks, Intoxicating Drink and Immoderate Dancing

Up at Storybook Glen, the back-office staff of the Referendum had been growing restless. For the most part they had been ordered to stay up there, in order to prevent rivals from sneaking in and taking over their hard-won premises - in particular the Doric Country Alliance was concerned about the intentions of Mr. Quillan's rowdy supporters on the upper floor of their palace. But when the backup teams saw the stream of revellers heading for the free concert down in Brigadoon, they decided to follow their social instincts. Party premises were abandoned, along with all the stockpiles of leaflets, window-stickers and rosettes. In no time at all, Storybook Glen's buildings, both large and small, humble and grand, fell silent. The Three Little Pigs wandered around forlornly, while their Wolf slipped ever deeper into depression. Goldilocks, Snow White and Cinderella sat, faces like thunder, lips pouting, waiting for bears, dwarves and other flunkies to turn up.

No sooner had the last campaign activists disappeared into the trees than the manageress of the theme-park came out with a huge bundle of keys and a wheely-bin. She reclaimed her premises one by one, and tipped into the wheely-bin all the rubbish left behind. Then she locked up. She chivvied the Little Pigs into emergency repairs to their houses, slapped Goldilocks out of her hysterics, chased Snow White back to make the seven empty beds, and set Cinderella to the task of scrubbing down the floors of the fairytale castle, where Jimmy Thompson's people had contrived to spill beer and trample egg-mayonnaise sandwiches into the parquet flooring of the ballroom.

'And good riddance,' she muttered, shaking a fist in the general direction of Brigadoon. 'Now we can get back to keeping the bairns happy.' She cast a baleful eye over the car-park, which was full to overflowing with garish Minis, badly-parked camper-vans and all the other preferred forms of transportation for festival-goers. The police, who were supposed to be in charge of traffic-control, lounged at the entrance, mentally calculating their overtime payments. Briefly, the manageress wondered whether she could offer the police officers temporary jobs, to plug the resource shortfall until she had recruited another set of dwarves and coachmen and bears. By the looks of them, most would easily fit the bill.

When the party activists reached the village, they threw themselves heart and soul into the ever-increasing rowdiness. Various wannabe bands had popped up on the stage, and then disappeared back into well-deserved oblivion. In desperation the DJ had been texting around all of his contacts, to see if some Big Name could make it out here. He had had word that U2 were interested, as were One Direction. But he had no confirmation yet from anyone. He started spinning disks, and that looked like it would keep everyone happy for an hour or so.

Everyone, except possibly the residents of Brigadoon. Those who had failed to gain entrance to the dance-floor, since they had no tickets, began to congregate in front of TESCO, nodding to each other, as acquaintances after a long hard day. Those of the residents who had done some partying now found themselves quite exhausted. Harry had popped some pills that he'd been passed by a friendly young man, and was spinning languidly on Jean's arm. Charlie, now Fiona's pillar of strength, stood with her in the phone-box, working out how to apply on-line for a passport - they had decided they were going to seek their fortunes in Canada.

From the schoolhouse, Sandy Macmillan appeared, slightly flushed and out of breath.

'Man,' he whispered to James Maclaren, 'this is a fair wee party, is it not?'

'Aye, man, one of the best,' agreed James Maclaren enthusiastically.

'I see only Lustful Looks, Intoxicating Drink and Immoderate Dancing,' said Archie Beaton in disapproving tones.

'Aye but,' asserted Maclaren, 'a grand do all the same. But, Sandy, man,' he continued, 'where have you been all day? We haven't seen you at all.'

'Well,' explained Sandy, 'I've been in the schoolhouse with Mr. Lundie. Oh, now there is a man who has been touched again by the Spirit of God!'

'Is that so, Sandy?' Some of the older generation, women more than men, began to gather round.

'Aye, so,' confirmed Sandy, 'he has been discoursing upon all the lustrous sermons of the Reverend Ebenezer Erskine, word by divine word, and explaining them to some of the fine gentlemen who have come to visit us today.'

'*The Wind of the Holy Ghost*?' asked Mrs. Mackintosh eagerly.

'Aye,' said Sandy with pride, rubbing his hands.

'Not *The Wise Virgins*?' demanded Archie Beaton incredulously.

'That too!'

'And *Ethiopia Stretching Out Her Hands*?' said others. 'And *God's Little Remnant*? And *The Plant of Renown*?''

'Aye, every single one of those,' Sandy nodded to general admiration. 'And the fine gentlemen seem keen to stay on and listen to more. At least, they dared not deny Mr. Lundie his pleasure. Now, if you'll excuse me, the dominie has asked me to run an errand to this fine shop. Our ostrich seems to have run off into the wilderness and we can no longer rely on it to bring us God's gifts.' He darted through the automatic doors of the store.

'Well,' said Mrs. Gilfillan, 'is that not a grand thing? Perhaps we should make our way up there and listen to what Mr. Lundie has to tell us. We are missing the moderating influence of the Word of God in this village, since Mr. Forsyth left us.'

Lustful Looks, Intoxicating Drink and Immoderate Dancing

'Woman,' said her husband urgently, 'we'll not go up there, not if we want to - you know -' He raised his eyebrows and looked around cautiously.

'Oh,' said his wife, flustered, 'aye, John, I was forgetting.'

'And what would you be forgetting, Mary Gilfillan?' asked Mrs. MacReekie solicitously.

Mrs. Gilfillan blushed.

'Come on, you hussy,' coaxed Catriona MacReekie, 'out with it. You can surely harbour no secrets from friends who have known you all your life?'

'Well,' said Mrs. Gilfillan shyly, 'John and I were thinking about paying a visit to that magical place on top of the hill there, that Storybook Glen. Just a wee trip, mind, and not staying long.'

Those within earshot fell utterly silent. Even Harry Beaton slipped back into consciousness. 'No,' he gasped, 'don't do that! The Curse, the Curse!' Jean mopped Harry's brow and he faded back into his drug-induced torpor.

'What can you be thinking of?' demanded Archie. 'Have you forgotten the Curse, what will happen if you leave the village? Then God will hide us away for ever! That is what Mr. Forsyth agreed with God when he brought us under His good protection!'

'Well,' said John Gilfillan slowly, putting an arm around his wife's shoulders. 'It is my opinion that Mr. Forsyth did us a great wrong when he made that agreement.'

Another horrified silence descended. Even the raucous noise of the party seemed to recede into the far distance, into another century altogether. After a moment, there was the sound of the glass door of TESCO sliding open and then shut again, as Sandy Macmillan emerged, bearing four bottles of Buckfast and six tubes of Pringles on a two-for-one offer. He was smiling when he emerged, having found out that he now had two hundred and twenty points on his Clubcard, something that would yield two golden guineas at the end of the next quarter. But the smile fell from his face when he approached his neighbours and saw their consternation.

'What's the matter, friends?' he asked, putting down his groceries with great care.

Brigadoon Revisits

Archie cleared his throat. 'John Gilfillan here was just saying that he considered Mr. Forsyth's actions over-hasty. "Wrong" was, I think, the word he used. John wishes to leave the village.'

Sandy was aghast. 'Leave the village? But that would mean –' He did not finish the sentence.

At that moment, Malcolm MacReekie cleared his throat. 'Catriona and I were thinking of moving to Marbella,' he said.

'Yes indeed,' added his wife belligerently, 'we have arranged a holiday there with some new friends of ours. And of course we can afford it now. Aye, we might even stay on and get a retirement apartment overlooking the sea. I hear they're built to quite a high standard these days.'

'And I,' said James Maclaren, 'had the Caribbean in mind. For have I not just won a free cruise there?'

'And I've been considering The Oil,' admitted Sandy Macmillan, absent-mindedly opening a bottle of Buckfast.

The confessions started to pour out. Jean and Harry were hoping against hope to find happiness in Edinburgh. Andrew Campbell mentioned that he had laid plans to fly to Tappan, New York, with Ms. Ashton.

'Father!' exclaimed his younger daughters in unison, horrified by this parental confession. And then they admitted to a burning desire to adopt a more modern life-style in Pumpherston.

More and more of the residents of Brigadoon came past. Tommy Albright admitted that he was returning to America with his new love, Elaine Stewart, to found a Dance Academy and perhaps break into Saturday night TV. Charlie Chisholm Dalrymple brought Fiona along and stood as far away from Tommy as was physically possible, before revealing their destination of choice – the frozen wastelands of Canada. Meg Brockie announced merrily that Warren Newcombe had agreed to marry her and let her have as many of his children as possible. Jeff said nothing, but looked on with some amusement.

Finally, Archie Beaton sighed. long and shook his head. 'This is a sad, sad day for Brigadoon,' he muttered. 'If Mr. Forsyth could see us now, if –' he raised his eyes and looked up the brae, 'if Mr. Forsyth could only hear us now. Surely he would say that The Backsliders are

Lustful Looks, Intoxicating Drink and Immoderate Dancing

now Characterized!' He looked around the group of villagers, most of them with their eyes downcast in shame.

'What Mr. Forsyth might hear and say is of no consequence,' argued Harry Beaton fiercely, rudely roused from his luscious dreams of mangrove swamps and tall and dusky fishermen. 'He is gone now. Father, it is time for us all to leave Brigadoon forever.'

Astonished, Archie Beaton fell back, melodramatically clutching a hand to his heart. 'It is my own son who turns against me, is it?' he gasped.

'Yes, father, it is, and you do not impress us with your play-acting. Every one of us has good reason to leave, though this place is our home. You too, father, do you not wish to leave?'

Mr. Beaton flushed angrily. 'You dare to ask me this?' he whispered.

For answer, Harry just smiled. 'You wish, as you have often muttered in your sleep, to seek out Mr. Forsyth and force him to an explanation for his desertion. Well? Do not deny it, father, I have heard you through the long, long nights, your prayers sound like mice pattering.'

Archie Beaton nodded slowly and then sat down heavily on the ground. Jean Campbell flew to his aid, for which he was very grateful.

'So,' said Jeff at last, breaking his silence. 'We all want out. Well, I can't say I care very much one way or another. But if we are to go, we all need to go at exactly the same time, it seems to me.'

Everyone was in agreement with that. They shivered, as if a cold wind had passed over their graves. Or was it merely that they were at last waking from a long nightmare?

'So we need to time it correctly, I'd say. Before midnight, just in case the village slips away of its own accord, like it does.'

'But after all these people have left,' suggested Fiona Campbell who had a heart of gold. 'We would not wish them to be carried off into the darkest of nights!'

'Would we not?' asked Jeff, more to himself than to anyone else. 'Hell,' he shrugged, 'you're probably right, Fiona. Now, if we only knew what time of day it was. My watch stopped working last week.'

Brigadoon Revisits

Young Hamish stepped up with a Blackberry in his hand. In the gloom, he peered closely at the screen. 'Exactly eight-seventeen,' he announced proudly.

'Say, you're some piece of work, kid!' said Jeff admiringly. 'Now, this hooley's supposed to finish at ten. Cops said so. So what say we let them all go home, and then we slip out right after. All at once, mind. How do we do that?'

'Line up on the banks of the river,' said Harry promptly, 'and all wade across at the same time, on the count of four.' He had given it considerable thought in recent days.

And so it was decided. Excitedly, all the women went home to pack, while the men-folk, as befitted their station, went down to MacConnachy Square for one last drink and a few eightsome reels. No one thought of Mr. Lundie, not even Sandy Macmillan, who sat alone with an open bottle and a tube of Pringles, dreaming of The Oil. The night-air cooled, and a faint mist appeared.

When ten o'clock came, sure enough the festivities drew to a close. Bono had sent a message of support, as had Sting, and One Direction had promised to dedicate a song at their next sell-out concert; but not one Big Name had actually made it as far as Brigadoon. Because of the coolness of the night and the clammy haar that was beginning to gather, the Square was cleared of party-people within thirty minutes, leaving only a tired bunch of politicians and their teams talking to the delighted officials from *VisitScotland*. Will Tuttle, having struck a clandestine deal with Barry Jones for the loan of a phone, tweeted nineteen to the dozen. Ms. Ashton had gone looking for Mr. Campbell. Stragglers from the TV and press were packing up their gear. So busy were they all with each other that none of them noticed, in the enveloping darkness, that the villagers were gathering in small groups down by the banks of the River Doon. Another ten minutes passed and the mist grew thicker. Jeff and Tommy anxiously counted the numbers - only Andrew Campbell was still missing. Should they wait? Ah, here he was now, arm in arm with the great lady from America!

Lustful Looks, Intoxicating Drink and Immoderate Dancing

All of a sudden, there was a great commotion as one - two - three - and then four ostriches burst out from TESCO's delivery-bay, where they had been hiding these past few hours, loped swiftly towards the hump-back bridge and bounded over it. The villagers watched them in silence. Then they picked up their possessions.

But the mist had come down. The far side of the river had vanished.

~ 30 ~

Very Smart, Troll, But No Smarts

'You! What's your name - Troll! Get your great big arse over here!' Standing in the glare of a floodlight, Bob Tucker had had enough. It was time to take control of the situation. Brigadoon? Not on my watch! No more pussyfooting. Newcombe had gone native? - so let him - he was history now anyway.

The Troll had taken on the role of supervisor in the small party of fifteen labourers who worked on steadily into the gloaming and beyond, without claiming any overtime, long after everyone else had knocked off for the day. He lumbered over to the Portakabin.

'What?' he asked gruffly.

'What what?' demanded Tucker irritably.

'What you want?

'What you want what?' Tucker shouted up at the Troll.

There was a pause. Then: 'What you want, Mr. Tucker, sir?'

'What I want, thicko, is for you to fetch me one of the coachmen, and then we get in that dozer over there and we go down and clear those hippies out of the way. That's what I want. That too complicated for you, Troll?'

'No, sir, Mr. Tucker, sir' affirmed the Troll. He turned laboriously and stomped off to grab one of the coachmen by the ear. 'You,' he growled, 'get in dozer, start him up!'

Very Smart, Troll, But No Smarts

The coachman, eager to at last get his hands on one of those big powerful pieces of machinery, scampered off and fired up the huge yellow beast. Since they had signed up, hours ago, he and his colleagues had been doing nothing but hosing the mud off the dumpers and dozers, and had had no chance to get behind the wheel. His three brothers scowled in jealousy, each wishing for the machine to veer out of control and crash and allow him the chance to take over.

The Troll reported back to Bob Tucker. The latter had in the meantime kitted himself out in a boiler-suit, and a black balaclava, over which he had pulled on his hard hat. He handed a larger balaclava to the Troll. 'Here,' he said, not unkindly, 'cover yourself up with this - we don't want to frighten them to death.' The Troll struggled to fit it over his head, but failed. The whole thing ripped to shreds. The Troll looked at it sadly, then chucked it away. His eyes lit upon a pile of black plastic sacks. He tore three neat holes in one with his sharp yellow teeth, and slipped it neatly over his head.

'Very smart,' said the Troll smugly.

'Very smart, Troll,' agreed Bob. 'But no smarts. Now let's go and clear those fuckers once and for all!'

He jumped aboard the bulldozer. The Troll clambered on behind. The coachman switched on the headlights, released the brake and slid the machine into gear. They tipped over the edge of the ridge and trundled down the slope. In the galre of the headlights, the small hump-backed bridge was slowly being enveloped in the curling fingers of the mist. Tucker the Tearless pointed at it and bawled in the coachman's ear: 'Aim straight for that bridge! And don't effing stop when you get to it!'

The coachman nodded eagerly, lost in an octane-fuelled nirvana. Nothing would stop him now, this baby would rock and roll ! The huge yellow machine bucketed and lurched and slithered across the muddy slope. The coachman laughed out loud with unrestrained delight. None of your girly pink-and-silver coaches for him any more ! This was just like on *Top Gear* ! Better even !

After about five minutes, they were within fifty yards of the bridge. At that precise moment, one - two - three - and then four ostriches emerged from the fog in front of them. The birds paused for a moment to check out the on-coming bulldozer, turned to their right and sped off up the hill towards Storybook Glen and freedom. Unable to restrain his baser instincts, the Troll leaped from the back of the dozer and set off in reckless pursuit, his vision impaired by the fluttering black bag. Bob Tucker did not notice this desertion: his eyes were firmly fixed on the mist which now surrounded the protest-camp.

Just as they reached the bridge, visibility was reduced to nil. The fog was so thick that Tucker could not see anything at all. The headlamps were on full, but the effect was like a light playing over a cinema-screen, reflecting back only flickering whiteness. No matter.

'Keep going!' yelled Tucker. The coachman needed no encouragement. On the more level ground at the foot of the hill, the dozer slowed down, but there was no way of telling where they were, no reference point within that thick fog. Despite the utter lack of screams and satisfying sounds of breakage, Bob supposed they were even now flattening teepees and shelters made of branches and humpies of tarpaulins and networks of tunnels. The protestors must be fleeing for their lives. Benefit-fraud bastards - he'd show them!

The machine ploughed on and on. Every so often a small tree would pop out of the wall of fog, and for that split second Bob would instinctively duck. The next instant there would be a slight bump as the tree vanished beneath them. Over the uneven ground they bounced, the coachman wild-eyed, his mouth in a rictal grin of delight and terror. Before the irresistible onslaught of the bulldozer, all the frail barricades in the protest-camp must surely be falling, splintering, smashed forever. In the night, unseen and unheard, the detritus of society was surely contemplating its destruction under the Engine of Progress. He, Tucker the Tearless, had seen to that!

And then all of a sudden, in a moment's silence, the Engine of Progress toppled over a low bank. With a huge splash, it came to a dead stop.

In that moment of sharp deceleration, Bob Tucker was thrown over the front of the dozer and plunged into the shallow waters of the River Dee. Some moments later, he surfaced, chilled and dripping.

Very Smart, Troll, But No Smarts

'What the - ?' he gasped. He looked around, baffled; outraged. And then he shattered the still night air:

'Effing Brigadoon!'

THE END

Printed in Great Britain
by Amazon